A Nowhere Man

----------- fault lines of love

A Novel

Sudipto Chattopadhyay

First published in 2020 by

Becomeshakespeare.com
One Point Six Technologies Pvt Ltd.
119-123, 1st Floor, Building J2, B - Wing, Wadala Truck Terminal,
Wadala East, Mumbai, Maharashtra, India, 400022.
T:+91 8587995915

This book has been funded by WORDIT ART FUND
WORDIT ART FUND helps deserving
Authors publish their work
To apply for funding, please visit us at
becomeshakespeare.com

To,

My Dear Departed Father

Shrish Chandra Chatterjee

Wish you were here

&

My Closest Friends

Amit Purohit & Animitra Ghatak

Kindred souls, left much before their time

A Nowhere Man --- fault lines of love

The central narrative is structured on the edifice of a filmmaker's life. This character is deliberately left ambivalent and ambiguous. He does not even possess a name, nor is he the narrator.

Characters of different hues people this book. All of them revolve around the protagonist and depend upon him for their existence in the text. They are drawn from his personal as well as professional life, which often, merge with each other.

The narrative progresses through different modes. Life provides the impetus for cinema; characters from real-life become characters in a film script for a while and then again come out of the script to lead their own lives without the intrusions of a scriptwriter. The story progresses through conversations, observations and introspection.

It begins with a relationship on the verge of ending and then goes back to trace its beginning. The subplots are predominantly tales of love. Yet they become intrinsically related to the main premise. Some stories die midway; others are concluded or left hanging in the air. Yet they find fruition in the final denouement.

As each part progresses, the complexities increase. The text graduates to become a film script with the characters from the plot becoming characters of a fiction film.

Life becomes topsy-turvy in a bizarre turn of events, leading to a spine- chilling climax, so horrific in its excesses that revulsion is the dominant emotion at play.

In short, this novel aspires to paint the imperfect picture of the times we live and die in, often unnoticed.

Acknowledgements

I am grateful to many friends, well-wishers and family members who make my work possible through their unflinching love and support.

First my mother Deepa Chatterjee, my sister Smita Kumar, my brother-in-law Sandeep Kumar and my niece Sambhavi Prakash who keep on illuminating me even in the darkest hours.

Special thanks are due to those who helped create the book in its present form and to those whose insights made the material possible. Ranjit Maity for his zealous spirit in the early years of the book and Deiptimaan Chowdhury for giving it the final shape and constantly cajoling me to format and print the book. Thanks are due to Vishal Pawar for formatting the cover and typeface of the cover. I thank Myra Goswami, Ratnomanjulika Mukhoty and Barnali Roy for their opinions and support.

My thanks are also due to those many real-life people whose lives are sucked into the narrative (names, sex and situations changed). If they didn't do what they did, I could not have written this novel.

Finally, to my departed father Shrish Chandra Chatterjee who always wanted his son to become an author and film director, right from my childhood years. Thanks for allowing me to choose my path.

NOTE OF WARNING

This is a work of fiction. Do not seek any resemblance.

If you do, you just might find some

A Nowhere Man—fault lines of love

CONTENTS

12

'THERE IS SOME SOUL OF GOODNESS IN THINGS EVIL

WOULD MEN OBSERVANTLY DISTIL IT OUT"

------------- HENRY V.

SHAKESPEARE

PART ONE

IMPURE HATE

"THE HELL WITHIN HIM; FOR WITHIN HIM HELL

HE BRINGS, AND ROUND ABOUT HIM ..."

-------- PARADISE LOST.

MILTON.

PART - I

CHAPTER 1

The beginning was all-important. The revelation of the first few images were far more important than the plot, that was to follow. For him, the plot seemed pedestrian now. The plot was a mere construct; but images that flew unhindered did not need a circumstance. Their sheer shimmer arose like vapour from the heart. The premise followed that perfect beginning. From then onwards, it was a roller coaster ride. Words flew like darts on the keypad in a maddening frenzy to create the *mise-en-scene*.

A complete and absolute hatred for life, since it failed to offer a perfect beginning, over-powered him. After brooding for a while, he dropped the cigarette, instead of the tension fraught column of ash growing ahead of the fire. Wondering whether to extend the immobility or take a few brisk steps ahead to readjust to the narrative of life, he finally opened the window.

The immediacy of traffic noise below and the reflection of those moving lights on his glasses brought him back to his world of image and sound.

The computer screen blinked in the hues of midnight blue, luminous and wordless in the silent room. The table lamp reflected his face on the dark screen. His face cupped in his left hand. He lit another cigarette and on seeing the glow of the fire on the screen, wondered in which film they used this image.

The very thought was revolting. Even a moment of my solitude when I want to ideate hatred is not original. It has already happened in some film. Even this moment, when nothing happens in my life's story, is perfect. It is tainted by the repetition of an image borrowed from some film. Fuck it!

Then, with a wry smile and gentle indignation, he typed the words on the keyboard. Unprintable words, four letters, four foul letters. The indignation grew to become not so gentle when he remembered her. She could make my life's story possible, but now, this very moment, she is making it out with someone else. Fuck her!

With the predictable motions of a ritual, he opened the cupboard and brought out the bottle of whiskey - with hate suspended in the heart, without a perfect beginning yet.

CHAPTER 2

It was a wonderfully silent morning. His eyes opened, and the head turned right to look at the clock. The clock was smiling at ten. But there was no sound. Where has it disappeared from the universe?

Abandoning the thought, he stepped into the washroom. The paste on the brush, he concentrated on the brushing exercise. He hated stink in the mouth. That was why he was averse to kissing alien mouths. He loved teeth, as all erotic thoughts always began with a set of sparkling teeth. After pushing the toothbrush into the mouth and making a few vigorous moves, he felt alarmed. Except for the internal rhythm, there was no sound. The teeth clattered, and the jaws vibrated in perfect harmony. But there was no other sound. He pulled back the toothbrush and examined it carefully. It seemed impossible that he could have turned deaf in sleep. What then was preventing the toothbrush from sounding its normal self?

He looked at the mirror and examined the face carefully. He looked intently at himself and the then started laughing a silent laugh. His hands went up to the ears and pulled out the thick wads of cotton wool that he had inserted as earplugs, in states of inebriation, before he fell asleep.

As soon as he pulled the cotton wool out, the hangover started catching on. It filled him with the normalcy of noise - the water gurgling in the basin, the clock ticking, the air-conditioner burring, the heart-thumping, pit a pat. He felt relieved being yet alive and continued brushing noisily.

Albeit unwillingly, he also realized the trickery of goading himself to believe that sound has evaporated in this delusion. Was it to overcome his sense of guilt of being a silly cow and drinking like a pig, as usual, the night before? He wondered whether he was losing his sanity or this was a prank he was playing with himself.

Just then the telephone rang. He washed the mouth and, with the towel in hand, picked up the receiver. It was she. He used the drooling a hello, technique.

-- It's me, she said.

-- Yeah

-- Good Morning

- Mornin, mornin ... he drawled as he fetched a cigarette and lit it. He took the cordless down to the reclining chair.

-- What were you doing? She meekly enquired

-- Nothin in particular ... jerking' off. Every morning I get a hard-on that needs jerkin' off!

There was a studied silence at the other end.

He pulled up the legs on the chair. Suddenly he realized being only in undies.

-- You know what a fucking faithful soul I am when in love. All I can do is just jerk off.

-- Do you have to use swear words? You know very well that they don't suit you.

- I do it for shock value; to jerk off the middle-class morality you're loaded with.

-- I am middle-class ... how are you placed today?

-- Why?

-- No, I thought might be I could come over . . . for the script you know.

-- I don't want to meet you ... he got up from the chair and walked to the kitchen, filled water in a tumbler and lit the gas stove.

-- Oh . . . what are you doing?

-- Sitting on the potty and shitting.

He snarled noiselessly and broke into a vicious soundless smile.

-- I guess I'll hang up now.

-- Nay, Nay don't, just making tea . . . he put a spoonful of tea leaves on to the boiling hot water.

-- What's the point? You don't want to meet me.

-- You know damn fuckin well how desperately I want to . . . he poured the tea into the mug.

-- Well then, what time?

-- Now, this very instant... he sipped the tea.

-- That's not possible. I'll come around by twelve.

-- Why not ... I can reach you right away . . . Do you want to bet?

-- Leave the bets till I come ... cherry, cherry and she hung up.

Cherry my foot! He gulped the tea down. All I am left with is hate, and no beginning yet.

CHAPTER 3

Down below, the nineteen storied edifice was Abel's Inn, his favourite brunching place - very English and laid back; one of the very few places that served tonic with your gin. Gin makes men go impotent. Ah who cares, he thought, rather be impotent than give up the pleasure of gin in the sun. Anyway, potency was not of much use anymore.

As he downed the second drink, she walked in. She was still not very comfortable with the drinking bit.

-- Now you're drinking in the afternoon.

-- Just as I thought. I bet that this would be your opening line. Now that I have won my bet, I'll have one more.

-- It's not hilarious you know ... she said as she sat down.

-- Hilarious, my seams are bursting with laughter. What will you have?

-- A cola ... what were you writing? It drew her attention to the piece of scribbled paper on the table.

-- Nothing, nothing in particular. He picked up the scribbling and crumpled it in the left palm.

She extended her hand and opened his palm. She seized the piece of crumpled paper and read it. He ordered drinks and food.

-- You know you should write poetry . . . she said as she carefully put the paper inside her purse.

-- T S Eliot is not conducive to Bollywood cinema, madam . . . he laughed, lighting a cigarette.

-- Then maybe a novel, you have a way with words ... she sipped her cola.

-- Oh. you mean those quaint Indo-Anglican monstrosities with nostalgia dipped in *chutneys*, flavoured with *jalebis*, *samosas*, and pickles. Those lost lanes of Innocence, the Indian pastorals set in Kolkata or the sidewalks of Byculla or the backwaters of Kerala. Garrulous aunts and queer uncles, peopling your childhood. Those meandering lanes littered with poverty, through which you travel, to find your sublime address. The wafts of *ragas* and the rhythms of *talas* or more simply put, "third world esoteric *tadka* "for which the Brits may eventually crown you with a colonial award. A patronizing pat on the back! Sorry madam, I was bred on Browning, Joyce, and Shakespeare ... he gulped the drink with vindictive glee. I have no patience for such indulgences.

-- You say all this to show off and shock me. You seem to forget that not very long ago, in an inebriated state, you were eulogizing Rushdie, Roy, Ghosh, and Seth for their rapier-sharp sparkling prose and mastery over plot construction. I'm not as literate as you. But I've read some recent writings, and I know you've read most of them. A couple of them are quite nice ... she said affirmatively, biting on to her sandwich.

Oh, then I guess you mean the rooster lit brigade. They are to be found in bookstores at airport terminals. I refuse to touch such stuff. One dolt hit the jackpot and immediately a slew of the IITians and the business school brigade tried their hands at fiction writing with vapid outpourings of childish, churlish stories that reflect their schoolboyish effervescence. They are all so déclassé and written with the sole purpose of selling the film rights to Bollywood producers. Shee'h!! I'll never write such toady stuff even in my dreams. He finished with a flourish and deliberately clapped loudly to startle all those around them. Like any powerless potentate, this man thirsted for attention all the time.

-- You can be so nasty ... you seem to revel in nastiness ... Aasma wiped her lips with the napkin.

-- All great men were bitches . . . he asserted, fiddling with an unlit cigarette ... Pope, Wilde, Shaw.

-- So why don't you write a novel that stands out, from the others you run down, with devilish delight.

-- Coz I don't have any novel ideas ... he grimaced and reclined on the chair ... moreover, we have not found the perfect beginning for our script as yet.

-- You're content writing film scripts and making inane films ... you could be sooo good as a novelist ... as she said this, her eyes glowed with concealed pride . . . your sense of detail, your dialogues. Though much of the verse you recite go much above my head, I find it thrilling, almost like a piano recital.

I could be so good at so many other things dear. Only then so many poor fellas would run out of business ... he said smugly ... so I am content doing nothing ... that's conceit for you. Deep down inside he knew an essential vacuity was preventing him from creating any work of substance.

He laughed a short laugh and looked at her intently. Besides, your opinion does not matter ... you idolize me; therefore, you think such ... he shrugged. You cannot even dream of being my muse. Correct, she snapped back. Now shall we try and get back to look for a beginning?

A Nowhere Man—fault lines of love

21

CHAPTER 4

Observing her sitting before the computer with an anticipatory what next on her face, he was seized with an absolute desire to hug and kiss her.

In the period he was stalking the prey, it was easier. He could just turn around and say with great aplomb ... I yisse you. When her nose curled up in question, he would explain, yissing means hating. Whenever I get worked up, I say that to people. And each time he used to chuckle inside. She had not known the meaning of yisse. How could she, poor soul? She had not yet come across "The Superior Person's Little Book of Words." There, yisse meant to desire. Now that she was initiated, that trick would work no longer. Whenever he used a remote word, she would pick up the book.

All he could do was grunt and hiss. Her eyebrows arched; she assumed a position of fervent expectancy.

- Okay, Okay, I'm about to begin, so don't look at me like that. He repositioned himself above the table, took out the glasses and perched them in the left palm, resting it on the temple. How the hell can I look for a beginning when I'm burdened with the thought of making love? He jumped down from the table and rushed towards her. Coming near, he put both the hands on her shoulders. The muscles hardened on the edges of her shoulder. He immediately withdrew his hands.

-- All I do is touch you and you retract as if you're about to be raped.... he turned and began hitting at the table with clenched fists, as the jaws hardened.

She jumped up in a start, rushed and held his hands.

-- I never mind you holding me, please believe me ... she looked intently into his eyes . . . and stop pretending to be an SRK duplicate . . . . you never like him anyway.

-- Aasma, you love me? He placed his left hand gently on her shoulder again.

Aasma smiled and nodded in assent.

-- Be a little patient with me ... whenever there is this block, I get all worked up. For the last four days, we simply don't seem to find a beginning point. It's the first time such a thing has happened to me.

--- How about starting from the middle ... she asked innocuously? I mean, if that is all right.

-- Bright idea ... he lifted the head and walked away ... but

I'm afraid, won't work. I have a classical disposition, you know. The first image is the most important.
-- How about starting the story first and then set about creating the scenes ... she placed her left thumb on her lower lip.
No, No, I never begin with a story ... he kept on nodding vigorously... first the image and then ... suddenly he turned around and looked at her. He went close to her and kissed her lower lip cursorily.
-- How about beginning with a kiss?
She took a few steps back. She understood the signal. It was time to begin.
-- The kiss of the spider woman ... he hissed pacing up and down the room ... a kiss before death finally takes over ... he closed the eyes and moved around as if in a trance ... a woman kissing a dying man ... and then fire in her eyes, as she rises majestically. Fires burning all around ... a landscape devastated by violence ... the lonely woman walks through the wasteland as a gush of wind blows her hair... the illuminated cityscape shimmers in the background . . . the timpani rises ... a flash of fire ... write Aasma write ... we have found a beginning.
He rushed to the music system and shoved in a CD, and switched it on. It was Tchaikovsky's Symphony No 4. He switched on all the fans around to full speed. The chiffon and *tassar* curtains flew all over the place. The scene looked like a typical Sanjay Leela Bhansali film.
As he waltzed around the room, Aasma worked busily at the keyboards and words began marching across the screen. Ta ra rum pa ra rum ta ra rum pa ra rum ...

SCENE 1
A dark screen.
Music with a sense of foreboding.
The scene fades in.
A woman in her early thirties wearing a white saree with a red border, her hair open, holds a man in her hands. The man's face is in silhouette. The woman looks into the man's eyes.
Woman: You cannot leave me like this? I have no one else.
Man: My time's up. . . I have to respond to the call of the beyond....
Woman: I am left with death and destruction all around me ... what do you leave for me?

Man: Hope for the future. Another life, another chance, and a kiss before dying in your arms!

The Man lifts his face and kisses the woman, sobbing silently. Then he falls back in her arms--dead.

The woman looks at him for a while and then gently places his body on the ground. With great effort, she lifts herself and walks majestically across the dark stretch with burning pyres strewn across ... the sound of distant cries and whimpers of wolves. The cityscape shimmers in the background. A strong gush of wind brushes the woman's face and dishevels her hair. The woman gradually becomes a tiny spectre in a landscape of fire.

The Opening Titles

The music reaches a crescendo as the titles come to an end.

In a dark room, a woman suddenly gets up and gasps for breath. She is the same woman seen before.

A bright flash of lightning.

-- Well how was it? He contentedly bit into a bar of chocolate.

Aasma lifted her fingers from the keyboard and heaved a sigh of relief.

-- Trust you to come up with something so melodramatic . . . she swivelled around in the revolving chair.

-- The ordinary does not interest or impress me . . . he kept munching.

-- Well what next? Is this a dream?

He lifted both his arms in the air.

-- I don't know, I don't know.

Aasma quietly walked up and held his hand.

You know, I love you for this. You're terrific!

He winced within. This was the corniest thing he had ever written. He was sure of it.

I know I am. He said it smugly and lit a cigarette. And yet you love a bank clerk more than me.

CHAPTER 5

Now being convinced about a beginning, he began concentrating on the plot and character. Whenever at a loss, in trying to find meaning and substance in his work, he would allow perverse logic to take over with its accompanying grandiloquence and earn him brownies merely by babbling horseshit. Then he would begin his bathetic act of striking belligerent poses. Yet he would get critical acclaim for the same perverse logic he espoused in the garb of post-modernist art in a post-structural universe. His theatrics would always find admirers and lackeys to keep his ego satisfied with such a lie.

Popular Cinema always need popular idioms or clichés to make itself palpable to people. Why, he thought, was there the bloody need to explain everything? In difficult times, you need complex structures to create a truly satisfying work of art. Does communication become difficult when you use metaphors and metonyms rather than similes? Why are the common people such blithering idiots?

Conveniently the man chose not to allow the realization to dawn, that he too was becoming an idiot in his pursuit, to impress a vulnerable and impressionable mind.

--If they were not such idiots my dear, how on earth could you retain the supreme satisfaction of being a superior person ... his friend Soumitro Sanyal indulgently sipped his martini as he spoke.

They were at the club. Every Thursday, when he was in town and not out for a shoot, they would sit there in the evenings.

-- But that is at odds with my need to reach out.

--Precisely. You try too hard. You should just give up and relax ... there was a wicked smile on Soumitro's face.

-- It's easy for you, lording over your idleness. I need to do something constantly. Create, make things happen, ideate.

--Then don't waste your breath and ideate hatred. You do it so beautifully. It is simply so divine to hate everything, everybody ... saying this Soumitro lit his cigar.

-- If you feel so, why don't you kill yourself? That is better than such all-pervasive hate ... he stood up, with the drink in hand. I don't hate everything and everybody.

-- Simple . . . . Soumitro gulped the contents of his glass . . . very simply I hate death. That's why I can't kill myself. And you feel so much an inferior person while committing suicide. That goes against my grain.

--Such find grain you have . . . saying this, he burped loudly. Soumitro looked at him with a frown and hollered.

--Boy, were you brought up in a barn?

To this, both of them laughed. This was a joke they shared since their school days. They subjected anyone displaying a lack of Victorian manners or etiquette to this indictment. Both of them had not quite got out of their school-boyish obsession with vicious glee. The pleasure one derives from pricking frogs with pins in biology practical classes in high school. Soumitro had once poured concentrated hydrochloric acid on a lady teacher's bum during chemistry practical. As the lady writhed in agony and shame for the hole in her saree, Soumitro cackled. He had been suspended for a week from school.

-- Food and booze are two things worth living for boyo . . . saying this Soumitro attacked his steak. This is how I like my steak to be ... rare... with blood oozing. Indians fry their steaks.

-- And what about sex? He enquired as he munched his well-made steak . . . having sex is no fun? I thought you were obsessed with sex too.

-- Egad sex is never to be had. Inferior people have sex. Soumitro wiped his mouth with the napkin. Superior people relish talking and thinking about sex. Whenever I have sex with someone, my interest in that person dies.

-- I'm afraid I can't say the same thing . . . he sipped the wine to wash the meat down.

-- Yeah, you and your romantic aberrations ... don't you get tired of trying? You try to do everything from your misplaced notions of the ideal. And no such notion exists today. Everything is but a shadow, all relations a spectacle...... the smile gradually evaporated from Soumitro's lips as he spoke.

He got up as if in a trance from the table and walked towards the bar. There were not too many people in the dining room. Usually, on Thursdays, the club was quiet and unpeopled. He sat on the stool and swirled around.

-- You'll never know, you'll never know ... the power, the beauty and the glory of being in love.

--- For the nth time? Why are you deluding yourself...? Soumitro blew a few rings of smoke in the air.

He jumped off the stool and rushed near Soumitro with boyish delight.

-- I still believe in magic. When I look into her eyes ... the shimmering innocence . . . O coz, coz, coz, I am fathom's deep in love ... saying this he plunked on the chair.
-- I must get my shoulders padded again .... Soumitro smirked.
-- What for pray? He stooped ahead.
-- To ready it for your head and tears when she also leaves you.
To this, both of them laughed again.

CHAPTER 6

How could he tell her she was meant to be loved, because she was born? Or that it was because she smiled in a particular manner when she tossed her hair back. She would often wonder why he of all the people in the world, someone who was so special for her, could fall for her, of all the people in the world. She was too preoccupied in assuming a position of mediocrity. When he unravelled her extra-ordinariness, she was uncomfortable, at odds with herself.

There was a certain something that separated her from the rest of the world. Any attempt at a definition would spoil the mystique of her uniqueness. He was otherwise so logical, so argumentative. That was why she expected explanations and when he failed to do so, thought it to be his infatuation, which might pass. Perhaps this scared her. What if he ceased to look at me one day like this? What if he finds out the real me? For all her knowledge, she could not see the real her and therefore she was afraid. The reality in her was there for him alone to see and cherish and set apart from all the other loves. Or so he thought, with his grandiose notions.

All he could do was to offer a meek explanation. You inspire me, you see. This was never satisfactory for her. In which way, she would ask and repartee matter-of-fact, I virtually do a stenographer's job. And again, he would try to convince her how vitally she contributed to work. Without your suggestions, I could never get a frame of reference. This she would dismiss with as if you would not have done all this if I had not come into your life. Yeah, maybe in a very different manner. This would go on till he had to shut her up. One day he thought of a brilliant line – would a blind Milton be ever able to write a Paradise Lost without a stenographer? So even a stenographer has good use ... ha, ha ... checkmate! He relished at this ability to have the last word and laugh.

At other times, he would pretend to get offended and wear a martyred expression.

That's what you think of me, trying to seduce you like those typical film folks? I won't even touch you. Saying this he would march to one corner of the room like a petulant child. Then she would smile naughtily, walk up to him and place her hands on his shoulder. . .. you won't touch me? You're tired of me, bored with me. So many beautiful women want to be touched by you. Look, I told you, I'm not

worth it. She would use the words to tease him.
He would turn to look at her with tears brimming in his eyes. She would get unnerved. Hey? What's the matter with you? Why are you doing this? She was not yet, well versed in this theatre of the absurd.
I wish I could explain. And he would draw her to the mirror. Look at yourself and look at my eyes. Isn't this true? Isn't this true? She would just close her eyes and shiver in silent thought.
O Aasma ... O Aasma was all that he could say and sigh.
He could never dare to pronounce the truth... the great pretender he.

CHAPTER 7

His office was a precise arrangement of chaos; almost a metaphor of his mind. The outer chamber was a normal reception, neatly arranged by his secretary. But it was inside where all the fun happened.

All sitting arrangements were on the floor, beanbags and rugs were strewn across. A few wooden steps with a flight of three or four steps on which were heaped cushions, files, the laptop and an assortment of ashtrays. Across the floor were stacks of shooting-stills, typed scripts, and teacups.

Once Kalpana, his secretary had taken the initiative, garnered enough courage and stepped in to set everything to order. He barked at her. Please leave me in my disordered world - the outside is yours; there I don't interfere. Leave me in my domain. Get thee to a nunnery! He exclaimed, and she withdrew. Kalpana was a plain-looking quiet girl, a self-evasive soul who never interfered or intruded. She just did her job and never gave him a cause to complain about any spelling errors. He hated spelling mistakes.

She was a trifle confused about his expletives as she never understood their frames of reference. Otherwise, his oddities did not bother her. Unlike her previous employer, he had never made a pass at her. With him, she felt safe. He was almost paternal with her, always enquiring after her needs. Even when he scolded her, on occasions when she was late in getting what he wanted, there would be a tone of informality. It touched her when he said, "take care, child". She was an orphan, living alone in a hostel. However, there was no sentimental effusiveness in their relation. It was a matter of fact. Though, he wondered occasionally whether she had a lover.

The paternal was the dominant character trait in his personality. With associates, assistants and sundry members of the coterie, he was always assuming positions of fatherhood. Though hardly a few years their senior, he loved playing the role. Giving sage advice, getting concerned about their problems, often taking on responsibilities, he would find difficult to shoulder later. Although they liked this quaint caring, they would occasionally smirk behind his back and find these grandiose notions, comical. Behind his back, they would make fun of him, much to the delight of enemies. He had more than a fair share of enemies, of people who hated and loaded this man with bullshit.

He realized all this but eventually did not care.

Walking into the office, he saw Kalpana neatly arranging sunflowers at her desk. She smiled at him and said the routine good afternoon.

-- Any message or telephone calls Kalpana ... he kept the car keys at her desk.

-- No sir, Oh, yes sir ... Kalpana stuttered. She had a stammering problem.

-- Make up your mind child ... he whisked through the mail on her table.

-- Actually, yes Sir ... Mr. Ve-Vensimal called up ... asked you to ca-call.

-- Oh, the frog .... Yeah, I'll call him ... where are the twins today?

-- Oh they . . . they've not come in as ye-yet Sir.

He stepped across her table and entered the room, lit a cigarette and plunked himself on a beanbag. He took the phone and dialled a number. Kalpana peeped through the door.

-- Ch...chai Sir?

-- You want to kill me Kalpana, with that horrid stew of a tea . . . he mumbled with the cigarette dangling between the lips.

- N . . . No Sir, I've arranged to make t . . . tea here, from t . . . today . . . Kalpana smiled sheepishly.

-- Such a darling . . . that's precisely why I love you so child . . . he took the cigarette in the left hand . . . Ah, hello, Mr. Vensimal what are your latest TRPs? Do we make it or break it?

Just then Dabloo stormed into the room and swished his hair across his baldpate. As he concluded the conversation, Dabloo paced up and down the room in fervent animation. As soon as he disconnected, Dabloo glided and sat in front.

-- Would you believe it, I composed this tune in my dream . . . saying this, Dabloo rushed to the corner of the room, picked up the guitar and started humming. He closed the eyes and allowed the melody to float in. Dilip, the peon, quietly tiptoed into the room, placed two cups of tea and stepped out.

-- What do you think? Dabloo asked agitatedly as he stroked his head.

-- Well I think it's a whole lot of bullshit ... no, no more like cow dung, all greasy and slimy . . . he smiled mischievously. Dabloo looked at him for a while and then silently formed a swear word suggesting fornication on his lips and placed the guitar aside. Then he moved forward and took a cigarette from the packet lying there and lit it.

-- It's like throwing pearls before the swine. I never know why I make you hear my compositions . . . Dabloo got up and started pacing up and down the room.

-- Becoz I'm your only hope of redemption ... he smiled smugly and pulled a pillow.

-- Bastard . . . Dabloo snarled and pulled his hair to cover his baldpate ... hey, will you be serious and tell me whether we retain this melody?

He could not control laughter at Dabloo's pathetic condition. Dabloo always got worked up over trivialities. The mad hatter music genius, he thought affectionately, has again come up with a gem. He loved being patronizing you remember.

-- Yeah . . . I guess it's kind of nice . . . he smiled almost reluctantly.

Dabloo broke into a wide grin and patted him vigorously on the back.

-- I knew you would like it. Any person with good taste is bound to like it. Now don't play tricks anymore. Just rearing to do some good stuff. Television bores me... Dabloo drank the tea in one gulp.

-- You bet ... he yawned . . . there will come a time, said Andy Warhol, when celebrity hood would last for only fifteen minutes. We've almost reached that stage. Only now it's twenty-three and a half minutes or an episode of a web series. Want some lunch? He rang the bell.

-- Sure, sure . . . Dabloo jumped up again.

Dilip entered the room and he ordered lunch for the two of them.

Yet we have to live, not for celebrityhood but to create works of lasting value . . . Dabloo started stroking his beard again.

-- Don't delude yourself with such notions ... he started playing with a paperweight . . . we have no immortality left for us. We work because we live. Others manufacture cosmetics or weapons; we manufacture dreams and melodies. Each to his delight!

Dabloo vehemently nodded his head and swished his falling hair from his half haired head.

-- I cannot agree ... Dabloo picked up a cushion and squatted on a rug . . . without a desire for immortality, there is no

impetus to create anything worthwhile.
-- Are you an amateur that you need an impetus? He chided
Dabloo . . . It becomes like mathematics after a while ... there
are set theorems and rules, through the standard application
of which you ......
-- And what about the soul? Dabloo butted in . . . don't you
need to invest your soul? I know you say all this just for
effect's sake. All your work is loaded with sentiment -
emotional outbursts of anguished souls.
-- My only interest is in the development of the soul. Little else
is of worth study . . . he said this with his nose in the air.
Ah! Ah! Ah! I caught you there . . . Dabloo jumped with a
wide grin . . . that is Browning. What's happening to your
script?
He smarted within, having lost this round.
It's getting written. You know very well writing is not as
simple as composing a little ditty.
He had to win the brownie points for the day.
-- There we go again. Dabloo grimaced.
Just then, Dilip brought in lunch.

CHAPTER 8

What is life but a process of waiting?

He shuddered at the thought of having fathered this pious platitude. It seemed so utterly trite, so incongruous with his veneer. Yet could he deny that truth sometimes manifests itself in such sentimental piety? He hated to think mediocre thoughts - or rather thoughts thought by mediocre people. Throughout the growing-up years with great effort, he tried to break free from anything and everything mediocre, or what is commonly cliched as middle- class moralities. For him, life was all about taking stances and striking poses. Vanity tainted him from childhood. He had always been the monitor in class.

Why do I need to try to attempt to shake off this mantle? Perhaps this is the real me, he thought and broke into a cold sweat. The day that becomes true, I shall cease to live.

Yet he was alive and contemplating on the fact that life is a process of waiting.

Waiting for most of the things that seldom or never happened; waiting for values, beliefs, dreams, aspirations all to become true - palpable, within grasp. Waiting for the spirit to awaken and become perfection; waiting for the soul to blossom and encounter its maker; waiting for love to become reality. The only awaiting that had the certainty of a reward was death. But that was far away.

He hated waiting but was left with no alternative. He had deliberately avoided an electronic clock in the room, only to hear the ticking of the mechanical one. With each tick, the history of life seemed to progress. The history of waiting for a Godot who might not even turn up. Was she becoming his Godot?

When you wait for someone, time becomes dual. On the temporal level it progresses forward, brushing each past second into time past. On the other hand, time becomes a static circle, within which you keep on rotating, in an eternal time present.

Aasma had this wonderful habit of never, ever being punctual. Eventually, when she would come, for an observer the scene would be comical.

He would sit with a sardonic expression, looking preoccupied reading a book or listening to music, paying her scant attention. She would nimbly come and sit beside him and look at him like a lost hart confronting a tiger. After a prolonged moment of silence, she would gently extend her palm and ask what the matter was, gulping each word. He would look up oh so casually and give a curt reply . . . nothing, why on earth should anything happen to me? Then Aasma would walk up to the laptop table and press her fingers on the keyboard and enquire, shall we start? Forget it, he would say and light a cigarette. You don't like my presence, she would say with hurt in her voice, should I leave? And he would snap back, yeah leave, leave like the rest of them. To this she would retort, what did I do, and he would say nothing . . . nothing really. . . only you fucked up my evening. Her eyes would droop and she would whisper, sorry, I am not worthy. And he would rush to her, hold her by the shoulder and shake her, I've told you a thousand times, love means never having to say that you are sorry. Saying this, he would hug her and she would submit herself. The love for such kitsch as love means ... always stood him in good stead in moments such as these.

What must she be doing, he wondered? Sitting with her bank clerk at some sleazy joint drinking tea and talking about things that the stupid oaf could never relate to. All Minal needed was the reassurance that she loved him. Or else he would get all worked up and stage an exit. She would run after him like a puppy dog and try to patch up on a crowded road with millions of passers-by piercing them with their stares. After making up, each would board their respective buses - the bank clerk homewards and she towards the Master's house.

Tonight, when she entered his flat, there was a twinkle in her eyes. She kept her purse and rushed forward.

-- There was a massive traffic jam, that's why I got held up, believe me. But there's great news.

-- Really . . . he looked at her in disbelief ... give me something more original.

-- I can stay over tonight . . . she smiled . . . told my folks that I'm staying over at Neelima's . . . we can work on the script right through the night.

-- You mean that stupid friend of yours with a theatrical father . . . his face contorted.

-- Yes, stupid people get along with stupid friends ... Aasma had learned by now to retort.

-- I never said you were stupid ... he tried to make amends.

-- You need not keep on reminding me I'm ordinary ... Aasma

had picked the cue . . . only you are the one who keeps on talking about my imaginary extraordinariness. I'm a simple person who likes to treat life on simple terms. You've known from the very beginning that I'm such . . . Aasma gasped as she said the last words.

He suddenly felt something growing inside the loins. Immediately he got up and switched on the air conditioner. Then he went to the cupboard, opened it and brought out a bottle of whiskey. Indulgently, he looked back at her and raised the left eyebrow.

-- You want a drink? He enquired, pouring a large drink.

-- You know very well how much I hate your drinking . . . she bit her lower lip as she spoke . . . yet you do it every day despite my . . . okay, pour me a drink.

Though wincing within, he was filled with a sense of delight. If she had a drink, she would be more malleable. He took special care and served her in a nice velvety crystal. Both of them tinkled their glasses and downed the drinks at one go. He poured another round. This too, Aasma had bottoms up and her visage contorted. He drank with the leisure of a veteran.

-- Shall we begin? There was a tinge of fire in her voice.

-- Begin what? He grinned innocuously.

-- I trust you, so don't come near . . . now there was a fire in her eyes as she swallowed her third.

-- I shall remain afar; far away from you forever . . . he hummed, pouring another.

She came close to him and put her arms around the waist as he looked out of the window at the cityscape.

-- Don't do this to me ... he said in a mild voice.

-- What have I done to you? She placed her head on his shoulder.

He cupped her face with the left hand, still looking away.

Why didn't I meet you earlier? Why didn't I meet you before you met him?

Why weren't you born earlier? His voice was mellow.

Drama! Drama!! The thespian in him started playing up.

She placed her finger on his lips.

-- But eventually, we met . . . the rest is unimportant for me . . . she kissed his left earlobe.

His body shivered as the head went up and eyes closed. The right hand clung on to the hanging thread of the Venetian blind.

-- O Aasma . . . my dream sharer . . . his eyes opened, turned and looked deeply into her eyes . . . how can I dream of further dreams without you?
-- But I am there with you, I am there for you ... saying this, she kissed his right eyelid.
-- With the break of dawn, you'll go away, depart as a dream . . . he closed the eyes again.
She turned her face away, unable to say anything. He placed the right hand on her shoulder.
-- I don't blame you, I walked into this fully aware of everything ... he sighed . . . I shouldn't have allowed this to happen.
-- It was beyond you or me to prevent this from happening. Destiny had it in store for us... she held his hand on her shoulder . . . didn't you say that the now was important? I'm here now, with you and for you.
-- You always win over with your commonplace logic . . . he smiled . . . what about our future?
Aasma placed her index finger on his lips.
-- That'll also become time present soon. I don't like complications. I am with you. I don't want to think of anything else.
She embraced and kissed him on the lips, warmly holding on to them. Her luscious lips melted in the mouth as he explored with the tongue. He felt every single tooth in her mouth, entwined the tongue with hers, left it to explore her gums, and brought it down into the cavity of her mouth sucked the air from her mouth by sealing her mouth with parted lips. Then his hands moved down from the shoulders, over the limbs, bent at right angles and caressed her breasts, encircled the nipples with two fingers on each side. Her hands moved over his chest, glided down to the trousers and stroked the genitals from outside.
 He was on fire. His hands swiftly came down to her navel and then turned and slipped beneath her skirt. Aasma quickly pulled her hand and held his hands tightly below her skirt, preventing it from moving.
-- Not now, not now ... she whispered ... what's the hurry?
He deftly pulled the hands out of the skirt and retracted. He turned away from her, went to the desk, picked up a cigarette and lit it. Aasma rushed towards him.
-- What's the matter? She embraced him tightly.
He opened her embrace, went and sat on the rocking chair.

-- Nothing ... you don't have to remind me time and again that you don't want to make love to me . . . he took a few quick puffs . . . I didn't take the first step.

He fixed himself another drink, pouring one for her too and extended her glass.

-- Who says I don't want to? She sipped her drink . . . I only said not now.

Let's not get into an argument, Aasma . . . he gulped the drink in one shot . . . shall we start work?

This was an excuse to impress her further with his nonsense. The woman had been dreaming. She wakes up beside her husband in the darkroom. As she switches on the table lamp, her husband's face is seen. It was not that of the dying man. Who then was this man?

SCENE 2

The darkness of the room.

The woman quietly gets up and goes near the windows and draws open the curtains.

In the blue spectre of moonlight falling on her face, beads of perspiration can be seen on the woman's forehead. She holds her chin with her left hand for a while and stares outside.

Suddenly she moves back to the other side of the bed. A man is lying on this side of the bed with his face angularly placed on the pillow. The woman comes near the bed and switches on the bedside lamp. The sleeping man's face is discernible in the light. The woman sits beside the bed and looks intently at the man's face and mumbles softly.

Woman: It's not you . . . it's not you.

The man's eyes open and he stares at her blankly for a while. Then he jerks his head and gets up.

Man: What's the matter with you? Aren't you well?

The woman gets up and sits on the bed. She presses her left hand tightly on the man's chest.

Woman: Hug me . . . hug me hard!

A smile breaks across the man's face. He extends his hands and holds her in a tight embrace.

Man: Madwoman! My little mynah! After all these years you've not got out of your girlishness.

The woman rests her head on his chest and closes her eyes.

Woman: I love only you. Only you ....

The man gently caresses her hair.

Man: I know that you do silly. That's why I love you too. Hey,

Shristi now get some sleep. Tomorrow I have a hard day ahead. You too have a shoot remember.
Shristi: No Manjul no! I want you to hug me like this for the rest of my life. I don't need anything else, anyone else.
Manjul lifts Shristi's face and cups it in his hands.
Manjul: What's the matter with you? Can't you come to terms with your happiness? Six years is a long time. You know very well I can never fall for another woman. And you're so hopelessly devoted. I know you'll never fall for someone for the next couple of lives. Now go to bed. Your director might not like to see your face puffed in the morning.
Manjul switches off the bedside lamp and tosses Shristi over to her side of the bed. Then he holds her in a tight embrace. Shristi's eyes glisten in the darkness of the night.

SCENE 3
Morning.
Dining Room.
Breakfast table.
Manjul sits at the head of the table engrossed in reading a newspaper and sipping orange juice. Shristi sits two chairs away, her hair curled in rollers, her left hand extended to the make-up girl who polishes the nails meticulously. With her right hand, Shristi lifts and then bites into a toast. Suddenly her attention is drawn to her nails.
Shristi: Strokes should be more delicate Shirley, more delicate. Or else these hair strand marks appear. Such a bother!
Shirley: Sorry ma'am.
Shristi: Don't be a sorry child, be sensible. I've told you a thousand times to put those false nails on ... but you'll never listen.
Manjul looks up from his newspaper.
Manjul: I forgot to tell you, darling ... this evening we've been invited to Mehra's for dinner.
Shristi: Oh Manjul, but I'm shooting till ten tonight. Be a sweetheart and excuse me.
The maid walks in with the tea tray and places it on the table. Shristi starts making tea. Manjul folds the paper, places it aside and cuts into his omelette.
Manjul: Sri you know the Mehra's ... they're very touchy. Must have invited a dozen others just to show off their filmy connection. Try to make it. We'll leave a little late

maybe.
Shristi extends the cup towards Manjul.
Shristi: That'll be all Shirley ... get the stuff into the car.
Shirley withdraws her hands from Shristi's palms and leaves.
Shristi: If you insist ... I'll pack up at nine-thirty. We'll leave from the studio.   Just pick me up from there.
Manjul: Thanks ... they mean big business to me you know.
Shristi gets up and comes near Manjul.
Shristi: I know, I know ... now give me a pecky, pecky!!!
Shristi extends her right cheek to Manjul and fondles his hair. Manjul kisses her cheek.
Shristi: I have to fly now ... Oh, the scene I'm doing today. You would turn purple with envy.
Manjul: A steamy bed scene with Sanjeev at the most ... aah!
Shristi rushes out of the room with a flourish, waving at Manjul. Manjul sips his tea and mumbles in his mind.
Manjul: At times I feel like calling her a bitch. But I can't ....
She's so damn perfect.
....

 -- These characters have begun speaking like you ... Aasma observed lifting her fingers from the keyboard.
-- You mean I speak such trite stuff? He sniggered.
-- I mean they have the same hoity-toity demeanour. She tapped the tip of her nose with the little finger of her left hand... don't you feel all this demonstration of lovey-doveyness is a bit superficial?
-- Exactly ... he thumped on the windowsill; his trick was almost getting caught, and he had to find a way out ... they are superficial people, caught in a superficial life. This will be the great tragedy of superficiality. This is the trauma of our times ... enmeshed in our trivialities, we relish the thought that our lives are tragedies when we enact a farce. He felt thoroughly satisfied at having come up with this invincible hogwash.
You stretch things too far... she got up from her chair ... always exaggerating little insignificant things.
He leaned dramatically against the windowsill and lit a cigarette.
Insignificant! What do you mean? Is there anything significant left in our lives? Do you mean the love we profess for each other is for real? The last line had to be his.
She looked saved into his eyes. You mean it is not real?
 --Bah! ... He said and turned the eyes away. At least, he had

saved the day.

CHAPTER 9

The Studio was a mad jamboree of hustle, bustle, further noise, glad stares, fetid smiles, people and more people trying to please. He hated every moment of this prostitution.

As the car moved in past the gates, opened by the grinning gatekeeper, he shuddered at the thought of having to spend the next ten hours here. Among fools, magnificent fools, all of whom he had to endure with a grin and the typical display of modesty -- folded palms.

Dilip sprung out of the front seat beside the driver and opened his door at the rear left. Kalpana sneezed, and then looked at him apologetically.

- Sir, I should be back at the office to complete the correspondence ... nervously Kalpana sifted through the papers in the file lying on her lap.

-- Why must you forsake me in this jungle, child? He alighted from the car.

A cluster of people immediately surrounded him. Giving up hope, he waved at Kalpana, and then at the driver, to withdraw. With wanton abandon, he switched on to the act of gracious benefactor, as the chorus grew into a cacophony of buffoons.

--Some coffee for you Sir . . . the forever wanting to please production manager Vipul enquired. --Hey boy, Vipul hollered, run and get special coffee ... remember... without sugar.

The production boy Nanoo sized up Vipul with a stony, authoritative glare.

-- You don't have to remind me about Sir's coffee ... Nanoo said in a quiet voice ... I've already asked for it.

-- Sir how have you been? The young aspiring actress Sheila asked with a lipsticked smile.

He turned to look at her. She was garishly dressed in a shiny green outfit in broad daylight. There was lipstick on her teeth too. Has she chewed the stick, he wondered?

-- You never even think of me ... Sheila complained in a disgusting singsong voice.

-- Why on earth should I think about you?

Sheila blushed purple and crossed her eyebrows.

-- You are never considering me for a role ... I am dying to work with you ... I'll do anything.

-- Anything? He looked at her with arched eyebrows and then turned around.

A group of fidgety young boys walked up to him. Garnering great courage one of them spoke up.
-- Sir!!!
Before they could speak any further, he silenced them.
-- Meet my assistants and leave your photographs . . . he started walking down the garden path followed by a bunch of assorted shapes and sizes led by Vipul.
He stopped by a vanity van and opened the door. Inside the van, a young girl was sitting in front of the make-up mirror and getting made up by a make-up man. This was Rashmi.
-- Hello Sweetness! He smiled mischievously.
It startled Rashmi. Regaining her composure, she smiled and came up near the door.
She craned her neck out and announced...Good Morning . . . I'm almost through, will be there on the sets in ten minutes.
-- Take your time ... I still have a lot to do before we shoot ... he closed the door and walked ahead.
The moment he entered the sets, there was flurried activity all around. The speed of work suddenly seemed to go up. Electricians shouting and running around with lights and wires, the art department people organizing furniture, several people greeting with warm smiles and hands lifted to their heads and him responding with alacrity. Almost in fast motion, he thought, pulling a chair and sitting down. A film set was like a circus. The constant urgency to speed up things to keep the show running baffled him even now.
The assistants whom he affectionately called Pico, Tico or the twins, rushed with the script. Pico handed him over the script. He wiped the glasses with a handkerchief and smiled at them.
-- How are things this morning?
-- Fine, fine ... we should do two scenes today ... both of them piped in unison. He concentrated on the script.
Nanoo brought in his coffee and handed it to over with loving care.
-- Would you like an omelette and toast Sir ... Nanoo whispered conspiratorially? He looked up at Nanoo, smiled gently patted him on the back.
-- Not now ... but do get my cigarettes.
Nanoo sprinted out of the sets like a deer. This chap is so attentive to my needs. What would I do without him?
This thought suddenly reminded him of Aasma. She must be rehearsing at her dance academy. My ballerina dances like a

dream; he fondly remembered and kissed the left thumb silently. When she is dancing, she truly feels liberated. Bereft of thought, only concentrating on energy. The eye of the fish, he always briefed her; Arjuna's *lakshya*, the coveted goal, was only the eye of the fish seen reflected in the water. Become the greatest dancer. You must be nothing but the best.

What can I gift her with? Nothing but a dream in her heart. A dream to reach beyond, become the star shine in a million eyes. He could only nurture and preserve this dream for her. He must prepare her for the passage of flight. When she truly spreads her wings, he would release her like a dove held in warm palms. When she would soar the skies, his spirit would meditate in silent prayer. He would have to let her go one day if his love was true. His heart ached with the thought. He relished the calmness his heart assumed while thinking of her.

-- Hey director where are you lost?

He got out of the reverie and looked up. It was Avinash, the hero of the film. A smile crossed his face.

Avinash pulled a chair and sat beside him.

-- Hi handsome . . . he patted Avinash's shoulder ... Avi, what's the matter with you?

-- Nothing, nothing ... Avinash shrugged his shoulders.

-- I can feel it . . . you are not fully here ... he scratched the forehead ... nowadays you don't respond to that electric moment in a script. I've known you too long enough for comfort.

Avinash hastily lit a cigarette and took a few quick puffs.

-- I guess you're right . . . you know after my sister's death things seem to go haywire . . . Avinash bent his head . . . I can't handle it anymore.

-- Avi, I had known your sister quite well ... he spoke with concern. She was a very strong soul. She would never want you to crumble like this. You were almost like her son. He patted Avinash on the back. Now, boy, you have a special ability to find the right place for the right nuance. You know exactly where to punctuate a script. Please don't let me down.

-- I am trying, I'm trying ... Avinash threw his cigarette and smiled . . . you know, your faith in me sometimes frightens me.

-- Let me share a secret with you . . . he winked ... I'm writing

a new script. A fantastic character I'm working in for you.
- Most unfair of you, you always write the best roles for Avinash . . . Rashmi chirped as she came and stood beside him.-- Don't be greedy Rashmi . . . he scolded her ... in this film, you take the cake. Avi is just a bystander. He is sleepwalking through his role. I've never known him to be so ghastly.
-- Don't give me that sop . . . Rashmi's lips pouted in mock anger . . . after several years of coaxing, I've landed myself with this role. Whereas Avinash has been there in every single film you've made in the last six years.
--   Haven't   you   heard   of   Toshiro   Mifune   and Kurosawa? Avinash haughtily lifted his collar . . . Oh, I almost forgot. You have not been initiated into Japanese cinema. But I'm sure you know the Govinda and David Dhawan Jodi here.
-- Spare the poor soul . . . he gently chided Avinash, as Rashmi looked trifle bewildered . . . Indian actresses are not wont to experience such delicacies.
--I regularly see all the DVDs you recommend . . . Rashmi protested arduously.
Pico, Tico rushed towards the trio and screeched to a halt near Rashmi's toes.
-- We're ready sir .... Pico said in a contralto.
He feigned the arrogance of a decadent monarch, with the nose up in the air and the glasses perched on the bridge.
-- You should have been at the opera... he spoke with a smack of disdain.
--As you say, Sir . . . Pico smiled dutifully as Tico hollered ---
Full Lights!
The circus was about to begin.

CHAPTER 10

Minal was not a bank clerk.

He was an officer with a nationalized bank. What made him poor was the fact that he had to support a large family. He was a lanky young man, rather on the darker side, with tinted spectacles, through which his eyes shone like fish. A mop of hair covered his forehead and bounced as he walked. He had a slight stoop, the shoulders fringed forever. He spoke in a husky voice, elongated each word and always accented the last syllable. Aasma found his voice erotic – Minal always, always sounded as if he had a perpetual cold – the slightly wet manner of speaking.

Why the bloody hell can she never be punctual Minal wondered, as he kept on looking at his watch, time and again standing at the bus stop. Most definitely, she would jump down from the bus gasping for breath and look at him like a lost dove. Today I shall surely give a good piece of mind. And a good piece of his mind was at the present moment, seething with rage. He hated this thing about her. Never would she be on time. As such, they spent so little time together. She would hardly be with him. It would either be her rehearsals or some important writing assignment. Especially nowadays, she was spending most of her time with that accursed blob. He winced at the thought of himself suffering at the crowded bus stop. In all probability, she must be navigating around in that bloke's car, whilst the conceited bastard is gibbering away some outlandish rubbish. He has held her captive with his words.

As she hurriedly got down from the taxi and rushed towards him, Minal started to walk away. Aasma caught up with him, with a few brisk steps.

-- What's the matter with you, I'm only fifteen minutes late . . . you see there were no buses. I had to catch a taxi. . . Aasma panted as she tried to keep up with his steps.

-- Nowadays you always travel by taxi . . . you've moved up in life... Minal looked away from her.

-- Don't be mean . . . she tugged at his shirtsleeve . . . okay, baba I'm sorry.

Suddenly she remembered his grand assertions that love means never having to say that you're sorry. She brushed the thought aside.

-- Sorry, sorry, sorry . . . of course in love you can say sorry a thousand times ... she repeated vehemently.

-- I never said you couldn't say sorry ... Minal snapped back
. . . you should say sorry and feel sorry for what you've been
doing with me.
--   What have I been doing with you? She asked
incredulously.
-- Don't play with me Aasma, don't play . . . Minal hissed ... I
have none of your lofty arty-farty notions. I simply know that
I love you and want to stay with you whenever that becomes
possible for both of us. But now that also seems to be
impossible.
-- Why do you say such harsh things? She snuggled up to
him . . . you know very well how much I want to stay with
you.
-- Don't lie Aasma, in the name of Allah, don't lie ... All that
you want now is your career, - your dance and your writing
and of course your Master, your Ustad, the mother fucking
bastard, the perennial babbler.
Minal crossed the road in a flash. Manoeuvring between
speeding cars and buses, Aasma crossed over. They were in
front of the coffee shop. She tightly clasped his hand.
-- Please don't say such things. Aasma's eyes were moist . . .
don't you want me to be successful? If you don't trust me, I'll
even go behind the purdah, never even come out to face the
world.
As the waiter served coffee, Minal sipped from the cup while
Aasma looked at him with concealed hurt in her eyes. Minal
smiled and kept the cup down.
-- Yeah, I'll put you behind purdah if that would keep you
away from him.
-- What do you have against him? Aasma gently replied . . .
he's my teacher, almost like my father.
-- I never knew that fathers and daughters got to fucking
around ... Minal remarked.
The coffee spilled from Aasma's cup as she banged it down on
the table. She got up from the chair and hastily made her
way through the tables and chairs in the crowded coffee
shop.
A cold whiff of wind brushed past her nose as she stepped
outside. With brisk steps, she jostled through the crowded
pavement. She felt like running, but could not because of the
people all around. People, people everywhere she thought,
how I hate people. I just want to be left alone, absolutely
alone. I don't need anyone – not Minal, not my friends and

certainly not him.
All this trouble for him alone. Why did she have to meet him? Why did she have to perform so well that night? Why did he have to come backstage to congratulate her? Why did he have to put on his charm? Why did she have to be impressed? Why did he have to ask her out for coffee? Why did she have to agree? Why? Why? Why? After all, however crude it may have sounded, Minal was certainly not wrong.
As Minal caught up with her finally and kept apologizing again and again for his behaviour, Aasma resolved never to meet him for the rest of her life.

CHAPTER 11

Soumitro was late. Gulping the second drink, he started worrying. This was yet another negative aspect of his character.

He always worried too much and got worked up. Unnecessarily, his sister would say. She was the only stable factor in his disordered life.

He resented the authority she exercised. Mere slip of a girl, he would think, years my junior. She behaves as if she were my elder, my guardian. Smriti would not simply bother.

Dada, she would chide, stop behaving like a child. And despite the concealed rage, he would nimbly obey. In private moments, he would holler at her, do you know my position? But in public when she chided, he would gently obey. After all, he knew, she was the only one who truly cared.

He fixed a third drink when Soumitro walked in. He looked distraught.

Shit, he thought, has he tried suicide, again?

I wish my parents were away, Soumitro said as he sat down. Such a pain they are, Soumitro gulped down the martini pining for his company.

If, only if wishes were horses, he chimed and held up the glass for a fourth. As the waiter poured the drink, he absent-mindedly looked at vacant space, I wish reality away. Yet it bites into me with the ferocity of a cheetah.

They detained me with their homilies, Soumitro spoke almost apologetically. The servant had brought in the wrong variety of mustard sauce. Indians eat their mustard sauce differently from my bloody English mustardy father.

Can we please go further and order our steaks, he piped? As such, I am rather late. Tomorrow is an early rise, oh hell!

On such trivial thoughts you dwell, Soumitro gasped, the season's not good for rhyming any further.

Oh, father, that was a clever pun, he said, putting an end to all such inebriated meandering.

Red herrings, Red herrings, Soumitro scowled.

They ended the evening, both pretty drunk.

CHAPTER 12

Smriti walked into his apartment and threw a fit.

How can you afford to live in such a hell? She wondered loudly. Where are the servants?

I have none, he meekly answered. Well, you better have some, she concluded. Or else, I have to reduce myself to all this scrubbing. Sure, sure tomorrow he said. Not tomorrow, she ordered. NOW!!! Well, he said, gulped the words and stuttered, I manufacture dreams; I cannot conjure servants you know. He quietly lit a cigarette and withdrew to a window.

Smoking shall be the death of you, she screamed. I would have almost fallen out of the window he said with a startled expression. Your screaming has this unnerving effect.

It would serve you right, she retorted, better fall and die than cough and die.

But eventually aren't we all destined to go up in smoke dear sister, saying this he winked.

Don't try to be caustic, she chided.

He grimaced and shrugged; I was only trying to be cosmic.

Such a perfect comic you; always looking for opportunities for verbal horseplay, huh!

With gentle indignation, Smriti began dusting the furniture.

He plunked himself on a sofa and felt very secure looking at the sister's attempt to bring some order back to life. Don't be so harsh prey on my poor furniture, they have not received such thrashing for a long time you know.

Don't order me around, she snapped back, I know what is best for you and this house. Whose lipstick is this? There was a tone of incredulity in her voice as she picked up a lipstick from the assorted mishmash lying on top of his desk. He winced and turned the other way to avoid her catching the expression on the flustered face. What lipstick are you talking of?

This . . . she thrust the lipstick right under his nose. So now you're bringing them over to the house, and desecrating the place, chichi! She threw the lipstick into the wastepaper basket.

She had caught him with his pants down.

Hey, hey, he tried to "manage" the situation. Is there any lipstick on my collar? I must have sat in the make-up room with my papers and carried that godamn stick by mistake. Grant me some better taste at least. He lit a cigarette with a flourish. I will never entertain women who leave their lipsticks lying on my table. I hate the taste of lipstick.

He loved Aasma's strawberry-flavoured lipstick. He stole it from her purse one day, while she was away in the washroom. While downing drinks in the evenings, he would pop up the stick and taste the tip. It would arouse his spirits. How would the shrink interpret this, he wondered?

Smriti check all my collars, he pleaded innocuously ... I am not one of those cinemawallahs with insidious intent.

Even your collars would all test positive in the Eliza test. She smirked and nudged him gently.

He embraced her. Stop worrying about me, he mumbled, you're my kid sister. I should worry about you Smriti.

She looked at his eyes. I worry even more about you than for my one-year-old daughter, damn it! Tears welled up her eyes and he brushed them off. You're all alone. Why are you all alone?

He just smiled and thought about Aasma. If only if, I could tell you, dear sis, what agony lies concealed in my heart!!

For a change, his voice rang true.

CHAPTER 13

Aasma sat beside the telephone expecting that it just might ring any moment. To prevent her Amma from guessing, she pretended to be engrossed in reading a magazine. She had not yet bought her mobile phone.

Had he forgotten her? Her vanity brushed aside the thought. After all, she was the one to have forsaken him. She had done the right thing, she asserted in her mind. There was simply no point in furthering this relationship. She had defied her parents for Minal's sake.

Though Minal belonged to the same community, right from the outset Amma disapproved of him, for reasons beyond Aasma's comprehension. He is a wastrel, an illiterate ragamuffin, Amma had pronounced disdainfully. He is a qualified chartered accountant, Aasma would argue to no avail. With her nose perpetually in the air, Amma would scoff, must have cheated in his exams. Such a wimp, and just imagine you'll have to live with his ten brothers and sisters cackling all around like geese in that chawl that stinks of stale beef. Your mother-in-law would ensure that you read Namaz five times a day and force you to live in purdah. We did not bring up our daughter for all this. We would not mind if you marry a liberated Hindu, but not that scum.

For some strange reason, Amma adored him. Such a polite man, well versed in social graces.

Amma's face lit up with a smile as she spoke and such a fine thinker. Thank your stars that he likes you. If only he were from our community, I would run with a marriage proposal. I wish you could see through his veneer Amma, Aasma sighed as she thought, and yet looked at the telephone and pleaded it to ring.

I will never call him. But why doesn't he call me up? What must he be doing at this time of the night? What else but drinking himself silly, she chided herself for asking the stupid question. Minal is correct for me. He arrived first in my life, he's my age, we've shared so many sunsets, I've fought with my parents for his sake, I feel sexually aroused by him, I like the smell he exudes, I like his eyes, I like his husk, I like his touch, I love him, period!!

Why then was she waiting for the telephone to ring? Aasma had no answers and hated herself for this. Amma walked into the room and positioned herself theatrically on the bed. So, you are waiting for that clerk's call, she chirped and arched

her eyebrows. Amma opened a small silver tin box with great care and put a clove in her mouth. Do I have to keep on telling you that without *riwaaz,* you'll never be able to accomplish perfection? And to think I spent all my energies since your childhood to enable you to achieve perfection.   What fine qualities you are gifted with child, if you only realized that, then you wouldn't be frittering it all away. Such graceful limbs, wafting in the air like a dove, Amma got up and began moving her limbs to the strains of the unheard melody. I thought I would be able to fulfill myself through you someday.
Aasma got up and began moving to the door.
Why haven't you called him up?
Hearing Amma, Aasma took a sharp turn.
Is this any way to behave with a gentleman?
Did you speak to him? Aasma enquired curtly.
No why should I, Amma walked up to Aasma. Don't hurt him, she put her hand on Aasma's shoulder, he cares for you.
 I don't, Aasma brushed off Amma's hand, and reacted like a rattlesnake. I don't wish to discuss this further. I'm leaving now and will come back after an hour.
As Aasma left the room Amma wondered why things happen the way they do.

CHAPTER 14

The news of the murder befuddled him completely.

 He felt so numb that he could not even lift the mug of tea held in hand, to the lips. The front-page headlines blurred before his eyes. What must be poor Soumitro's condition, he gulped down the cough that had formed in the throat and the words, Oh Shit, escaped his parted lips.

While Soumitro was recuperating from his appendicitis operation, at a nearby nursing home, the servants had murdered his parents at night. Robbery, it seemed to the police department, was the apparent motive.

Why didn't Soumitro call him?

How could he in such a state ... such a foolish thought. He regained composure and quickly changed. He did not bother to take a bath.

Soumitro's house was swarming with relatives of all different dimensions. The hysterical outbursts of Soumitro's elder sister could be heard as he alighted from the car.

Soumitro was alone in his room. He was sitting on the sofa in kurta pajamas, smoking a cigar. He did not remember ever having seen Soumitro in such attire. He sat down quietly and lit a cigarette. He could not speak.

Soumitro broke the ice.

-- It would have been nicer if I had stayed in the house.

-- You could not have prevented it.

-- No, I don't mean that way.

-- Then? He enquired with a tinge of doubt

-- I could have had the pleasure of having my throat slit as well. They would not have spared me surely.

-- Just consider the possibility. You would not have been able to indulge yourself thus, in retrospect. You don't have to make things comfortable for me this way... he rebuked Soumitro.

-- I'm not making anything comfortable my dear . . . Soumitro spoke languorously, punctuating each syllable, with the cigar clenched tightly between his teeth ... I'm just contemplating what could have been a perfect death.

Soumitro's sister's wailing could be heard intermittently from the adjoining room, a baleful waft of ten syllables punctuated by the momentary silence of sighs and then the voice scaling a further octave.

-- That's competition for many a soprano ... Soumitro observed as the servant brought them tea. Do you think I

should observe all the rituals that a Hindu death entails? Soumitro poured the tea from the pot as he spoke. Tea from my father's garden ... can only be served in moments of mourning.
-- Don't be irreverent in such moments ... he was trifle annoyed. I am not prepared for your clever ones today. You seem to forget that I also knew your parents. Especially your mother was very fond of me ... as for the rituals, do what your conscience tells you to.
-- My good fellow ... Soumitro sipped his tea . . . you don't seem to realize that my conscience has taken a temporary vacation. I should be feeling sad, but I'm not. I'm beyond tragedy.
Soumitro got up and impatiently paced up and down the room. He kept quiet, observed Soumitro's restlessness, and lit a cigarette. Soumitro went near a window, stood looking out for a while at the garden outside. The *Gulmohur* tree was in full bloom. A squirrel dared to perch itself on the windowsill and look askance at Soumitro.
Soumitro's eyes glowed as he whispered ... I wished my parents away. I simply wished them away.
The sun set soon after that.

CHAPTER 15

Break for lunch, he announced and moved towards the chair on the studio floor. He positioned himself comfortably on the chair and lit a cigarette as the assorted crowd began moving out from the floor. Avinash walked up to him.

-- Let's go to my vanity van and have lunch there.

-- You carry on. I'll join you in a while ... he said lifting the clipboard with the shooting script. Avinash smiled and walked away. Avinash knew the signal. He wanted to be left alone. Nanoo, the production boy brought him a glass of chilled *nimbu-pani*.

-- Some lunch for you Sir? Nanoo meekly enquired. He nodded in the negative. Nanoo slipped away.

It has been five days since the murder. And seven days since he last spoke to her. So finally, this was the end, the curtains down . . . fin, finito.

He never wanted to end with a whimper. He had meticulously planned out the *mise-en-scene* with suitable alternatives. He had even orchestrated the background music and dialogues for the final encounter. Like the director in The Truman Show.

Nothing of that had happened. Nothing needs to happen. She was just a phone call away.

What if she refused to relent this time around? This script would never get written without her. It was his duty to eat humble pie...

Whom are you deluding Johnny, his other self questioned? Haven't you written all along before she came into your life? Yes, but ... with her, it's always ... shut your gob, the other-self snapped back. As such you were writing bull crap of a script. Don't give excuses; don't clothe your desires with all this aesthetic mumbo jumbo of two minds working in harmony to create music of the spheres. Plain and simply you desire her presence, in flesh and blood, in the now. You wish to hold her, kiss her, and enter her. Your dick is dictating your heart.

This is a ridiculous proposition he shouted aloud and quickly realized the faux pas. Luckily for him, the floor was empty now except for a pair of pigeons. They flew off, hearing the sudden exclamation.

He got up and entered the set. It was a hot and stuffy interior of a bedroom. They were filming a scene with Avinash alone in the bedroom. There were three walls in the room. The

fourth had been dismantled to set up the lights and cameras. He went and sat on the bed. It was elaborately done up in sky blue linen – a round bed with a net hanging from the top. The bedspread was satin material with delicate frills falling from the sides.
The monstrosity of a linear existence was more dismal than the linear narrative in a popular film.
His foolish heart ached as the hand clung to the linen bedspread, a drowsy numbness pained the senses, feeling her proximity on the bed, sensing her smell. She was but a phone call away but a Milky Way separated them.
Such distances he was shy to travel.
He was caught within the finite matrix.
Pico, Tico walked in, wiping their hands together, on their respective handkerchiefs.
We are ready sir, they sang together.
He turned and promptly asked --- Is readiness all??

CHAPTER 16

Minal ran his fingers over Aasma's forehead with the dexterity of an accomplished pianist.

It soothed her overwrought nerves. They were both lying naked in the darkroom.

It was Minal's friend's flat. He had managed the keys. She had bunked her dance classes. They were both deliriously happy after making love, twice in quick succession.

My nipples blossom like flowers whenever Minal touches me, Aasma thought as she put her hand on his hairy chest. Her hands went down Minal's stomach and her fingertips touched his flaccid organ sleeping after a prolonged orgasm. Suddenly she remembered the fire growing below someone else's trousers when she touched him.

His bloody trousers, why, oh why do such impious thoughts cross my mind, she cursed herself. Her fingers retracted.

Minal smiled. He was at peace. With Aasma held in his embrace and the silence that enveloped both of them in the darkroom.

---Empress . . . he whispered in her ears . . . when you become a famous danseuse, will you keep me as your secretary?

Aasma clung on to his naked body almost fervently searching for his shirt to grasp more tightly between her shivering fingers.

---Let us get married tomorrow Minal ... she spoke between her gasps ... I want your child. I don't want fame.

---But I want it ... Minal smile sparkled in the darkroom ... I want to be known as the spouse of the famous star. When they ask me in the interviews what you do, I want to say that I sleep with her.

Aasma boxed his chest as Minal laughed silently.

---By boxing me, you'll arouse me a third time ... Minal turned Aasma to his side as he spoke.

---I want to live with you, cook for you ... Aasma bit Minal's left earlobe ... let us run away to another city.

Suddenly the image of someone kissing her left earlobe flashed past her mind. Aasma screamed aloud.

Minal sat up on the bed and cupped her face. A sharp shaft of light fell on Aasma's nose through the slit in the curtain.

---What's the matter with you? There was anxiety in Minal's voice. Did I hurt you ... I'm sorry I could not see in the darkness.

Aasma regained her composure.

---I squealed in delight, Aasma responded. That was a weak excuse, only a fool would believe it.

---My God, Minal heaved a sigh of relief ... I thought I had squeezed your arm in the darkness. Why are you so delighted?

---Because it's just like old times ... Aasma bit her tongue as she spoke.

---I wish we could run away, but you know I have responsibilities that I cannot avoid.

Minal had resolved not to bring up his reference or even his name today. When she mentioned running away, for a trifle moment, he had crossed Minal's mind. But Minal brushed away the thought. This evening is going to be picture perfect. She loves only me. She cannot afford to love anyone else. Whatever happened was because she was ensnared by that man's hypnotic presence. Even grudgingly Minal had to admire his facile charisma.

As Minal entered Aasma for the third time, she began thinking about the first encounter.

CHAPTER 17

It was a warm December evening. Aasma had performed before an audience for the third time. She was full of sweat and flooded with bouquets and feeling suffocated backstage, when her presenter briskly pushed away from the crowd of admirers, held her by her hand and marched her to the make-up room.

A waft of cold air and his smile greeted her when she walked in. She fell into her chair and began breathing heavily as the attendant thrust a glass of water into her hand. She gulped it at one go.

He was seated on the sofa, reclining and bemusedly watching the flurried expressions fleeting across her face. She was not her usual self when she saw him first. Thus, she would console herself later, in her moments of frustration.

He was cool and composed. After she settled herself and the who's- who introductions went by, he spoke.

---What do you study? He asked very softly.

---Pardon me...she leaned forward.

He lifted his right palm, asking her to relax.

---I asked you what you are studying. This time he spoke in staccato, loud and clear, with a smoky base voice.

---You didn't like my dance ... she sounded a trifle hurt.

---If you want me to utter the same inanities which the jostling crowd did, then I must say you were brilliant, out of this world, etc, etc. But I'm afraid I can't do that. The very fact that I was waiting for you in your make-up room ...

---Oh, she is just a child, doesn't realize the importance ... he stopped her presenter with a swift movement of the palm. I asked you what you studied to know what kind of a person you are ... can we go somewhere quieter for coffee?

Aasma was flummoxed by such a hasty proposal. She could but afford just to nod meekly.

It was her first visit to a five-star. As he waxed eloquent on her being the finest performer of her generation and the silence of the lotus in the pond before it pops open, an image from Kobayashi's Rebellion, she was amazed that cold coffee cost five hundred bucks over here.

CHAPTER 18

---Hello...Amma spoke hesitantly, as he answered.

---Is that you Amma? How are you?

---Existing...Amma said curtly.

What bond existed between them neither could fathom. But Amma knew that she could presume upon him.

---Is anything the matter ... he asked anxiously.

---No, no ... she has not yet returned ... Amma choked as she spoke ... I thought maybe...

---I have not met her for more than a week ... work is stuck ... he dared not to tell Amma that his life was stuck too.

---She keeps on complaining that you don't pay her enough. It's not worth working with you.

 He winced within.

---Well is that what she's told you? But she's not returned as yet ... It's past ten ... his heartbeat grew faster as he spoke.

---I'm worried ... Amma had resolved not to cry as she spoke.

---Have you tried Minal's? He asked hesitantly.

---Are you in your senses? Amma burst out ... I feel like puking even before I do such a thing. Has she no shame left? Her Abboo has just passed away; we are still in mourning.

---Don't get agitated Amma ... please ... he pleaded. Am I not there for you?

---I have lost all hope ... Amma cried. Why does she have to torture me like this? Shameless girl, doesn't she know what sacrifices I made for her? You know very well how difficult it is for a girl from our community to take up dancing. But I encouraged her, only because I knew she was born to dance, not like a nautch girl but as an artist. And all she does is waste her life with a pimp.

---Patience, dear Amma, is the mother of all virtues ... he tried to explain. Only you know what I'm going through.

---That's why I feel sadder ... Amma hollered. She spurns your love for ... you love her perhaps more than I do.

---I feel blessed Amma ... he cried silently after putting the phone down. At least, Amma knew the truth.

Here there was no play-acting.

Though he and Amma were consummate performers in their own right, both of them succeeded in pulling off their masks, to share their common sorrow at that moment.

CHAPTER 19

Did he want to make the kind of films he was making?
He had questioned himself on this account several times, but no answers seem to emerge eventually. What then was the point in working without a goal? Television provided the money; films were meant to provide something else. What was that something else? It was not merely dramatic structures or characters with their sempiternal angst or ennui. All those could be found in the written script.

What could he as a filmmaker add whilst translating a script to screen? *Mise-en-scene* said his teacher, was the truly cinematic contribution. Now the moot question was whether to create a *mise-en-scene* of desire or expiation.

How to achieve this without any abstraction was the next question that followed.

Cinema abhors abstraction. Every image has to be concrete, have a definite form and as such be de-adjectified. This posed a further problem. Though the definitiveness of the image to a certain extent resolved the spatial complexities, within a frame, within a shot—what about the temporal dichotomy when two images were juxtaposed; joined to create the *mise-en-scene*?

Adding up time in a linear pattern creates a narrative structure, the *mise-en-scene* of desire. A non-linear representation of time subverts the narrative and the *mise-en-scene* of expiation emerges. But that does not become palpable to an audience hungry for a story and that form of cinema is denounced at the box office. Satisfaction, however, was, in the creation of the latter. But box office adversity prevented that and he had to be content by creating only a series of dramatic encounters.

That's not cinema, that's not life. Why does something have to 'happen' in cinema? Why does something have to happen in life? If nothing happens, in both the spheres we get restless, impatient. All the work he had done so far seemed worthless. He resolved to abandon the script freshly started. He was beginning to forsake previous stances.

She was continuously driving me to dramatic forms. I was deviating from my goal and filming theatre. Now I shall write a film bereft of patriarchal notions of form, he resolved firmly.

But his fingers refused to move on the keyboard.

There was a horrible emptiness that filled the stomach, as he got up from the chair, to move to the cupboard and fetch a bottle of whiskey. The monotony of daily rituals, of smoking and drinking, evoked a strong sense of nausea. He was helpless. This is what happens to you when your life is without a story, he reasoned. Is this not a boring life? The poor audience has every right to get annoyed and feel affronted when the same happens in a film. The narrative is a must. He tried to resolve the conflicts without realizing it consciously.

Poetry is the only liberated form. Maybe even pure music. And, of course, dance.

Maybe that's why Aasma felt liberated from reality and he was bogged down by it.

CHAPTER 20

Smriti and Srijeet presented the perfect picture of marital bliss.

He had never seen two people so much in love before. Their devotion to each other was almost distracting. Often, he would say in jest, that such a situation happened only because Srijeet had surrendered himself completely. To this, Srijeet would vigorously nod his head and laugh vehemently. Smriti would get all worked up and accuse him of being partisan to the brother-in-law.

---All you men are incorrigible ... she would utter disdainfully and plunk the coffee mugs in front of them.

It was a Sunday afternoon.

They were lounging at Smriti's house. It was the only sunny side of his life. As Smriti's daughter, Pimpu, took her first few uneasy steps across the room, they chatted the afternoon away.

---Dada you are very unfair to us men ... Srijeet complained ... in all your work, women are seen so much stronger.

---Well, I can't tell the critics, but I can confide to you ... he whispered conspiratorially. You see, amazons who've threatened to bash my head and make fine pulp of it, if I did not make demi-goddesses out of them on screen, have always surrounded me. The finest in this category is your not so charming wife ... he winked at Srijeet who inadvertently broke into a cackle.

Smriti looked up from her book and cast a regal glance at them.

---Well I refuse to react to your gibberish.

---Spell gibberish ... both he and Srijeet hollered in perfect unison. This was a shared joke. This was the way they chose to rile Smriti and get even with her.

---I shan't bother... Smriti shook her head haughtily and began reading again.

---Of course, to critics I have to give a different version ... he turned to Srijeet. I tell them that women have been the dominant influence in my life, the centripetal force of my existence and all such horseshit.

He noticed Pimpu lifting the cell phone and speaking into it and ran after her.

---Well I can see yet another woman dominating your life ... Srijeet spoke with a warm smile ... this little brat.

---Wait and watch, she'll be the one to size him up . . . Smriti

commented with malicious glee.
---Oh, I would be her loyal servant ... he lifted Pimpu ... she's my only hope of redemption. I don't mind the world calling me a female-dominated pig, for her sake alone.
Srijeet held his arm as Smriti quickly wiped her tears.
---Dada, why don't you get married again ... Srijeet hushed with emotions dripping from his voice ... we also want to see you happy.
---Stupid people ... he slapped Srijeet on the head ... how do you dare to think I'm unhappy when Pimpu is with me ... such delirious joy, few people are wont to have ... saying this he touched his head.
She will continue what I've left undone ... he prayed in silent thought.
They had Black Forest for dessert to celebrate the occasion.

CHAPTER 21

Avinash was a bundle of nerves, poor fellow. All worked up and hysterical. It was two past midnight. Avinash secretary Ashutosh had frantically called him up, apologizing profusely for the midnight intrusion. It seems the poor fella had no way out.

He held Avinash's hand firmly, as the crumbling star clenched the wrist and was shaking uncontrollably. His teeth were jittering as he foamed at the mouth.

Simple, the doctor pronounced. It was an overdose of drugs that did Avinash in. He prescribed a few medicines and walked off rather impatiently. Imagine someone calling you at three o'clock with their problems. You film folk make me sick, the doctor scoffed. Such aberrations ... this guy deserved to be spanked, a perfect moronic hulk.

He took the doctor aside to assuage his frayed temper. This guy must have been coming or about to come when the phone rang. Coitus interruptus could indeed be irritating.

You better jerk off or else the sperm can turn to stone and cause greater irritation; he casually advised the miffed doctor. The doctor's jaws fell. He was flabbergasted. Hurriedly, he picked up his bag and ran to the door. What a nightmare, the doctor heaved in the lift, walking straight into a den of degenerates.

Ashutosh scurried off to fetch the medicines. Avinash was slightly better. He firmly held on to the curtains of the French window opening up to the terrace.

Avinash's penthouse apartment on the twentieth floor was a sight to dream of. However, the owner did not seem very proud of it. The place was littered all around with junk like furniture. Avinash had this fetish for automobiles. He had tyres, car seats and dashboards strewn across the living room. All very expensive -- the dashboard of a Merc, the seat of a Peugeot, the tyres of BMW, and all very uncouth.

He went up to Avinash standing beside the window.

---Come with me Avinash ... he escorted Avinash walking in a daze, to the bathroom. He filled the bathtub, took off Avinash's robe and pushed him into the tub...just relax; I'll get you something cold to drink.

He asked the servant to serve Avinash *nimbu-pani* with lots of crushed ice. This was his standard remedy for all malaise. Whenever there was a hangover, he readied himself such a drink. The tangy flavour of lime-juice energized his senses and reactivated the brain cells. He snapped open his cell phone and dialled a number. The phone rang for a while.

---Is that you Alisha ... sorry to bother you at this hour ... no, no he is not dead ... just had an attack ... be reasonable; your presence might help ... you know what he's like ... I know you care for him regardless of whatever you might say ... okay, okay ... but I seriously think he needs it... look I could also not bother but ... now you are being harsh Alisha ... no, it's not just because my film is not yet over ... I care for Avi ... he's a friend Alisha and I can't forsake him even if he's wrong ... you cannot too ... now stop this nonsense and do as I tell you ... shall I come to fetch you?

In the car, Alisha kept quiet right through. By the time they reached Avinash's apartment, Ashutosh had administered the medicines and Avinash was sleeping. Alisha entered the bedroom. He and Ashutosh stayed outside. He affectionately put his hand on Ashutosh's shoulder and Ashutosh started crying silently.

---I can't take this any longer. It's been going on for too long ... ever since Madam's death ... Ashutosh wiped his eyes and looked downwards.

---I understand ... it must be the most difficult for you ... poor Avi cannot handle his life ... helpless without his elder sister.

---But she always asked him to be strong ... Ashutosh protested . . . always asked him to stand on his own feet. I was the witness ... I was ...

---Life does not obey rules my boy... he heaved ... not everyone can handle failure. But I am amazed by your resilience. You have stuck to him through thick and thin. Even Alisha deserted him.

---Don't say unkind words about her ... Ashutosh pleaded . . . she couldn't take it anymore. I couldn't desert him out of gratitude. Whatever I am today is because of him. I was a sheer nobody from the streets ... he made me.

---Therefore, you choose to descend to hell with him? ... Alisha observed closing the bedroom door.

They had not noticed her.

A flustered Ashutosh excused himself and went away. Both he and Alisha moved to the terrace and looked down at the streets below. Nobody spoke for a while. He handed Alisha a cigarette, which she lit with a quaint lighter.

---I remember that was a present from Avinash ... you have still kept it with you.

Alisha turned to look at him. There were tears in her eyes.
---I wish our childhood days were back again ... she softly sobbed. I've known Avi since childhood. It was so simple then.
He held Alisha in a warm embrace and prayed for Avinash's well-being to a non-existent God.

CHAPTER 22

Life without Aasma was becoming gradually bearable, liveable. It was almost a fortnight since they had last spoken. The sting was losing its sharpness. The tragic was now elegiac-
That has passed
So, may this.
Grief is like a pendant stone at first hanging down your neck, a constant reminder of your sorrow. With time, that same stone gets transferred to a pebble in the pocket of your sweater. Whenever your hand goes into the pocket, the sharp stone now a pebble, still stings you and reminds you only occasionally of the enormity of the grief. But normal life goes on otherwise. --- living and partly living. The history of lovers revealed that moments of happiness were, always transitory. Love is caught in a flux of time and hence yields itself to mortality. Suffering was permanent, before and beyond him. Suffering escapes the clutches of time, almost magically. Maybe because it happens only within. Love had to happen without, simply because it takes two to love. It was bound by the dichotomy of temporal opposites. Suffering breaks the chain of opposites by its isolation, its uniqueness, its aloneness.
For now, he wished to be left alone. To meditate about ... what? He had forgotten what to meditate about? He broke into a cold sweat. My mind becomes a *tabula rasa* ... nothing is written on it. He felt weak, as despair started catching up. Become mellow, he ordered despair ... become melancholy, he requested. But it did not obey orders and grew beyond control. He began cringing and desperately wanted to avoid despair. He pined for company.
When he dropped in at the recording studio, Dabloo was a bundle of nerves, swiftly swerving his long hair across his bald pate, in states of extreme agitation.
-- No, no, no ... Dabloo vigorously shook his head. That will simply not do Rukmini; you've got the pitch all wrong.
Rukmini immediately pulled out the pitch pipe from the purse and blew into it to check for herself.
--Dabloo, I think you were wrong ... she said authoritatively, putting the pipe back into the purse, I'm in perfect pitch.
Dabloo rushed towards her and almost fell over her. Rukmini pulled back a few steps. He watched bemusedly from inside the recording room. They were both, on the floor.

-- Who is the music director . . . Dabloo shouted ... who is the music director, you or I?

-- Obviously you . . . Rukmini retorted with a smirk.

-- Then, when I'm saying you are not in pitch, you are not in pitch, Dabloo blasted. Is that okay with you? Dabloo arched over Rukmini who retracted angularly.

As he watched them going through the frenetic gestures in fast motion, he recalled those days when Dabloo and Rukmini were not at war.

....

You must try her out, Dabloo held his hand and pleaded ... she is a gem.

The best in the last twenty years? He arched the left eyebrow out of habit. You said the same thing about your last girlfriend. But frankly, I'm not too impressed; he said lighting a cigarette and offering Dabloo one.

Dabloo grinned sheepishly. You always come up with smart ones. But I have chiselled Rukmini's voice to perfection. I can lay a bet.

With a swift motion of the right palm, he silenced Dabloo. Will she go to bed with you if I give her one chance to sing?

Dabloo slapped him suddenly. All you can think of is fucking. I am not degenerate like you. It's okay if you are not impressed but I still maintain my stand. She's the brightest pupil I've had. And yes, I am promoting a talent, Dabloo swished his hair over his baldpate, I care two hoots for a pervert's opinion.

Rukmini sang brilliantly and he was adequately impressed. After the recording, Dabloo appeared as pleased as someone who could shit after two days of constipation. That was the beginning of the end.

....

The end has not yet come. I shall see to it, that together, they create some more eternal melodies, he resolved. He walked into the recording floor. Both of them had thrown a tantrum each at one another and sat with puffed faces. Everyone else had frozen to silence.

He went to Rukmini first and put a hand on her head.

-- Patience ... he whispered . . . you have to obey.

-- But I ... Rukmini protested between sobs. He promptly placed a hand on her mouth and looked firmly into her eyes. I said patience ... for my sake. Then, he walked up to Dabloo.

-- Don't make an ass of yourself ... he reprimanded Dabloo ... everyone is watching.

I don't care . . . Dabloo's voice was choked. Who does she think herself to be?

-- You have made her feel this ... he hissed. You created the impression that she was god's gift to humanity. Now you'll have to endure your Frankenstein. Please get on with the recording, please ... if you don't, I'm not your friend anymore . . . he issued an ultimatum and started to walk away.

Dabloo looked lost for a second. Then, he quickly regained his composure and jumped to his feet. A smile reappeared on his face.

Rukmini . . . Dabloo shouted . . . we shall start afresh.

He turned and winked at Rukmini. She scowled back.

CHAPTER 23

Kalpana jumped up from her chair as he walked into the office. He was appearing after ten days, the longest break Kalpana had seen him take from the office. Ostensibly, he was busy with the shooting and other assorted assignments. At least that's the explanation he had offered to her over the telephone. But Kalpana knew otherwise. Never before, since she joined, she had seen him missing office while in town, for more than two days. And he was very much in town for over a month. Kalpana sensed there was something amiss. What the matter was, she dared not ask.

He walked straight into the room, without the customary pleasantries of how have you been my child, missed you so much, etc, etc.

-- Ch- chai Sir? ... Kalpana meekly enquired.

-- Ca ... coffee please . . . he replied without looking up from the heap of correspondence.

Kalpana felt hurt for the first time. Never before, he had made fun of her stammering. She had left her last job on this count. She resolved to do the same. She had never expected him to behave so ungallantly.

She marched up to her chair and faintly asked Dilip, the peon to get a cup of coffee. She wiped her tears in her handkerchief and bit her nails. Maybe he was in a foul mood. But that did not give him a right to shatter her illusions. To her utter surprise, Kalpana realized that she had grown fond of him. Was she falling ... just then, there was a gentle knock on the door. As Kalpana looked up, a gentleman entered.

He was dark and disdainful, wearing a tie over a full sleeve shirt. What was peculiar about his appearance was that he had left the top two buttons of his shirt unbuttoned. He had a thick moustache, a quaint voice and the eyes of a butcher.

-- I have an appointment with Mr. ...

You're Mr. Parmeswar Pandey . . . Kalpana interrupted the butcher . . . he's expecting you.

Parmeswar Pandey glided into his room and halted. As Parmeswar looked around for a chair, he briskly beckoned Parmeswar to sit on the floor. Parmeswar gently glided down.

-- You'll have to excuse me for a minute... he said without looking up from the files. I've not been here for quite a few

days and have to catch up with . . .
-- That's perfectly all right . . . Parmeswar piped as he surveyed his prey ... take your time. Parmeswar kept his file beside him . . . you're an Aries I presume.
He looked up and smiled.
-- You've done your homework pretty well Mr. Pandey . . . he said putting away the file.
-- What do you mean by that? Parmeswar asked meekly ... I could not quite get you, Sir?
-- I mean you googled about me before you came . . . he pulled a cushion.
Dilip brought in coffee.
-- Care for some coffee? He casually asked.
-- Black and strong . . . Parmeswar replied.
Dilip nodded his head and withdrew.
 -- Sir, I know next to nothing about you ... Parmeswar folded his palms and played with them as he spoke . . . I am from a different line of business.
-- What then, made you search me out and want to meet me so urgently... he lit a cigarette and blew the smoke ... after all, a call from the minister saying that a certain mister so and so wants to meet you, can be quite unnerving for us lesser mortals ...
--The other night, my wife and I happened to watch an episode of yours on television ... Parmeswar chimed in a singsong voice. She liked what she saw and requested me to meet you.
-- You are here at your wife's behest? He laughed.
-- Incidentally, I don't watch much television. But that episode engrossed me and I thought it would be a great pleasure to meet you.p
-- How did you guess my sun sign? Are you my Facebook friend?
-- You have very visible Arian traits ... Parmeswar said in a matter-of-fact tone. I can tell you so many other things besides that, if you please.
-- Like what? He sat up and leaned forward.
-- Like your favourite colour is red; you're in love with a Muslim girl with a name beginning with A, you like eating pomfrets and Italian food, your brand of whiskey is ....
-- Wait! Wait! He exclaimed ... are you an astrologer-- No... Parmeswar smiled and pulled down his chin. I merely get these vibes. For instance, otherwise, you would think that I

learned about your divorce from a gossip magazine?
Holy shit! He gasped, that's not on google.... I had made sure
to avoid that part of my life
Parmeswar wore a benign smile on his face.
Dilip brought in Parmeswar Pandey's coffee, black and
strong.

CHAPTER 24

-- I was bewildered by this man ... he confessed, sipping coffee at Soumitro's house.

-- What were his intentions? Soumitro enquired, lighting up his extinguished cigar.

-- I couldn't make out. He wanted to discuss some business. At least that's what he said over the telephone. But he didn't utter a word about work. Just chatted, made certain revelations and walked away. He could have found out everything else about me from other sources. But, but . . . how did he know about Aasma? Apart from you nobody ... he was rendered speechless.

-- Is he a mystic? Soumitro asked in an incredulous voice. Does he wear beads and a toga?

He nodded in the negative and kept down the coffee cup.

-- Impeccably dressed in formal attire ... tie shie and all you know ... speaks in a singsong voice with an affected manner, ends his sentences with a salutary Sir!

-- Doesn't seem very safe ... Soumitro nodded his head ... try to keep away from him.

-- There is no proximity ... he asserted. So, the question of keeping away does not arise. His eyes are perpetually droopy, expressionless.

-- This Parmeswar Pandey seems to have cast a spell on you... scoffed Soumitro. You have been talking about him for the past twenty minutes. . . Soumitro observed, looking at his watch.

-- Almost an episode... he laughed. Now for the next ... he twitched eyebrows. What's news with you?

-- Your life seems to be divided up in episodes, commercial breaks, scenes, intervals, TRPs, and box-office . . . admonished Soumitro.

-- Can't help ... professional hazards you know. Any clues so far? He changed the topic.

-- None whatsoever ... Soumitro grimaced. The police will not investigate unless I offer them money. I shan't bribe them to find out who slit my parents' throats. Will such discovery bring them back? Soumitro lifted his arms questioningly.

-- How's your sister? Sensing an awkward situation, he again changed tracks.

-- Her usual hysterical self . . . Soumitro replied in a resigned tone . . . somehow managed to send her back. She refused to leave her poor kid brother in such a state. Sometimes I

wonder how I can endure such inanities.
-- Endurance is the virtue superior souls are blessed with . . .
he announced majestically. This is what the religious texts
keep on referring to as moksha. You rise above your
environment and become non-reactive.
-- Stop this holy shit ... Soumitro snapped back. I want to
reactivate my life. Do you think that I should migrate?
-- There is no easy escape ... he replied sagely. The mind is
its own place ...
-- Please save your school-boyish Miltonic effusiveness for
your sycophants... Soumitro said in disgust. They will like to
hear such precious pearls of wisdom. I'm seriously thinking
of leaving the country.
He rose from the sofa and propelled to the garden
outside. Soumitro was amazed but followed suit soon
after. Both of them stood in the garden silently for a long
while. It was a starless, moonless night. The August winds
blew through their hair as two grumpy middle-aged men
groped for words. In the end, he spoke.
-- I have a strong feeling that your life is going to change
Soumitro. Go to your tea gardens for a while. You will surely
rediscover yourself.
Soumitro knew that this was not the time for a wisecrack. He
whispered near his friend's ear.
What about you?
He smiled.
-- I shall wait for the tide ... I shall wait for the tide.

PART - TWO

LOVE AS KITSCH

HAMLET: I DID LOVE YOU ONCE

OPHELIA: INDEED, MY LORD, YOU MADE ME BELIEVE SO

HAMLET: YOU SHOULD NOT HAVE BELIEVED ME....
I LOVED YOU NOT

----HAMLET

SHAKESPEARE

PART II

CHAPTER 1

Before boarding the flight, I remembered her. We had exchanged telephone numbers the first time we met.

On an impulse, I dialled her number. I didn't know what to say. Felt weak hearing her. The usher was urging me to disconnect my cell phone and climb the flight of stairs. I stepped aside on the runway.

I: I am leaving

She: Where?

I: For Work. I will be back in a week.

She: Hmmm . . .

I: The lights are blinking . . .

She: What?

I: I mean the other flight is taking off . . .

She: Thanks for the coffee . . .

She thought of thanking me for a week after we had coffee.

The usher rushed to me and urged me to board the flight.

I: Bye . . . c'ya around . . .

She: Will call you . . .

I was on cloud nine, as the aircraft soared through the clouds.

I: (in my mind) It can never happen again. I am too old for all that. It doesn't befit my station in life. Especially, after all that I've gone through.

I realized soon enough that I was wallowing in self-pity. I blushed at the thought that anyone could still have this effect on me.

I: (in my mind) The boy inside me refuses to grow up. Why does this cloying sense of insecurity goad me to seek out the other? Why can't I ever find fulfillment within myself?

Low self-esteem was not the answer. On the contrary, my behaviour displayed great conceit. Maybe that's the reason why people resent me.

 For the life of me, I could not fathom why the public opinion was so sharply divided about me. One group reviled me, the other revered.

I had this dual effect on people. Some thought me to be a glib talker, a cunning, manipulative bastard under the veneer of a genteel charmer. Others were floored by my dazzling, mesmeric presence. It was not that I did not enjoy this adulation, but what troubled me more was the fact that

people misunderstood me so easily.
I: (in my mind) She too might do the same.
Again, my thoughts came back to her. Her presence enveloped my consciousness right through the tour and I was desperate to get back.
When I returned, I resisted the temptation to call her. What would be the excuse? I had no work with her as such. She was too young to become my friend.
I: (in my mind) I have just met her once and was not foolish to fall in love with her at first sight.
Oops, I had uttered the forbidden words unknowingly. I bit my tongue. But then, I had not uttered it; I had just thought of it.
She called me a day after my arrival and was extremely hesitant to speak. Hearing her voice, I held the cell phone between my ear and shoulder and performed a jig - silently of course. Just to think of it, I was the so-called pallbearer of high art.
I: What's the P.O.A?
She: P. O. A??
I: Brunch or lunch?
She: Whatever . . .
I: What's your favourite colour?
She: Blue
I: (in my mind) Juliette Binoche (loudly) The mood of languor
. . .
She: What?
I: I like lilies . . .
She: Orchids . . . but they are too expensive . . .
I: (laughing) No Orchids for Miss Blandish . . .
She: I saw you on Times Now . . . do you always speak in riddles???
By the time we met for lunch at Abel's Inn, with great effort, I regained composure. As she came up to the table where I was seated, I looked up with studied ease from the book I wasn't reading and beckoned her to sit down. She was ill at ease, not yet accustomed to social graces. She could not make out what I meant by starters and asked for a glass of water. I whisked at the waiter and ordered two Bloody Mary's.
She: If you don't mind . . . . I think they've served me some stale juice . . .
I: (smirking) That's a delicacy here . . . stale tomato juice . . .
She: I feel dizzy . . .

I: Have the steaming soup . . . that'll do you good . . .
The tangy mulligatawny soup made her feel better. Then, we spoke about rhythm for a while. She spoke animatedly about the tala-structures and their permutations, as I watched her spell-bound. Her eyebrows danced, her eyes danced, her ears danced, her nose danced, her lips danced, her chin danced, as she spoke.
I felt tranquil after a long, long while.
When I spoke about poetry, I noticed the deep admiration in her eyes. I recited Tagore and Browning. She immediately placed me on a pedestal, from which I was to fall later.
We wound up lunch at five in the evening.

CHAPTER 2

The next few encounters were over breakfast, lunch, high tea and dinner. After that, I invited her home one Sunday morning.

She was dressed in light blue and wore a plain black shawl over her shoulders. I made tea and scrambled eggs for her and put the telephone off the hook and switched off the cell phone.

I: (reading)

Having unclothed my soul
I now revel in the glory of nudity
Reality can no longer fetter my wings
For you chose to make me fly.
When was it last you looked skywards
Observing flight, the sheer artless waltzing
Through vacant space, kindred spirits
Enjoying motion without the finality of touch.
If only you allow your thought
To meditate upon the magic of the moment
Divinity will surely smile within us.
In the unbecoming of our previous lives
We have lent each other light
Time is now camerized
Beyond transient myths.
This constancy can only be ours.

I read to her some of my writings. Hesitantly, she told me that she had studied literature for her graduation besides learning dancing.

I: I could never muster enough courage to learn Odissi as it is considered unmanly . . . you know I'm a good cook . . .

She: Really . . .

I: I will cook for you today . . .

She: Only if you allow me to help you . . .

As we chopped and peeled the vegetables, marinated the pomfrets, she spoke about the right methods of preserving the aroma of spices in cooking. This she had learned from her Amma. When we ate lunch together, it rained. Both of us were surprised and delighted by the winter rain.

I: Why don't you work with me?

She: Like what?

I: On my scripts . . . you are a student of literature . . .

She: But I know next to nothing about cinema . . .

I: You know all about rhythms . . . that's most important . . .

She: But . . . but . . .
I: I've made so many mistakes in the past . . . wouldn't mind another one . . . will you . . .
She: The pomfrets were out of this world . . .
I: My recipes are my own . . . just like my films . . .
She: My Amma regularly watches the chat show, you host . . .

I: Oh, that's a time pass for me . . . allows me to pull people's pants down . . .
She: What will I have to do?
I: Nothing much . . . just be a bouncing board for ideas . . . most of them are so intimidated by me . . .
She: Even I am . . .
I: Bah!!! You treat me like a . . .
She: Like what?
I: Boa constrictor . . . (laughing) will you???
She: Why me?
I: I was married once . . . Pimpu my niece is the reason why I live . . .

I drove through the rain, both of us listened to Bach. We speeded down the traffic-less Sunday streets. I dropped her at the five-point junction. I wanted to drop her home. But she had to meet a friend here. As she got down from the car, she agreed to my proposal. I watched her cross the streets and run down the pavement to catch up with a young man whom I came to know about much later.
The young man was Minal.

CHAPTER 3

When Amma spoke to me for the first time, I felt uneasy. She expressed her desire to meet me with great trepidation. Someday, I assured her, very soon, I would meet her. She could not stop talking enough about me. Amma felt happy for her daughter. She also seemed to be worried about her but did not mention anything. I came to know exactly what is that was disturbing Amma, much later.

Amma spoke in a theatrical tone, punctuating her sentences with gasps, sighs and a burst of sad laughter. She seemed to have suffered much in life. At times she sounded ancient, her voice burdened with age. At other times, she sounded like a young girl, full of zest, full of life, chirpy, ebullient and laughing uncontrollably when I made certain acerbic remarks. For a long time, Amma was just a voice. She had seen me on television and adored me.

The circumstance in which I met her for the first time was extremely awkward.

That morning I received a call. Aasma was panting at the other end. Her Abboo had just suffered a cerebral attack and was being rushed to the hospital. Would it be inconvenient for me to . . .

Without wasting words, I rushed to the hospital.

Aasma stood shivering outside the glass door of the I.C.C.U with Neelima and a few relatives by her side. I looked inside and saw the doctors trying to resuscitate her Abboo and immediately knew, nothing more could be done. As I stood beside her, Aasma firmly clenched my wrist. I saw Aasma's father dying before my eyes.

Nobody could muster enough courage to go home and break the news to Amma.

The onus fell on me.

As I drove towards their house, I resolved to take care of the poor child. I meandered through the lanes not knowing where to go. Neelima told me where to stop.

Anticipating the worst, Amma sat like a stone. I walked into the room alone.

I went beside her and held her shoulders firmly. Amma knew what I would say next and put her hand on my mouth. Luckily, I did not have to pronounce her widowhood to Amma.

CHAPTER 4

I came to know about Minal from Amma. She was concerned about her daughter's well-being.

Minal had sealed his fate by misbehaving with her family. Amma hated the very sight of him. I now understood why Minal was not present either at the hospital or at the funeral. Amma had issued strict instructions that he should not be sighted at any family gatherings. According to Amma, everything about Minal was wrong. He was vain, ill-mannered, a cheat, lusting after her beautiful daughter and misleading her. He would ruin her daughter's budding career.

I did not mention any of this to Aasma. I also did not feel the need to be jealous of or resent Minal. After all, Minal was not my rival. I would form my own opinion when I meet this bloke.

She introduced Minal to me at one of her recitals. Both of us had sat side by side, during the performance. But I had not noticed Minal. I was too engrossed with her fragile presence. Later, backstage Aasma did the formalities. It occurred to me then, that I had seen the fellow before, at the five-point crossing. There was no mention of their nature of friendship. We had coffee together at the cafeteria adjoining the auditorium and I found Minal to be taciturn. Sensing an impending uncomfortable situation, Aasma bade farewell and left with Minal. When I volunteered to give them a lift, Minal curtly refused.

Though I felt slighted, I did not display it. Instead, I smiled and waved them good-bye.

I: (in my mind) These two little kids do not deserve my wrath. As such, they are enmeshed in their complexities and insecurities.

It was not in my nature to be so overtly outgoing, bending every rule in the book, to please her. What prompted me to make an exception for Aasma, I could not fathom.

Nay, nay, take control of your senses, my good man, I cautioned myself. Lay off her for a while. Do not make an ass of yourself again. While giving sage advice to Dabloo, I spoke of reason as a virtue. I had admonished my bald friend for being foolishly sentimental.

In my own life, I was committing the same mistakes but had no control over it.

The intellect becomes dulled when one is driven by

obsession. Love stories are always fascinating tales of fools. And to top it all, it was outrageous that a middle-aged man, who had been cuckolded, be smitten, besotted, by a mere slip of a girl??!!
I: (in my mind, indignantly) Her knowledge of the language was slight, her pronunciation atrocious and her sentences gawky.
I cherished snobbery, albeit privately. For the outside world, I wore the mask of a benevolent man.
I: (in my mind) Don't be mean. There is still time to redeem yourself. Be gracious and accept that words are not the only means of communication. The intellect does not necessarily reflect itself through the spoken word. And her command over the native tongue was formidable. She had read the major poets and could reason very well.
My mind was blank for a moment. As my senses came back, I understood that all the while, my sub-conscious self was advocating her cause. The very thought was revolting.
I: (in my mind) I was not even in love with her. She was the little dove who accidentally chanced upon my palms. As is my nature, I had volunteered to nurture her and teach her how to fly.
Ironically, I was getting attached and sought bondage with someone whom I was meant to teach the meaning of freedom.
I: (in my mind) I must distance myself from her.

CHAPTER 5

The moment she entered my apartment I sensed she was fidgety and had gauged I was not in my elements. She was clever enough not to push for explanations.

I made coffee for both of us and offered her some biscuits.

We made small talk for a while. She spoke about her favourite composer; I spoke about my love for gossip and my favourite hobby - riling people on television. Then she took the first step and broached the topic.

She: When would we start our collaboration?

I: Now,

I replied in the affirmative and showed her the way to the desk. Then I posed two strange questions to her.

I: What would be an example of Tautology?

She: Dunno what that means . . .

I: Perfect wisdom . . . what would be a suitable example of an Oxymoron

She: Cruel Kindness?

She enquired almost apologetically.

I: Well that is what Wren & Martin teaches you. But it is too obvious and suitable. . . Perfect Love . . . (laughing) love is imperfect by definition

She was baffled when I told her that these two questions contained a riddle, that she would have to solve someday.

Then, we started on the first venture. We got along like wind and fire, the sail and the wave, the moon, and desire.

Before either of us realized it, the script was over. How did we manage it, we wondered in unison? When we had begun, there was no ostensible story in hand. Just a few characters and their passions. Together, we fashioned a torrid love story out of it.

The day we finished; she was deliriously happy. For her, it was the first major achievement in life. As I tossed chocolate into my mouth, she announced . . .

She: I'm staying over tonight . . .

I almost choked on the chocolate.

She called up Amma and informed her that she was spending the night at Neelima's. Then she called Neelima up to confirm her story, in case Amma cross-checked. When Neelima enquired where she was, she whispered to her friend that she was with Minal. I heard what she said but chose to overlook it. I felt, she was succumbing gradually to my overtures.

I brought out a bottle of rare French wine presented by Srijeet and Smriti.

Ceremonially, I even cooled it in a bucket of ice. She made dinner. I made the salad and sauces. Then we tinkled our glasses. The scene was almost imitative of Hollywood kitsch. That did not matter. We munched chips and sipped the wine as we watched a favourite film of mine - "In the Mood for Love". She had not seen it before.

Around eleven at night, Dabloo called up to inform me that the music maestro, his guru, had just passed away. I consoled Dabloo but decided not to trade the transient happiness of the night with grief and hung up shortly.

The splendid September night was passing away. As the film ended, she held my hand. Tears shimmered in her eyes, accentuating her beauty. I smiled at her and nodded in knowing. Neither could speak. We ate in silence. Then, I went and stood beside the window. She quietly walked up to me and rested her head on my back and held my hand again. We stood frozen for a while. I reassured myself that I would not take the first step.

She circled her arms around me, lifted her toes and kissed my cheek. I closed my eyes. She kissed yet again. Even death could not be so absolutely perfect.

Is this what they mean by intimations of immorality, I wondered. As she relentlessly, mercilessly, smothered me with kisses, the soul flew away from my body. Disembodied thus, it quietly observed that something as trite as carnal knowledge could evoke a thought, pure in its abstraction, in its non-definiteness.

Then again, mortality interrupted the soul in meditation.

Maybe the wine has gone into her head, the devil reasoned. Maybe she has been sexually aroused. Why was she pleading me to open my eyes, when I savoured every moment of the blur that covered my eyes and saved me from the feelings of guilt associated with any sexual encounter with her.

I want to see happiness in your eyes, she had kept on repeating. You deserve happiness and I know that I alone can bring it back for you. Please open your eyes and see my act of worship. For me you mean perfection, I will not let my perfection be tainted by sorrow.

As I opened my eyes, the world was still a blur. She wiped the tears, brought me to a sofa and made me sit down.

There she was, resplendent in her nudity.

I: Please switch off the lights!!!
We were two figures silhouetted by moonlight as my cigarette glowed and lit the tip of her nose. Her eyes were now bright, now dark. My eyes were now dark, now bright.
I remembered Blake. We were for once in an amoral universe, an unpeopled world of breath and touch, perfect with its imperfections. Was this bliss, true bliss, as ephemeral as this night?
 With the birth of dawn, the permanence of suffering would surely catch up again. Live in the now and act in the now, the rational self cajoled me. But I could not relent.
Tonight, I had to snatch away immorality. As I caressed her in bed, I cursed my hands for tainting themselves with time present. Mere mortal hands can't touch her soul. I writhed within.
She surrendered herself to me for one night. How could I explain to her that I wanted her for eternity? All I could do was request her to preserve this moment as memory.
I: You have the liberty to forget. If you don't want to forget, then, only then, kiss me when you wake up.
Saying this, I entered her. She folded her palms in prayer.
I woke up with her wet lips in my mouth. She smiled and got up from the bed. I wore my glasses and lit a cigarette.
Shyness had deserted her. She moved around the room, pulling back the curtains. I suddenly jumped from the bed and dashed towards her. As we fell on the ground, wrapped around each other, we laughed.

CHAPTER 6

As a matter of principle, we would always meet in private. She was not allowed to intrude into my world; I chose not to interfere with her professional life.

Both the parties concerned adhered to, the contract. Though this posed a lot of practical problems that was the way it was to be. No trespassing into each other's territory. This meant that we had to be discreet. That meant quite a few questions asked. Men are wont to be more possessive.

I seized every opportunity from then on, to hug her and kiss her. Very peculiarly, she started to avoid touch. I would grumble and growl. She would laugh it off. I don't like it wet, was all she could offer by way of excuse.

We kept no secrets. I mentioned my life to her. She confessed about Minal. I was mortified but had known the truth before. My male ego persuaded me to believe that soon, the insignificant other, would evaporate.

 Little did I realize that I was the other. The troubles started soon after. Over priorities initially, and then over trivialities. That was exactly when the end had begun.

Trouble boyo, Soumitro had cautioned. You are doomed, Soumitro pronounced prophetically when I confided for the first time. I should have kept you in chains. But then, how do you simply pin a fly down, Soumitro summed up curtly. Alas, I can't save you!!!

Rubbish, I pronounced grandly.

Eventually, she's going to be mine.

PART - THREE

LOVE AS DEATH

"AROUND US FEAR, DESCENDING

DARKNESS OF FEAR ABOVE

AND IN MY HEART HOW DEEP UNENDING

ACHE OF LOVE "

----- ON
THE BEACH AT FONTANA

JAMES JOYCE

PART III

CHAPTER 1

Two months had elapsed since he last met her. He felt ashamed for still surviving. That is the punishment for all your lofty notions. So much had happened in the past sixty-one days.

And yet, he still refused to die.

The dividing line between maudlin and melancholy is indeed very thin.

He could not yet decide which side he was on. Loneliness devoured him and that caused anguish. This, in turn, resulted in the sighs and tears. The pathos emerged out of a selfish need - the need for human contact. The proclamations of the saints - that you come alone, live alone and go away alone, did precious little to ameliorate sorrow. Why does the heartache thus pine for touch, for sight? No answers.

Historical context changes the tragic to the bathetic. That was more in tune with the times.

 He could neither alter the course of history nor the course of life. He stood at the crossroads, the perfect fool - wise with the knowledge of his essential foolishness. His life's story had come to a pause.

The trouble was that he did not wish to go anywhere. He wanted to be left abandoned, standing, bereft of touch. Touch me if you can, he playfully beckoned life.

Life gave a mighty push and he fell with the stars into the abyss unknown.

There was lipstick on her teeth as well. He ordered her to go and cleanse her lips and teeth. As the unknown woman washed herself in the washroom, he could not get over the cloying sense of amazement.

He had dared to defy Smriti's orders and had brought an unknown woman to the apartment. He decided to make love in the living room.

He was sufficiently inebriated to see her in a haze. As he switched off the lights, she asked for a name. He got all worked up and switched the lights back and asked her to depart. The poor little creature stood intimidated, frozen with fright. He cooled down after a while and told her that the preferred mode was anonymity. She coyly answered that her name was Daisy and mustered enough courage to hold the right hand and put it on her right breast. His hand stuck like a magnet to the breast; motionless.

Daisy unbuttoned his shirt and then her blouse.

As they lay down side by side on the carpet, she put her head on his chest. He removed her head, got up, wore the trousers and regretted the decision. But what was done could not be undone.

He felt defiled standing by the window and smoking. Daisy had left. He felt like puking for feeling so miserable. Fidelity my foot, he hissed.

She has never adhered to it, why should I? He was not effeminate enough to embalm the genitals and keep it preserved for the sacred hole.

Not a hole, not a hole, grant me a soul ... he prayed ... O Lord, gift me a soul.

CHAPTER 2

He was mortally scared that Smriti might discover a strand of Daisy's hair on the carpet.

As he tried to manoeuvre the vacuum cleaner across the room, in a hurry, Smriti, Srijeet, and Pimpu arrived. Pimpu dashed forward with open arms as he pointed the nozzle towards her.

You will suck my daughter into the cleaner . . . Smriti screamed as he lifted the bundle of delight.

Are you doing all this to impress me? Smriti added haughtily.

He winked at Srijeet and bit Pimpu's cheek. She screamed and slapped him.

-- Serves you right ... she is the one who can jabdofy you ... Smriti squealed in delight.

-- You speak like Aurora Zogoiby . . . he commented sarcastically. I am impressed to see my sister going up in life.

-- Who is this Aurora? Srijeet enquired.

Arre, can't you see Dada showing off ... Smriti chided Srijeet.

Then she turned towards him ... yes, I have read Salman Rushdie, do you mind? You're not the only intellectual in town.

-- Whoever said that you have to be an intellectual to read Rushdie ... he retorted. You only need to be a snob.

-- Dada's caught you there . . . Srijeet piped in.

He laughed approvingly.

-- Both of you are always conspiring against me . . . Smriti complained in mock anger.

-- That man was simply Rushing to Die ... he changed tracks. With all the fundamentalists lusting for his blood. When they lay their hands on him, they shall make delicious Salmi kebab of him. Only his beard will prick the palate.

I think they will pickle him ... those satanic eyes dripped in brine and olive oil ... Srijeet took off on their favourite trip to the absurd.

Srijeet and he revelled in this.

-- You seem to forget that Rushdie is no longer a hunted man unless of course, you consider the latest one to be a fundamentalist . . . both of you are such whackos ... Smriti said disgustedly. I'm afraid my daughter shall become like the two of you.

-- Funcle ... Srijeet cackled ... a fatal combination of Father

and Uncle.
-- That sounds a bit too corny for my sweetness . . . he nodded his head in disapproval ... and also mundane. Pimpu is above the mundane. She is perfection ... his eyes shone.
Don't spoil her from such an age ... Smriti butted in.
The tone in her voice was suspect. She quiet enjoyed the attention he lavished upon Pimpu. One thing Smriti never doubted was his love for her, Srijeet and Pimpu. They were his world.
Gently she broached the subject and a sudden hush spread across the room. Srijeet shifted uncomfortably as he sat down on the sofa motionless with a cigarette in hand. Smriti had come to announce their departure. For once he resented Srijeet's brilliance. Why oh why he complained within, did Srijeet have to be more indispensable in the US of A than here? Why couldn't a blithering multi-national pay him half as much and tempt him to stay back in India? He had known for a long time, this was inevitable. It had to come.
It came at a time when he needed them the most.
Pimpu toddled up and pulled at his trousers gesturing that she be lifted. He smiled and picked her up. Smriti and Srijeet glided towards his sofa and sat on the two armrests with their heads bent.
He held Srijeet's hand.
-- I am very happy and very proud .... he reassured Srijeet.
-- You must come and stay with us ... Smriti sniffed.
-- Better be careful about what you say. It's a very lucrative proposal . . . he smiled as he spoke . . . I just might agree. After all, a mansion in Chicago deserves me more than you . . . saying this, he pinched Smriti's cheek.
-- And we don't have to pay for Pimpu's nanny ... Smriti smiled mischievously.
-- I'm sure she'll forget me soon ... his tone changed as tears welled up in Smriti's eyes. Srijeet firmly held his hand.
-- We shall never let her forget you ... Srijeet spoke with compassion, dripping from his voice. We shall never forget you. How can we? You are everything to us. We are so proud of you ...besides the Whatsapp is always there for our daily chats . . .
He was taken aback. The crucible in his heart was brimming over with gratitude.
This unbridled display of love fulfilled him, as he held both Smriti and Srijeet in a tight embrace. Pimpu looked up at the

three of them and started laughing.

They ordered champagne and drank themselves silly. As Pimpu clapped, he and Srijeet sang hoarsely songs from films. Smriti kept on insisting that he accompany them at least for a while. He promised a visit in six months. That night they stayed back at his apartment.

As he woke up in the middle of the night, the realization suddenly dawned.

From now on, he would be all alone. He broke into a cold sweat at the thought.

CHAPTER 3

Aasma stood silently at the balcony. It was a moonlit night, a classic setting for a serenade. Minal would never sing songs to her, she thought. Probably, if she allowed him, mister pretender might do even that for her. She was filled with remorse just by thinking about the extent to which he could descend for her sake. She had placed him on a pedestal. He had no right to fall from grace. She had pushed the man to this pitiable state where he begged for her mercy. He, of all the people in the world, whom she had worshipped like no one else before -- he who was once free of fault. Suddenly, she snapped back to reality and cursed herself for thinking about him.

He's done me so much harm, she reasoned. He's hurt me such. Memories of another day flashed past her mind.

....

She was speaking in a hushed tone to Minal when he entered the room. This was the ritual goodnight call. For all his poverty, Minal had a cell phone. Usually, he called. Whenever Amma picked up, Minal disconnected. Amma would inevitably realize and this bugged her no end. Amma would keep on blabbering till the time Aasma would get fed up and snap back. Today, she was at his place, with the standard excuse of, sleeping over at Neelima's. She did not want to take the risk of Minal's suspicion and therefore called up earlier than usual.

He fidgeted for a while, seeing her speak in inaudible tones. How on earth the other person can hear her, he wondered pouring the after-dinner drink.

Jealousy was fast catching up with him. He downed two drinks to work up to a frenzy. As she disconnected, he tried the 'I'm perfectly okay' trick. Sensing trouble, she tried her ploy of I'd better make a move. This irritated him further. He took pains to remind her that she had volunteered to stay back for work. She upset him further by saying that she wanted to leave because he was not in his senses.

Then the theatrics started.

-- What do you mean by that? He demanded.

-- Your eyes are red and your speech is slurring.... she replied coldly.

-- Yeah, it's all right by you to smooch your clerk on the telephone from my apartment ... He swaggered and spoke. And it's wrong if I have an extra drink.

As she tried to push and make her way, he grasped her hand ferociously. His eyes were burning. She had never before, seen this side.

-- You think you can get away with some innocent cock teasing.... he hissed snakelike.

She put her hands to her ears. This is not true, O Allah, please prove this to be untrue . . . she prayed to a God she had no belief in.

-- I'm staying back ... she pleaded . . . so please don't wake your neighbours.... her teeth started to chatter.

-- Now I'm a drunken devil to you.... he shouted back. The Rape of Lucrece; The Rape of the Lock. Saying this, he pulled open her hair tied in a bun.

-- Please, please ... she whispered ferociously. If I had known this, I would not have stayed back.

-- You threaten me with departure? ... By now he was deliriously drunk. Dare to leave. You can't function without me. You are an extension of me ... he pronounced operatically.

He reached out to kiss her. She vigorously pushed him away. He fell on the floor.

He was now on fire.

-- You prefer a bank clerk's kiss to mine ...he yelled getting up. You dare to call him from my place only because I allow the blasphemy. You bitch you owe your existence to me.

She could not believe her ears.

He was speaking thus.

He, who would quote Shakespeare, Tagore, Browning, Keats, and Eliot, was speaking to her like this? I must be in another world, another space, she kept deluding herself. I must be the one who's drunk and hallucinating.

All through the night as he kicked her, slapped her, tortured her, she kept on thinking this to be a nightmare.

This is not he; she sobbed and thought this is not the man I know. This must be some genie that has possessed his soul. As he screamed, screeched abused and barked like the lowliest of mortals, she recollected the Zen outbursts and those Vedic incantations.

....
....

Amma's hand on her shoulder, brought her back to the reality of the balcony.

Go to sleep and find peace was all Amma could say.

How could she forgive his slap on her face?... Aasma wondered . . .
He didn't love her enough.

CHAPTER 4

Dabloo and Rukmini decided to part ways. The personal relationship had reached a point of no return. Brinda had happened by then, in Dabloo's life. Dabloo had to prove to her that he was out of love with Rukmini.

He had argued with Dabloo that this should not be an impediment as far as their professional association was concerned. Dabloo vehemently ruled out the possibility. Brinda would make life miserable for him. After all, she too was a singer looking for a place in the sun.

As always, he sighed, poor Dabloo has mixed his madness with music. Rukmini was his music. Without her, none of Dabloo's melodies worked. Yet, the poor fellow knowingly, allowed himself to be pushed to a corner, where he had to abandon his music for so-called love. Even if, one believed for a moment the sham to be love, was it worth more than Dabloo's music? Alas, such was life.

They were a bunch of fools entrapped in notions of the ideal, where none such existed.

Rukmini and Dabloo were perfectly unmatched for each other; right from the very beginning. She was a brazen sexless creature, totally immersed in her voice. Dabloo was a ram, forever pushing for fornication. He was their bridge. Initially, Dabloo used to even hold him suspect. She can even love you but not me, Dabloo complained. He tried hard to reason that Rukmini was simply incapable of love. Maybe that was why she had the perfect voice bereft of a body.

It was Dabloo who had allowed Brinda to become the vixen she was now. In the initial phases, when Dabloo needed a shoulder to cry on, he had painted the picture of Rukmini as a she-devil, before Brinda's eyes. He proved to Brinda that Rukmini took advantage of him and then discarded him. Dabloo was the martyr at the altar of love. He gave his music to Rukmini and she, in turn, had forsaken him.

Brinda had begun to resent Rukmini from then on. Once, she assumed a position of permanence, Brinda played it up by being vindictive towards Rukmini. The bird brain she was, Rukmini could not quite understand Brinda's attitude and felt affronted.

All three of them were caught in an unhappy mess.

But the heart of the matter was something else. Right at the outset, Rukmini had made her position clear to

Dabloo. She would worship his music but could not be in love with him. Indeed, it would have been more suitable for her to play-act with him and take advantage of the precarious predicament that Dabloo was enmeshed in, the present. When Dabloo's affair with Brinda blossomed, Rukmini genuinely felt happy for him.

Poor Dabloo could not stop loving Rukmini, even after she told him off. For her, it was a matter of fact. For Dabloo it was a matter of dreams he had woven around her. He could not merely switch off his love. He kept waiting and hoping for the impossible. His love and malice for Rukmini grew every day. Dabloo's decision to fall in love with Brinda was a desperate move. He wanted to prove to himself, his slighted ego that he too would be accepted. He felt sick with this continuous rejection.

Brinda brought order back to his life. He had lived like a gypsy long enough. He enjoyed the attention she lavished upon him. He opened his heart to her. That proved to be his undoing. She took charge of his life and work. Brinda was a clever girl. She realized that as long as Rukmini was around, she would never be able to sing his songs.

She misbehaves with you, Brinda reasoned, does not accord you the respect you deserve. Rukmini pretends to know as much about music as you do. Dabloo was more than ready to buy her logic. Brinda was speaking nothing but the truth, the whole truth. Rukmini spared no chance to humiliate him. People had started to assume that he was only capable of composing songs for Rukmini. This was a slur on his genius and detrimental to his career. I can even make a frog sing, Dabloo asserted in his mind. I must put a stop to this nonsense and throw her out of my life and music.

The brat she was, Rukmini too refused to bow down before Dabloo. When he reasoned with her, she did not wish to listen to logic and decided not to budge. Both of you are incomplete without each other, he argued. Rukmini vehemently nodded her head – a trait she had imbibed from Dabloo, and answered that life would go on irrespective. Dabloo would still have his music and anguish; she would still have her voice and pride.

Poor fools, he cried out. Where will he find the felicity of your voice and where will you find fecundity of his melody? Suffer in hell, both of you dog-headed fools!

Had he instead paused to think for a while and realize who

the real fool was, life would not have been so difficult. But then fools like him and Dabloo seldom did realize such simple things.

CHAPTER 5

-- What are you doing for lunch tomorrow? Parmeswar Pandey asked in sing-sing, over the cell phone. He was driving towards the studio.

-- Nothing in particular . . . he replied. Are you inviting me? He was curious to unravel the mystery of Parmeswar's pursuits.

-- I'll send someone over to collect your passport ... Parmeswar replied in a genteel manner.

-- So, you're taking me somewhere where they need to check my antecedents before they let me in Mr. Pandey? I'm impressed ... he said in zest ... where is this exclusive club?

-- No, I thought maybe we could lunch at the Hilton, Sir .... Parmeswar spoke casually.

-- Don't tell me Hilton has opened an exclusive restaurant where they need to check the passport? He enquired innocuously.

- I was referring to Hilton London!! Parmeswar chirped.

He pressed the brakes and screeched to a halt.

-- Now, now ... he gasped. Isn't that carrying things a bit too far? I'm sure you're no Onassis, nor am I, Fellini.

-- I don't know either of them, sir. Suddenly, I felt the urge of having lunch with you in London and dinner in Paris. We'll leave by the midnight flight if that's all right by you.

His saner self, asked him to refuse the invitation. He accepted it. He had to probe this mysterious man.

 He had work, yet decided to postpone everything and have a lunch that would cost two precious days and a further day of jet lag. His shooting schedule would be upset, but then such outrageous invitations don't come one's way every day. Modesty prevented him from mentioning it to anyone. Not many could digest the fact that he was travelling across two continents to honour a luncheon appointment. That too with a gentleman he hardly knew and had no business with.

Parmeswar Pandey had just appeared out of the blue. Well not exactly.

The culture minister had called him and introduced Parmeswar. The man was highly connected. Was he from the mafia? His appearance certainly pointed to that direction. Yet Parmeswar appeared very transparent – a family man, a corporate demeanour, a luxury car, a definite business address. Parmeswar had not hesitated to leave his residence numbers behind. He had carefully noticed that there were no imaginary guns under Parmeswar's tucked shirts or the pockets of his trousers. His obsession with the absurd was prompting the desire to know the outrageous Pandey better.

My close friends call me P.P. . . . Parmeswar observed unlocking his seat belt.

They were aboard the British Airways flight, a couple of thousand feet above the soil.

-- That sounds a trifle vulgar ... he replied sipping the welcome champagne. They were travelling first class. He made a quick calculation of the return fare for two and estimated that the money spent could buy a hundred lavish dinners, at any five-star across the country.

-- Phonetically you mean ... Parmeshwar laughed a short, contrived laugh . . . pee-pee, as in soo soo for children ... a former Prime Minister was very fond of it. Had it daily as a medicine dose.

-- That is rather bawdy ... he remarked. Especially when you're sipping champagne ... a bit too boho for my taste. Now, will you tell me the purpose of our sojourn?

-- Parmeswar smiled beatifically ... why do you worry sir? We shall discuss work over lunch. Now let us talk pleasure.

-- We shall in effect have two lunches ... he replied. One during the flight and one when we arrive. Should we call that lunch then?

But of course, it'll be afternoon when we check-in at the Hilton ... Parmeswar sipped a fresh orange juice.

 He had noticed that Parmeswar did not smoke or drink. No minor vices for this man.

-- I have no major vices either ... Parmeswar looked into his eyes and spoke. He was startled and taken aback. This man could read his mind.

-- This is most unfair Mr. Pandey ... he grumbled with a definite tone of resentment ... you have no right to invade my thoughts, make intrusions into my private space. I expected you to be a gentleman and had therefore agreed to come with you. I have never done anything so outlandish before, especially going out with a stranger. Now I regret my decision.

Parmeswar Pandey bit his tongue and apologized profusely.

-- I am so sorry sir, but I simply got carried away. This is my fault. I can read a person's mind even without wanting

to. Please forgive this trespassing. I have never held anyone in higher esteem. I respect your intellect too much to even think of ... Parmeswar folded his palms.
-- You simply want to show off your prowess ... he smirked. But that can frighten others. You're zany Mr. Pandey.
-- And you sir, you are not utilizing your talents enough. You and I could make a fatal combination. Suddenly Parmeswar changed tracks.
-- Would you mind talking about your taste in women?
-- You know everything about it ... he said in a resigned tone. You've read my mind.
Parmeswar nodded his head vigorously.
I can only read the surface. With most people, I succeed, because their thoughts are afloat. You have too many layers, even for me. That is precisely why I am interested in cultivating you. At last, I have met my match!
Saying this Parmeswar clapped his hands in the air.

CHAPTER 6

After lunch, they took a private ferry down the Thames. At the Hilton, he was in for another surprise. Lunch had been ordered, long-distance, two days back. It was an elaborate affair, a five-course meal with three courses of wine.

The trip down the Thames that September afternoon was very refreshing. It brought back memories of another September night. The night eternity happened in an instant. It was the very same day. He turned his face away from the face-reader standing at the deck.

Parmeswar came and sat beside him. The man's intentions could not yet be fathomed. Even after sixteen hours, Parmeswar had still not revealed his motives. With his dainty well-manicured hand Parmeswar fetched out a cell phone and made a few business calls. It all sounded Greek to him, shares and scripps. After ten minutes, Parmeswar switched off the phone and put it back in his pocket.

-- It was important for me to be in London today ... Parmeswar chimed contentedly... else I would have lost a million sterling pounds.

He kept quiet and lit a cigarette.

-- Now we can come to matters of business ... Parmeswar clapped his hands and wiped his face with a handkerchief. The real purpose ... I think you are a genius, Sir . . . I want to be your friend.

He looked at Parmeswar, a bit dazed. This man had brought him to London to propose friendship. Had he gone out of his mind or was he gay?

-- Neither ... Parmeswar chirped and immediately bit his tongue ... oh sorry, sorry I didn't wish to ...

 He started to laugh. The realization dawned that now he was completely at Parmeswar's mercy.

-- Actually, if we team-up. I can earn a million dollars in a matter of months. You combine business acumen with great artistic skills.

-- Alas, they do not go together Mr. Pandey ... he sighed. I seem to be out of touch with the times.

-- You are not meant to be sold like potatoes, sir ... Parmeswar announced confidently. You are an exclusive item for a niche market. I will sell you internationally.

-- Now I am a product in your hands?

-- Why do you take it in the wrong spirit? Parmeswar chided him. All great artists need business managers. I am volunteering to be one.

-- What do I have to do, pray? He meekly enquired.

-- We'll work together. I have decided to go into film production ... Parmeswar stood up ... now that we have finished business, shall I order some sparkling wine for you, sir? We have to catch the flight to Paris shortly. Or else we shall be late for dinner. You can sleep on the flight back home.

-- Dr. Faustus had sold his soul to the devil! He said in a hushed tone.

-- I am no Mephistopheles ... Parmeswar Pandey laughed merrily ... by the way, have you ever met the Devil? He is a rather interesting fellow.

CHAPTER 7

The script about the women's dream died a natural death with Aasma's departure. Thankfully so! Anyway, it was maudlin in its excesses.

Yet he hesitated to press delete. Let it remain, stored and incomplete forever. Why do all stories need completion? Some streams perish under the sand. Some events just fade away. In life, some stories cease midway.

But when you see a film or read a book you hunger for completion. You feel thwarted, slighted and cheated if there is no definite ending. Even something as trite as "and they lived happily ever after" or as maudlin as two lovers walking away to the sunset, satisfies your desire for an end. People refuse to accept an unfinished ending. It is as meaningless as halting before the orgasm. Climax, climax the mob rants in full-blooded fury. It is all a problem with narrative obsession. Sadly, even a poem has to end, music has to be rounded off, dance has to finish and painting completed.

To spite her, he would never complete the script about the woman's dream. The man dying in her arms would always remain a mystery. He relished the thought that Aasma would keep on guessing and never find out. Maybe, she would imagine her ending. This thought disturbed him. She has no right over my story. He felt extremely agitated and called her number.

He heard her voice and felt weak. Aasma kept on saying hello, but he did not reply. He disconnected. His mind was blank. He searched for words to fill his mind. There were none. He groped for thoughts. There were none. There was nothing before his eyes, no sounds entering the ears. Everything was a blur.

He opened his eyes and saw Smriti's anxious face hovering over. He was in an alien environment. He saw Srijeet beside Smriti. Smriti held his hand and patted it gently. As he attempted to speak, she put her hand over the mouth.

She explained that this was a nursing home and the doctor had asked him to relax and not to speak. They were all there to take care of him. The jing-bang was anxiously waiting outside and he would soon be okay.

He felt mighty pleased. His theatrical self felt relieved with the melodrama of a heart attack.

At last, this anguish found expression in a mild stroke. A severe heart attack would have been dangerous. This was just about all right.... cushy and nimbly painful. The only tragedy was that cigarettes were out. He felt suffocated. Smriti the dictator would not allow him such small mercies. Srijeet was a kind soul. But he refused to yield, petrified by the harridan of a wife.

They came one by one for the obligatory visit. Kalpana, Pico, Tico, Dilip, Nanoo, the vile Vipul, in one go. Then Dabloo plus Brinda minus Rukmini, then Rukmini alone, Avinash, Alisha and Ashutosh and finally Parmeshwar by a great display of ostentation – tulips and orchids straight from Holland, lilies and white roses. Once he arrived, Parmeswar fussed about the arrangement and drove the people at the nursing home, up against the wall. Eventually, he had to shut Parmeswar up. Parmeswar generously offered his villa at the hills or the beach-house for recuperation. He politely refused and went back home.

His stroke got reported in the papers. She must have read about it. She was surely practicing her suitable oxymoron cruel kindness.

Or was this a caesura? Of course, it was; he tried to console himself.

She came to visit him after seven days. Both of them were at a loss of words. Aasma fidgeted with a paperweight and he held an unlit cigarette between his fingers awkwardly.

As they searched for words to speak, he realized that the Bengali word *"abhiman"* was truly untranslatable. It did not mean hurt, nor did it mean anger or the vapid rise of the ego. The closest one could come to grasping the essence could be irreparable hurt caused to the heart by unknowing hands. Both felt that they were wronged.

Both wore *"abhiman"* in their hearts.

It was a hopeless situation. He felt that it would have been better if she had not come.

Aasma wished she had not come.

The silence kept on growing, till it enveloped both of them. Like lost souls in purgatory, they awaited the redemption of departure. Aasma walked up to the bedroom, checked the medicines, came back, went up to the kitchen, made two cups of tea, served one for him, drank the other, read a magazine. He sat on the sofa and played with his unlit cigarette, lit the lighter, fiddled with it for a while. She came and sat beside him.

Aasma touched the tip of his little finger and his heart ached

again.
-- So ... she said finally.
-- So? He replied.
Again, there was the meaningful pause, the caesura.
They both contemplated on the mistake of ever having met. They both regretted their meeting. They both resented their loving. Yet none could dare to speak. In the end, Aasma got up and left.
As the door clicked, words were about to burst from his lips. Modesty and vanity prevented expression.
On the bus back home, Aasma decided to marry Minal.
Life was slipping away.

CHAPTER 8

Boyo,

You bet I've found life. In this jungle that is euphemistically called a garden, I have rediscovered myself. I am beyond grief and hurt. Life has begun and tons have happened. Thanks, would make a lesser mortal out of you, so I shan't. Indeed, I've gone for a sixer. Now, where do I begin? Knowing you, you want to devour the gory details, so here it goes.

When I arrived, my taciturn manager condescended to drive me to the place I rightfully inherited. There was little or no conversation, except the statutory information about labour unrest and militant threats. Just to think of it, the bastard gets paid to serve me thus.

As I arrived at the bungalow, the servants were paraded in front of me with the salutary salaams. Then I went for a bath. After which, I went for a walk in the shrubbery, generously called the plantation. That is where I met him.

He is employed as a foreman in my garden. He is a qualified agricultural engineer from Punjab Agricultural University. His name is Dipon Bezborua. He is about twenty-six, tall, yellow, with chinky eyes. He has a quaint smile. We got talking. Dipon spoke at length about the problems of the labour force. I could not at that point, discern the tinge of political didacticism in his manner of speech. To me, he was the only civilized person among these natives. I invited him to dinner.

I noticed that he was a heavy drinker. Dipon gulped down eight pegs of premium whiskey with admirable ease, whereas, me poor me, felt drunk with four. He spoke about his years in the hostel in remote Punjab, the hostile environment where North Indians resented the North-Easterners. He informed me about his schoolteacher father and the suffering the native Assamese faced in the hands of these degenerate Bengalis owning almost a third of these smaller estates.

After dinner, as we graduated to wine, he finally got high. He started to sing and got more and more aggressive. There was a strange beauty in his aggression. It was mesmeric like the ferocity of the tiger. I indulged him. He wanted music. We shifted to my bedroom.

I played him my kind of music. That excited Dipon. English music, he said, was something that made him wild. He started to dance, as I sinfully thought that, I had vanquished a potential rebel. I was by then sufficiently inebriated. That was the moment when he took the liberty of kissing his master-Me!

I was flabbergasted. Believe you me, totally flabbergasted. I had never experienced this side of life before.

And now hold your breath . . . the wonder of wonders, I enjoyed it. Yes, I did. I who denounced sex, even in its more comfortable refuge, enjoyed the forbidden. I bit the apple. What pleasures unknown, revealed themselves before my eyes!!! Dipon filled me in the fullness of the night. Every conceivable way, he satisfied my mortified flesh-hungry for touch. He became me. Like a silly puppy, I promptly fell in love with him. I know here you will try to deconstruct my mind and trace seeds of the homosexual embedded in my subconscious self. Maybe I was a homosexual without my knowing it. Vanity prevented knowledge.

As I type this letter, he sits beside me and winks. He knows all about you. Pardon me, but I have sinned by confessing about my only friend in the universe to him. He wishes to meet you. We are both naked now, with no secrets between us.

I had never imagined that life would take such an unusual turn. Maybe, I was till now, unsure about my sexuality. The wonderful thing is that I feel no remorse, no guilt in waking up to this truth. This is no forbidden fruit. This is reality confronting me head-on, and I humbly bow and accept it.

Your reticent and haughty friend has finally found himself. May you in your way.

Love Soumitro.

The mail stumped him. Why did life around him have to be so melodramatic? It was almost Dickensian in its excesses. Almost everyone around him, except for Smriti and Srijeet, were on a perpetual merry go round. Too many coincidences like Hardy, too much grief like Dickens. Why weren't there Shavian and Kunderaesque characters peopling his universe?

At first, he cursed Soumitro under his breath and then felt happy for the bloke. After all, having known a person for the last thirty-five years of your life, it is not a very comforting thought to suddenly realize one day that he is gay. But then, come off it, Soumitro himself did not know that he was gay.

Eureka, he shouted, I have eventually found the oxymoron. Off with 'perfect love'; welcome the word 'gay'. This one word contained the absolute irony and did not

need two words juxtaposed side by side for ironic effect. The dictionary described gay as happy, "with wanton abandon". They even – in days of yore, had a restaurant by the Ganges, which was named GAY. In Victorian English, poets often used the word.
He had never known a gay to be happy. In a heterosexual universe, gaiety means sadness. Which blithering idiot could have christened the sexuality thus? In the politically correct environment of today, such people prefer calling themselves queer. He thought that this terminology was cornier. To hell with it!!
He feared for Soumitro's impending doom. Dipon Bezborua would be, he predicted, the nemesis of Soumitro's life.

CHAPTER 9

As they waited in the departure lounge, incessant tears dripped from his eyes.

He held Pimpu tightly, as Smriti kept on wiping the tears with her handkerchief, and admonishing him in undertones for behaving like a silly fool.

In extremely rare moments such as these, his veneer gave way. Now he was exposed, a silly, stupid, child. Even Srijeet wore a stolid, sombre expression. Only Smriti was struggling hard to make it look normal.

-- We are not going away forever ... she muttered. Promise me you won't smoke or drink too much. Pimpu in her native wisdom must have guessed. She clung on to his collars and howled. Smriti slapped her back.

-- Stop it, you are behaving like your Mamu ... Smriti scolded Pimpu.

Just then, Parmeswar Pandey appeared from the middle of nowhere and uttered the usual niceties. He introduced Parmeswar to his sister, brother-in-law, and Pimpu.

Parmeswar, as was his wont, promptly predicted that their flight would take off twenty minutes behind schedule.

As Parmeswar chatted up with Srijeet, Smriti pulled him aside, and instructed him to have the medicines on time, smoke and drink less, eat fat-free food, keep the place clean, keep the income-tax lawyers informed, pay bills on time, wind the mechanical clock and generally take care.

The flight was twenty minutes late. When they finally walked towards the departure lounge, Pimpu refused to let go off him. Smriti had to pull the wailing child and then hug him. She managed to contain her sobs and made him promise to keep her informed. She threatened him with death if he failed to report to her every day over WhatsApp.

As the three of them receded to become tiny spectres', Parmeswar placed a palm on his shoulder. He controlled the tears and put on the mask. Such effete sentimentality stinks, he reasoned. He, the great crusader against maudlin excesses in cinema, was indulging in it, in private life. What a hypocrite me! I feel like kicking my face but can't lift my feet that high!

-- You must condition yourself to departures ... Parmeswar chimed. They will be a continuing part of your existence. Another one will depart. He swiftly turned and shook off Parmeswar's hand from the shoulder. Why the hell should this man pass judgment on every situation? By indulging Parmeswar he had committed a mistake.

-- You'd be better off as a Druid fixing magic potions in boiling cauldrons ... he commented brusquely. Parmeswar smiled his beatific, idiotic and utterly irritating smile.

-- I am no soothsayer Sir ... saying this Parmeswar clapped his hands in the air. I cannot change the course of destiny. I can only see it unfold in front of my eyes.

-- Then you must also have seen that sometimes in time future, I'm wringing your neck, he replied nastily.

-- Heh heh heh! Parmeswar laughed in staccato. You will do nothing of that sort. We shall soon start a film together. This film shall catapult us to international fame. We must order our tuxedos right away. Parmeswar hurriedly started dialling his cell phone to order his tailor.

As they drove away from the airport, he observed that it was a starless night. Melancholy enveloped his heart. Parmeswar had insisted on driving him home. So, he had to ask the driver to follow them.

-- Your problem is you love too much ... Parmeswar's drone broke his reverie.

-- Oh yes, my charioteer ... he mumbled . . . please stop playing Krishna.

-- But I have to ... that is why I suddenly walked into your life. I must teach you to be more dispassionate. Or else you'll suffer.

-- I love therefore I am ... he pronounced grandly. Now, aren't we getting a bit too personal?

-- I am a businessman sir. I don't get annoyed so easily ... Parmeswar's face shone with a smile. Don't cling on, don't cling on.

-- Please stop the car, this very instant . . . he growled. As the car screeched to a halt, he alighted.

Thank you for the lift, Mr. Pandey. He slammed the door.

Love is not Time's fool he asserted firmly. Anyway, such wisdom is lost on you. Count your stocks and shares and don't call me anymore.

-- We shall meet for dinner tomorrow . . . saying this Parmeswar whizzed away without waiting for his jibe.

He stood on the dark road, speechless, thoughtless and seething with rage, as the driver pulled up.

CHAPTER 10

Avinash and Alisha had both reached the nadir. The relationship could not descend or progress any further. Several times Alisha had decided to abandon him. Avinash had this magical quality of bouncing back into her life. But it had by now, reached the point of no return. There were simply no further roads to explore. No more divinities, no more recantations that could even remotely sanctify their togetherness. Avinash had to be cast off from her life.

Alisha had gone through the routine rituals of mending to make her love survive. But it had come to naught. Eventually, she had no alternatives left but to forsake him. Alisha had often wondered what made Avinash the wimp, he had reduced himself to become.

She had known him since childhood, much before he had acquired all these fancy frills of stardom. They went to school together. His sister was Alisha's favourite teacher. The lady had brought Avinash up in a very no-nonsense manner. They had a quiet upbringing, very much grounded in reality.

Their romance never suffered the sting of the unreal. Being in such proximity since childhood, they discovered the pangs of adolescence together. They explored each other's bodies quite naturally. Their minds were extensions of each other's souls and their hearts – when they found out they had one, were one. There was no ceremony to announce their love. It was a foregone conclusion. Even Didi knew it and accepted it like the simple solutions her sums provided.

She grew up to become an architect, he an actor. The fringe benefits he acquired with his stardom spoiled it all.

Avinash ceased to be human when he became a star. The narcissist took over and Avinash stopped loving his Didi and Alisha. Initially, the two women in his life rationalized that this adulation was hard to digest, for a middle-class person. Then they started getting perturbed.

That was the time when Avinash got hooked on. That was also the time when Ashutosh entered his life. The negative and positive happened together. No angst or ennui prompted Avinash to savour such devilish delights. It was merely a passing fancy that grew to become a fetish. The drug devoured Avinash as much as the adulation of being the fragile number one. Insecurity crept up.

The only saving grace was that by that time he had acquired

Ashutosh as property. The poor boy was pulled up from his station in life as a mere production assistant, to become the secretary of Avinash, the unvanquished. Ashutosh sought to protect him with the alacrity of a pet Doberman. The only difference was that he was a timid rabbit in his own life.

Yet Ashutosh stood by Avinash through all odds; even when Didi had virtually given up. Even when Alisha decided to leave, Ashu could not leave. Alisha realized the selfless sacrifice this innocent boy made for the demon. She would often speak to him, asking him to come over and stay with her instead.

Who will look after him if I go over and stay with you? No one will look after him, was all that Ashu could manage to gasp. Alisha almost felt guilty at not having loved Avinash as completely as Ashutosh. The simpleton had abandoned reason and loved.

When Avinash went through the crisis, and his mentor and guardian angel, the filmmaker called her, Alisha had agreed to respond for one final time. She had assured him valiantly that she would try. Indeed, she tried and failed. Avinash refused to give up hell. Alisha had no aces left up to her sleeve to play. One moment further and she would die.

Avinash was lying on the floor, blue in agony, Ashutosh was pumping his chest in a vain attempt. Alisha resolved to quit for good. She stood up and looked at Avinash one final time. Then she stormed out of the room through the corridor to the lift. Ashutosh ran after her. As she entered the lift, Ashutosh held her hand and sobbed bitterly, pleading her not to leave. She shook off his hands and closed the lift door.

A feeling as heavy as death burdened Alisha as the lift descended.

CHAPTER 11

Rukmini and he were ensconced in silence for quite a while before he finally agreed to speak.

To his did you know you were a perfect bitch, Rukmini replied that only a perfect bastard like him could make that out. He and Rukmini shared the rare perfect friendship of no give and no take.

-- If only you had loved Dabloo, things would have been so much the simpler . . . he meekly reasoned.

-- You seem to forget my dear ... Rukmini retorted with alacrity, in that case, I would have had to be a hypocrite and suffer perjury. I love his art and not Dabloo.

You love Dabloo . . . he chided her. Or else, you would not have been so grossly over-worked when his appendicitis burst.

-- Alas ... whispered Rukmini, Dabloo will never understand that. Anyway, hush, you dare not mention it to him. If he comes to know, he'll compose four more immortal songs on that count for me and then burden me with further ingratitude.

-- Can you tell me why are we all doomed in our private hells? Why can't there be laughter, the normalcy of sunshine, in our lives any further? Why does it always have to be dark and brooding?

-- Because you choose to make it so ... Rukmini chirped. My life has its share of sunshine. All this doesn't affect me anymore. I find it too petty. I have elsewhere to go. I'll never be stuck in the darkness.

-- A star needs a dark sky to shine in ... he retorted. How can you escape the darkness?

You men are incorrigible . . . Rukmini snapped back. You always seek the masochistic pleasure of tragedy. If it is not there, you feel let down, disheartened, cheated. You go out with a torchlight seeking darkness and sorrow. You love to lick your tears. And all this in the name of high art. Down the ages, people like you pompously push the shit that 'Our sweetest songs are those... .' down people's throats . . . ugh!'

He laughed uncontrollably at Rukmini's outburst. Rukmini picked up a cushion and threw it at him.

-- See, you too can laugh. Only you choose not to ... then she walked up to him and held his hand... my heart fills with joy when I hear the sound of music. Nothing else is important then. It's bliss for me. I rise above the mundane and become my song.

Rukmini broke into a contralto and sang with full-throated ease.

The mist lifted from his heart.

-- How do you solve a problem like Rukmini?

-- Very soon I will reach the top ... Rukmini hummed. You cannot catch me and pin me down.

-- Won't you miss your mentor, forever, swishing his hair across his baldpate?

-- I guess you're right ... Rukmini conceded.

CHAPTER 12

At the registrar's office, Aasma was in two minds. Before the thought could get the better of her, she hurriedly signed the papers. Now she and Minal were finally together- united in holy matrimony. Both she and Minal were against a religious ceremony involving the Qazi and Quran. A paper ceremony suited them better. A paper that could fly in the wind; could be torn; could be burnt.

The marriage was a hush-hush affair conducted in the absence of their respective families. She had Neelima and another friend as witnesses. Minal had his cousins. They went out for a quiet lunch, which had to finish quickly as Minal had to rush back to the office. She promised to meet him in the evening.

When Neelima held her hand and asked her what it felt like now that she was married, Aasma had no answers. The burden had not yet lifted from her heart. She bade Neelima an abrupt farewell and jumped on to a bus. She got off at the next stoppage and tried his cell phone. It was not connected. He must be home, Aasma surmised.

Even when she rang the calling bell, Aasma did not fully realize what was happening.

As he opened the door, she rued her decision. He ushered her inside the apartment without a word. Dumbstruck, she sat down like a zombie on the sofa. The innards of her body were revolting, but she could not gather the strength to get up and leave. He came and sat beside her. He slept on her lap and wept silently. She caressed his greying hair.

He got up and kissed her. Aasma's lips were trembling as she was being undressed bit by bit. Then he undressed and pulled her to the carpet. He held her in a tight embrace and promptly fell asleep. Her eyes were wide open, but the mind was blank. Her vision blurred, and she dug her nails on his back. He woke up after an hour and found her to be senseless. His back was bleeding.

The water sprinkled on her face, brought her back to her senses. He had removed the clothes from the room. Fear crept up her heart. Would he keep her hostage forever?

He lifted her and took her to the bedroom. He placed Aasma on the bed and climbed on top of her. It seemed that she had forgotten the use of language. He gently entered her and lay motionless, looking into her eyes. Those looks pierced her soul. She was bleeding inside. Untold agony ripped her heart. He just did not move an inch, nor bat his eyelids. He was frozen in time till the climax.

With great effort, Aasma pushed him out of her. She stood up, located and wore her clothes.

He lay motionless on the bed. Aasma bends over him and kissed the forehead.

-- This is the end. From now, you must write your scripts alone.

Aasma felt like a bird on the streets.

122

PART – FOUR

HATE IN THE WOMB OF LOVE

"SWEPT WITH CONFUSED ALARMS OF STRUGGLE AND FIGHT

WHERE IGNORANT ARMIES CLASH BY NIGHT!"

--------DOVER BEACH

MATTHEW ARNOLD

PART IV

CHAPTER 1

In Dipon, Soumitro found his perfect foil.

In public, they kept their hierarchy intact, for the sake of their respective reputations.

Behind closed doors, Dipon made sure that Soumitro did not exercise any authority over him. In sober moments, Soumitro was talkative and aggressive, while Dipon was taciturn. In inebriation, Dipon was the aggressive, agitated orator, while Soumitro wore a benign smile. To Soumitro's childishness, Dipon responded with care; to Dipon's melancholy, Soumitro expressed more than adequate concern. They took over each other's lives.

It was a comfortable situation as they were situated away from the city and prying eyes. They never made their affection obvious. They were both the same sort and so it did not appear unnatural for the owner of the garden to take a fancy on his most educated employee.

On weekdays, they spent the evenings together – drinking, listening to music, making love, having dinner and bidding each other goodbye, precisely in that order.

Weekends, they drove out of the garden and checked into forest bungalows. They had a wild time together. Going out fishing, swimming in the streams, nude, making love on boulders, and having a bar-be-que and behaving like teenage kids. This rendezvous continued for three months till the time Soumitro was beckoned by his sister to return to the city on matters of urgent concern.

He hated the thought of going back. He had no choice. He hated that more.

When he broke the news to Dipon, the fellow just got up and left. Much as he would have liked to follow him, Soumitro couldn't. They were in the office. Later that night, he coaxed and cajoled his lover and promised to come back in a fortnight.

Dipon drove him to the airport. The place was a humble apology for an airport. Only two flights took off from there. The incoming flight had not yet arrived. Soumitro's departure would be delayed by about two hours. For the first time, Soumitro felt quite happy with the delay. Usually, he hated sitting in the lounge – delayed flights were a regular feature at this devil-forsaken airport. Normally he would while his time cursing himself and reading comic strips.

They went for a small drive. In the middle of nowhere, Dipon stopped the car, hugged Soumitro and started kissing him vigorously. Soumitro willingly gave in.

As they rubbed their crumpled shirts clean, Soumitro asked Dipon whether he would live with him. He proposed migration.

Dipon was quiet for a long while. Eventually, he spoke.

-- You hardly know me Soumitro. Besides, it seems an improbable, rather impossible situation. I have liked you, I care for you, but my parents depend on me. You hardly know the whole truth. Your life and my life are too divergent. You hardly know my past. I cannot afford to be selfish, even though I love you. You hardly know my present. My life is not me alone, it is for my people. You hardly know what my future may be. I respect you; I have begun to miss you already even before you're gone. You hardly will accept the truth even if that is harsh, even if it turns against you. You hardly will believe it Soumitro. I can't even ask you to forget me for I can never forget you. You hardly would guess the intensity of my feeling; you have changed my life completely forever in the last few months. You will hardly be able to forgive me. I have brought a curse on you.

Dipon had never spoken so much, so vehemently. He was panting after the outburst.

Soumitro lit a cigar and held it out. Dipon took a few quick puffs and returned it.

Soumitro held Dipon's shoulder firmly in his clasp and reassured him that he was willing to take Dipon as is where is -- good, bad, ugly. They drove back to the airport.

The flight had arrived and the ten-odd passengers had already checked in. As Soumitro was about to turn, Dipon held his hands and spoke again.

-- If you ever come to know anything ill about me will you stop loving me?

-- No ... Soumitro replied looking into Dipon's eyes.

-- Even if you come to know that I am associated with anti-national activities?

-- What? Soumitro's hands slipped from Dipon's.

-- Yes. If you come to know that I am involved with insurgent activities, working with the Liberation Front. You'll not stop loving me?

-- No. I care two hoots for the country. I can run off into the jungle and live there with you forever. You mean that much to me damn it!! Soumitro proceeded to check-in.

He did not look back.

But he knew Dipon's eyes had lit up.

He resisted from looking at Dipon till he boarded the aircraft. From the window, he could see a speck waving his hands madly as the flight soared the skies. There was a sinking feeling inside Soumitro's stomach as the plane bumped its way through the clouds. He had just denounced his country for the sake of someone he had barely known for three months. He dismissed the thought, knowing that Dipon had played a practical joke on him to test him.

These natives Soumitro reasoned, regaining his haughty composure, can be such blithering sentimental fools.

CHAPTER 2

-- I just feel like spending some money on you . . . Parmeswar signed the cheque and held it out with a flourish ... do whatever film you want to make.

-- I feel flattered by the confidence you repose on me Mr. Pandey even though my last film bombed. But I am presently in no frame of mind right now to think of or start another film. He lit the first cigarette after the stroke.

-- Don't start just right now ... Parmeswar reasoned. Go somewhere, take a holiday and write a script. I know that my money is in safe hands.

-- But I don't want to think ... he beseeched. I have banished thought. I just wish to be left alone.

-- I won't disturb you. I promise ... Parmeswar pinched his Adam's apple. When you come back and find the time, give me a call. Shall I book your tickets? Just tell me, hills, valley or sea?

It was impossible to ward off Parmeswar. By now he had understood that this man could not be warded off or wished away. He failed to understand why this man was wasting his time and money on a person he hardly knew.

-- I shall tell you the reason later? Parmeswar smiled mischievously.

He knew at once that the mind had been read. By now he had given up. He knew the situation was well beyond control. He was being raped. He might as well lay back and start enjoying it.

Tch!! Parmeswar bit his tongue ... that is a very unkind analogy. I worship your talent Sir, therefore ...

He snatched the cheque from Parmeswar hand and rose to escort Parmeswar to the door.

-- Good night Mr. Pandey ... he curtsied before slamming the door.

-- I just wanted to tell you ... Parmeswar chirped, jutting his head inside the half-closed door ... this marriage will not last.

-- Which marriage? What marriage?

-- Never mind. You shall know in due time ... Parmeswar withdrew his head ... good night Sir.

He was in a quandary. Whose marriage was Parmeswar referring to? Dabloo had just married Brinda. But Parmeswar would surely not know of that. He had never mentioned Dabloo to him. Then again, he had never mentioned Aasma also. And yet Parmeswar knew. Similarly,

he might have known about Dabloo.
Very frankly, he was also of the same opinion. Dabloo's rash decision had disturbed him. But he had chosen not to interfere. He was too troubled with his own life to bother about Dabloo's hamartia. He knew very well that Dabloo had married Brinda to spite Rukmini. That Dabloo did not achieve the desired effect was another matter. Initially, out of natural compulsion, he felt sorry for Dabloo. By then he had decided to cast off the mantle of an agony uncle. He did not bother and even attempt to prevent the marriage. Marriages are made in heaven, he reasoned, cackling with laughter. They manufacture the accompanying suffering in hell. Dabloo was cast into the inferno. He derived Parnassian pleasure seeing Dabloo battling against the lashing waves and sinking in time future. The phone rang. He rushed to pick it up. It was Soumitro on the line.
-- I'm back ... Soumitro announced grandly.
-- You deserve to perish in hell ... he hollered back. After all that has happened, you come back. I'll never forgive you for not coming during my stroke.
-- I'm not film-folk you remember? Soumitro replied caustically. I don't get enamoured by such trivia. Anyway, good news I've won Dipon. He loves me crazy.
-- I have lost Aasma ... he replied plaintively.

CHAPTER 3

Smriti was scared stiff with one thought. What must my brother be doing with his life? Pimpu kept on reminding Smriti – with her perpetual drone Mam … Mu, Mam … mu, of her foolish, foolish brother; an intellectual before the entire world, a fool, an utter fool for her.

All through he had kept on making mistakes. Recklessly falling in love with any tart that came his way and getting hurt in the bargain. She did not mind the aberrations. They were a part of his artistic existence. He could not be judged by conventional terms of morality. But it bothered her when her brother kept on repeating his mistakes. His marriage was a colossal blunder. It ended very messily. Even before that ended, he was involved in another sordid affair, which wound up with the beloved sleeping with a common friend. She knew of all this but chose to remain ignorant. For all the brazenness, he was shy in front of her. She decided not to lift the veil.

She had sensed trouble this time around too when she read his expressions. But again, she respected his privacy too much to intrude. Some sixth sense told her that he was not keeping well. This worried her no end. When Srijeet came back from work, he sensed that his wife was not in good humour. He guessed correctly, the thought that was worrying her, and called up long distance. Unfortunately, the Whatsapp call was not getting connected. Smriti understood that Srijeet was trying Dada's number. It was okay for her to worry about her brother. But why was Srijeet so attached? She had no answers.

The only point of contention in their marital life was who loved Dada more. By birth right, Smriti thought she did. By sheer emotional contact, Srijeet retorted he did. He is my brother, Smriti argued. But I can feel his agony more, Srijeet retorted. Now there was a third contender who could not speak much. All Pimpu could do was cry hoarsely, Mam – mu, Mam-mu. She loves him more, both of them agreed.

For the life of them, they could not fathom why Dada was wasting his worth on trivialities, faking realities.

You are meant for more; you are meant for much more. We can't see you wasting your life on persons, on situations dear brother! You have to rise above that circle of deceit called relationships.

CHAPTER 4

When he entered the office, it seemed like the set of a birthday party. In her sweet girlish manner, Kalpana had arranged for an elaborate welcome. The staff had pitched in their resources and made the arrangements. He was touched. Kalpana, Pico, Tico, and Dilip presented him with flowers. Kalpana even went to the extent of doing an aarti, garlanding him and putting the auspicious vermilion mark on his forehead. He felt ashamed at not having thought about these people who depended on him for a living. For their sake at least, he had to work.

He called Kalpana inside and asked her to arrange for Parmeswar's cheque to be deposited. It was lying with him for over a fortnight. He dictated several letters to her and enquired about her well-being. Kalpana's face glowed and she unabashedly confessed how much they all missed him. Pico, Tico requested him to visit the studio as everyone was anxiously awaiting his arrival. He told Kalpana to ward off all requests for interviews. After a while, he expressed a desire to be left alone. Dilip brought him coffee and they all withdrew.

As he ploughed through the pending files and mail, the door swung open and he looked up. He was flabbergasted to see Amma standing there. He quickly got up and escorted her inside. He closed the door behind them. Amma looked at him sternly. He felt distinctly uncomfortable and wondered how she had managed to locate his office. Amma seldom travelled outside. Amma's expressions betrayed hurt and anger. He fumbled for words and just about managed to ask her to sit down.

-- I never imagined you would forget me . . . Amma complained in a voice suffused with sorrow. You promised that you would always keep in touch.

-- Amma ... he faltered . . . I was not keeping well.

-- I know that ... Amma replied . . . I read about it. I wanted to visit you, but she would not let me.

-- How did you make your way?

-- I had no option ... there was anxiety in Amma's voice. I had to meet you. . . why couldn't you prevent it?

--Prevent what? He enquired.

-- The marriage ... Amma gasped.

-- Which marriage? He could not understand what she was referring to.

-- You mean, you do not know ... Amma questioned incredulously . . . you don't know, she has gone and married Minal.

He could now understand which marriage Parmeswar was referring to.

-- When did it happen? The words formed themselves in his mouth. His heart had started to sink again.

-- On the 14th of last month .... Amma replied. I came to know about it just a day back.

The last time he had met her was on the fourteenth of last month. Now things became clearer.

She is a marvellous woman ... she came to me for the last time, gave herself to me on the very day she got married. Was she human?

-- I did not know what to do, where to go to ... Amma continued. You were not available on the phone. Please do something ... Amma pleaded with folded palms.

-- What can I do? He replied helplessly throwing up his arms ...what could I do?

-- Her life will be destroyed . . . Amma wailed . . . don't you love her anymore? Please save her from sure destruction.

-- Has she left the house?

-- No, no ... she did not even tell me. I forced Neelima to spill the beans. What will happen to her career? I mortgaged my earrings to buy her dancing bells and pay her fees at the academy.

Amma could hardly breathe and started to pant heavily. He offered her water to drink. She held his hands and cried and requested him to meet Aasma for her sake.

-- You are too much a part of her ... Amma asserted vehemently . . . for her to reject you.

-- Alas ... he sighed ... I wish that were true. But it is not dear Amma ...

-- The fault is yours ... Amma chided him. Why didn't you pay her, her dues? My daughter is very money minded.

-- What dues? He questioned in a choked voice. He could not understand.

-- She tells me that she has stopped working with you because you don't pay her properly. She'll chide me if she knows that I speak to you.

He had no answers to this. He had never imagined that Aasma would stoop to this level to justify her predilections. So, it was after all a commercial transaction? He did not have the heart

to tell Amma the truth.
-- Please pay her well and she will return to you . . . Amma pleaded innocently. She hardly knew what she was implying, albeit unintentionally. Aasma needed to prop up a reason for a departure from his life.
He reassured Amma that he would do the talking. He escorted her downstairs and asked the driver to drop her back. He stood on the streets for a while, benumbed by what he had heard. As the traffic zipped past and the cacophony continued, he felt that it was not worthwhile living and loving in a cruel world of lies, deceptions, and falsities.
Aasma could do this to him? Why not? After all, she alone had the liberty to do anything with his life.

CHAPTER 5

That evening at the club, the tables had turned. He sat quietly listening, while Soumitro gushed forth about how his life had finally acquired meaning. His taciturn demeanour did nothing to dissuade Soumitro's flamboyance. The man was too preoccupied with his own love story, to pay him any attention.

Despite his predicament, he felt happy for his friend. Soumitro had eventually found a vocation in life. It was a purposeful existence. He did not have the heart to snap the happy man back to reality. For so long, Soumitro had done just that to him. Soumitro filled him in with all the graphic details of this unusual courtship, regaled him with anecdotes about his queer relationship. After their martini and steaks, as they graduated to wine, he spoke for the first time.

-- How do you propose to make it tangible? He queried after much thought.

-- Simple! Soumitro announced grandly. All we have to do is migrate. I have already started to make the provisions. For a start, I intend to sell off my garden.

-- Do you think that will be a bright idea? He inquired hesitantly. Given the present context of insurgency, who would want to buy a tea garden with mounting debts and labour unrest?

-- Well, in that case, there is always the option of distress selling. Nothing could stop a Soumitro possessed. I don't give a damn if I lose. I shall still have enough to see Dipon and me through, for the rest of our lives.

-- Are you comfortable enough with the idea of living your life with another man? It is all right sleeping with him under covers ... I mean such things do happen ... but living with him. Isn't that a bit too quaint?

-- Of course, it is quaint ... Soumitro answered indignantly ... that is precisely why I want to do it. Indians have these strange notions despite the fact half of your gods were either gays or fucked cows.

-- No recorded god in the recorded pantheon ever did things to cows ... he protested. Well, some did have rather strong male bonding, he conceded. But never was there any direct reference to homosexual activity.

How ignorant can you get, Soumitro seethed with rage and clenched his cigar firmly between his teeth. Even something as contemporary and as horrendous as those myths propagated by Hindi cinema celebrates the concept of male camaraderie more than man-woman romances. All this concept of ' *Yaari*' or Bromances stinks of depraved covert homo-erotica.

-- Why are you on the offensive? He enquired bemusedly lighting a cigarette. Even mainstream Hindi cinema has become rather gay-friendly with the success of the slew of gay filmmakers' brigade. Tell me something ... was this lying dormant in you for so long and has now erupted with the slightest push?

-- Am I wearing a green tee-shirt announcing glad to be gay and wear pink pajamas along with it? By now, the vicious had taken over the rational Soumitro. One fine day I discovered love. Accidentally it happened in the arms of a man. I don't find any reason for you to be neurotic about it. Would you rather prefer the asexual me?

He had no answers to that. How could he deny that happiness glowed in Soumitro's eyes for the first time? Was he being prudish just because Soumitro was such a dear friend? He had often seen people who argued vociferously for sexual liberation, freak out when they discovered their sons to be gay or daughters to be lesbian. Sex and love were, after all, matters of private choice. Could iconoclasts like him be converted to become conservative in homophobic environments?

-- On the contrary . . . he changed tracks ... it is fashionable to be gay in today's world. All artists, models, painters, dancers wear it like a badge. Gay activism is treated with great veneration by the media.

-- I don't bother whether you call me gay or not ... Soumitro spoke dismissively ... I happened to fall in love with a person who showered me with the affection I never received before.

-- So finally, you've come around to accepting the existence of love? He had scored victory finally.

-- Yeah.... Soumitro murmured begrudgingly ... you were right. The power, the glory the, etc of love was not bull-crap.

-- Divinity has touched you, my friend. Live with it and be happy.

Thus, they resolved a fifteen-year-old conflict.

CHAPTER 6

After Amma's knowledge, their meetings had become infrequent. This bugged Minal no end. He could not meet his lawfully wedded wife because she had a cantankerous mother to contend with. Aasma tried to reason, but all logic failed. If indeed Amma had come to know, there was no further need to hide. Aasma could do little by way of explanations. For the life of her, she could not make Minal see enough sense. If she acted rashly, Amma might just have a heart attack and die.

At times like these, Aasma felt the need of him. In a moment, she banished the thought. If it were not for him, Amma might have come around to accepting Minal as an inevitable choice. In a way, he was responsible for Amma's stubbornness and refusal to yield. From behind some invisible curtain, he was pulling the strings. She hated the control he exercised over Amma. She resented the fact that life would have been simpler if she had chosen him instead.

Life perhaps would also have been more meaningful for both of them. They were more compatible with each other. She shared more common traits with him than with Minal. Their spirits blended effortlessly with each other; their dreams coalesced. Minal was more remote, distant; except for the body, except for the first touch. Minal was the first man to touch her. Aasma hated herself when she felt that Minal was not the only man to have touched her. He had touched her deeper.

Minal was impatient. By now he was exasperated enough to agree to leave the family for her sake and set up home. But Aasma was not ready. She still valued her dancing more. In dancing, she truly found herself. More than her love, more than even him. She could give him up but not her dance.

He did not want her to give up her dancing, Minal did.

Apart from him, she had no access to that magical world of conjuring images. Aasma wished she had some. Then the pain of abandoning him would be less perhaps. Minal opposed this as well. He wanted to possess her. This irritated Aasma. She was not to be possessed. She found it too shallow. To be enveloped by one man's consciousness was more than she could tolerate. Yet that was all Minal yearned for; total possession of body and soul. She could not give him that.

That was precisely how the differences started. Initially, they yelled at each other and made up. Then the subtleties started playing up. Each little move of hers irritated Minal. Each digression of Minal from his original promises of – I won't interfere with your career, exasperated Aasma. They even started to loathe each other. Sometimes Aasma wished that she had a shoulder to cry on.

But, but, now, he was far away. Almost in the realm of thought.

 Aasma shivered at the thought of having forgotten him. Yet she did not dare to confront him. At the end of it, Aasma realized, she would have to relent. But she was not prepared for it.

Not for now .... Not for now.

CHAPTER 7

After the daily ritual of a film shoot, Ashutosh was driving Avinash back home. Avinash rolled a joint, lit it and asked Ashutosh what he felt about the last shot of the day. There had been much adulation at the studios but that he could not take that seriously. Driving effortlessly down the streets, Ashutosh observed that Avinash's performance had been lousy, to put it mildly. Why then did the audience still like him, Avinash enquired. Ashutosh replied that they preferred the mask Avinash wore. The reality stunned Avinash for a moment.

Then he began cribbing about this meaningless repetitive life. Ashutosh suggested that a break from the routine would do him good. And most definitely, an immediate patch up with Alisha would be the ideal thing for him. Avinash scoffed at the idea and threw the cigarette out of the window.

Inside the apartment, they ordered dinner, took their respective baths and settled down with the drinks and smokes. They were discussing Ashu's imminent departure, the next morning.

Ashu had not been home for a long time. Even since the death of Avinash's sister and Alisha's departure, he had to single-handedly manage Avinash's affairs. This meant shooting schedules, dates, costumes, script sessions, taxation, temper, tantrums, laughter, and tears. Each night Ashu had to put Avinash to bed after Avinash lost his consciousness.

Ashutosh came from a small town. His sister's marriage was about to be finalized. So, he had to leave. Avinash got all charged up and promised to attend the wedding in person. It would create a sensation, he felt. But deep within, he resented Ashu's departure. Ashu reassured him that he had set up everything and would be back after a week. Avinash did not take kindly to the idea.

As the smoking and drinking continued, the normally timid and shy Ashu started to open up, much to Avinash's discomfiture. He had no choice but to endure. Avinash himself had allowed these liberties. He needed someone to speak the truth on his face. Ashutosh was his court jester who could rile him with impunity. He could pull the cigarette from his hand and take puffs, snatch his glass and take a sip. Initially, Ashu used to feel hesitant, shy. Avinash would take pains to train him to become equal. Snatch the cigarette he would command like a professional dog trainer. It was lonely, living in hell. Avinash needed to drag down someone to the hovel.

-- I have even lost the capacity to feel ... Avinash tried to offer by way of excuse ... I cry a hundred times when my mother's die on the screen ... but when Didi died......

-- You were not there even ... Ashu snapped back ... you were lost.

Avinash got up from the sofa, swayed across the room to the balcony and pulled the curtains back. The stars glittered above the dark city.

-- I hid behind these curtains.... Avinash confessed...I tried to cry, but tears never came.

Ashutosh rose and started to swing along with the music. Avinash languorously turned around. Seeing Ashu dancing, he lost his cool.

-- You fool ... he shouted ... you stupid fool. You dare to dance when I'm telling you about Didi.

-- Didi didn't leave you ... Ashu laughed a mad laugh and swirled ... you lost her. You were too caught up in your world. I could never do that to my mother.

Throwing the burning cigarette from his hand, Avinash dashed towards Ashutosh and grabbed him by the shoulder.

-- I picked you from the streets ... he grunted ... I wanted someone to talk to ... what did I do to Didi?

-- You left her!

Unable to control his rage, Avinash slapped Ashu hard on the face. Ashu collapsed on the floor. What followed was an uncanny moment of silence. Having realized that he had over-reacted, Avinash sat beside Ashu and coaxed him to roll another joint. An adamant, Ashu refused to budge. Avinash gently patted him on the back and tried what he was best at – emotional blackmail. He called Ashu a little kid brother he never had and exerted his right over him. The trick worked as usual. Ashu got all charged up and started talking about a better future for Avinash, more meaningful roles, more acclaim. He proclaimed that the wanted to see Avinash in a passage of flight soaring high.

I'm afraid I might fall from there ... whispered Avinash ... please don't go.

-- I have to, I have to ... Ashutosh hopped across the room. I was nobody . . . you made me. Now, this life has become my addiction ... can't relate to those simple folks back home. I have to go back to them for once. But I can't . . . Ashu sat down crying helplessly.

Ashutosh felt that he was trapped and there were no means to escape. Avinash offered a simple solution. Dramatically he arose and spread his arms. As Ashutosh looked at him incredulously, he smiled a dazed smile and asked Ashu to spread his wings. Ashutosh jumped up and scampered around the rooms singing like a little child, that he would spread his wings and fly through the night to his home and reach before dawn.

-- Oh no ... Avinash smiled cruelly ... you can't. I have clipped your wings.

Almost in slow motion, Ashutosh turned to look at his mentor, his master, with disbelief in his eyes.

-- That's what you think? Ashu spoke haltingly ... well, I want to show you that the wings you think you've clipped are still good for flying.

The duel had begun. The demon had overtaken Avinash by now. He goaded Ashu on in his dangerous game, daring him to fly like a bat through the darkness of the night. The world was topsy-turvy for Ashutosh. As he flitted between illusion and reality, through the haze of smoke and alcohol that enveloped his consciousness, Ashu could hardly recognize the man standing there and provoking him. His God had failed him. The devil was beckoning him to fly. He had to accept the challenge.

In a sudden fit of frenzy, Ashu rushed to the balcony. The tumultuous breeze on the twentieth floor ripped through his hair and clothes. He looked at his master for one final time, smiled obediently and flew off into the darkness. Avinash fell in a heap on the floor.

After this, there would be reality no longer.

CHAPTER 8

As providence settles on the limpid icicles of the moment, eternity becomes an instant. Truth revels to reveal itself in moments of magic realism. Harsh and bitter or sweet and mellifluous, it recognizes only one constant – time present. Seconds, minutes, minute moments, moments and drops of eyelashes, eyelashes, and clicks of camera flashes.

He understood that from now on, Avinash's life was being sculpted in the myths of media where headlines and columnists become each to each, an instant eternity. The hero had indeed had a tragic fall. There was now no escape for Avinash. The image had to fake triviality-underlying reality, be subjected to jargon, verbiage, and cartoonist's adage displaying replaying a providential rage.

From now on, moments would create and recreate in thousand shapes and typefaces, drowning in the reality of the unreal. Precisely from here did the sparrow fall, he fathomed – from Hamlet to Andy Warhol. Everyone was having a ball. Oh, what a ball! This was the time when the vultures could tear Avinash to shreds. They spared no effort. Apart from him, only Alisha was there. She was not expected to be there, having borne the brunt of Avinash's innumerable indiscretions. Nevertheless, she was.

His sorrow took a backseat. He spared no effort. Avinash needed protection. He had to be there. That was *dharma*.

They shifted Avinash to his apartment. After a while, that too was safe no longer, as prying eyes invaded their privacy. They had come to know, as they always do. Alisha voted for the hills, he for the sea. Despite fewer years of intimacy with Avinash, he knew the sufferer and the tormentor better. So eventually it was the sea.

But they had to be discreet. So, they chose a place away from the hubbub. It was a serene staid place, bereft of people and noises. The sea was rough, but that was okay as they were not exactly tourists seeking sunbaths. The hotel hardly had any inhabitants except for a few horny middle-aged men with their mistresses or whores. There was a gay couple also. That reminded him of Soumitro.

Avinash had been virtually reduced to a vegetable. The shock of Ashu's death was impossible for him to digest. He could not speak or walk. Most of the time, Avinash refused to eat. It seemed that Avinash wanted to die.

Alisha had abandoned work. So, had he. Oh, he cherished

every moment of playing the messiah again after a while. Alisha and he were hell-bent on seeing Avinash back on his feet. The winner had to bounce back, they asserted. Avinash had resolved by now that, life had no further meaning left,

In moments of solitude, when they agreed to lend the lost soul sometime, the enormity of Ashu's death caught up with them. The guilt burdened them. The poor fellow did not need to die, their rational selves argued. The suffering of Avinash sobered them, chastised them. Yet Ashutosh's sacrifice could be scant forgotten. He hardly knew Ashu, but Alisha had known him as a brother.

Avinash was in a state of all passion spent. He had nothing left in him to confront reality. In his states of delirium, he would only be able to mumble incoherently the mumbo jumbo that few or none understood.

When they took him to the sea, the macho man for all his strength was scared and wept like a child. Alisha feared that Avinash might suffer an attack. He ruthlessly argued that Avinash needed the waves. With waves lashing at him, Avinash jerked back to life. Avinash's limbs moved and he twitched his face. Alisha's face, angelic in its grace lit up instantly, His eyes shone. It seemed that they had achieved victory.

But life was not cinema. Nothing drastic happened. Avinash could barely move. Recovery was still far away. The only consolation was that the process had started. In every little act of faith, he discovered flashes of divinity. Death had finally brought Avinash and Alisha together. From now on he knew they would be no separation. Fulfillment even in others' lives brought him happiness.

After a long time, one love story had worked, found a resolution.

His own story was dying slowly. The absence of the acute agony that he had felt initially after Aasma's departure pained him. He could not come to terms with the blankness that surrounded the heart whenever the thought of Aasma flashed past the mind. He understood that he had deluded himself so long into believing that there could be no life without her. Life existed in the great beyond.

So long, cocooned in the microcosm of love, he had chosen to ignore the larger realities of life. The religion of love was no longer tenable. But that disproved his very theory of living and being. He had to start life afresh from zero and enunciate newer theories. He could not afford to live without a theory. That was a burden, pseudo-intellectuals like him, had to bear. Yet in front of his eyes love had manifest itself never as beautifully before. The revival of hope in Alisha and Avinash's story was there for him to behold and learn from. My theories may not apply to me, he reasoned, but they work in other's lives.

It is not total bunkum after all.

CHAPTER 9

Parmeswar was persistent in his pursuit. Even after knowing the man intimately, he could hardly gauge the mind. This baffled and irritated him. After hearing the fantastic stories Parmeswar had recounted about his own life, he discounted most of them. They were the ideal material of the picaresque. The man had built his fortunes by taking uncanny risks. Parmeswar's mother drove him out of the house, in his teens, for his errant ways. His mother was an iron-lady, who ran schools and took no nonsense even from the first son, a rare phenomenon in Hindu households from the cow belt. Parmeswar had hoodwinked his mother's friend and managed five hundred pounds and a ticket to England. There, in turn, he conned a relative into providing shelter and a job. Thereafter he found a better job and accommodation and promptly snapped ties with the relative. He impressed upon his spinster landlady, a cranky Irish woman so much so, that the old lady left her little fortune for him. This money he used judiciously and multiplied it at the markets, using his mysterious sixth sense. After that, he returned to India.

Using his powers of hypnosis and prowess as a glib talk, he won over a few influential girl-friends. He played them, one against the other, and benefited in the bargain. This whetted his appetite for money and women. Both he gained in number, at an alarming speed. Then he put the brakes for a while and seriously practiced the occult.

Having empowered himself with black magic, now there was nothing that stopped Parmeswar's ruthless conquests – he won over anything and anybody. The filmmaker was his latest target. Somehow here all the tricks did not work. At last, Parmeswar was impressed with an adversary. Therefore, Parmeswar kept on persuading him to relent and be vanquished.

He relented but was not vanquished. He accepted the money but did not sell the soul. Parmeswar Pandey's normal enticements did not work – money, food, and women. He partook of the first two, judiciously avoided the third. But he digested without burping and thanking. Parmeswar bit his tongue and racked his brains to conjure new tricks.

One day he commented that Parmeswar needed subjects, not friends. Parmeswar was slightly taken aback but adequately impressed. Very articulately he had exposed Parmeswar's grand designs. I love winning the battles of the mind, Parmeswar confessed.

You love possessing souls and defecating on them, he retorted.

146

PART – FIVE

THE LOVE – HATE SCRIPTS

"...WE ARE SUCH STUFF

AS DREAMS ARE MADE ON ..."

-----THE TEMPEST

SHAKESPEARE

PART V

CHAPTER 1

He thought of a novel way of getting Parmeswar Pandey off his back. He was no longer interested in making full-length features. He intended to make a series of short films. There was no commercial market for such films and hence Parmeswar would be dissuaded and withdraw. Then he could pursue his thoughts and conjure something of substance.

This script was to be different from his other work. He felt relieved having chosen to veer from his usual path.

Parmeswar thought it would be a brilliant idea and thanked him profusely for having thought of a unique marketing proposition. His only request was that the series be made in odd numbers - three, five or seven. That was a fetish. You can even make nine if you want to explore the nav-rasas, Parmeswar suggested, Or else the seven deadly sins; alternately the five senses; or at least three-fold path. This man was certainly not the standard, by your leave, uncouth producer.

Parmeswar's sang-froid made him shiver. It also provoked thought. After all, it was not a bad idea. He only had to choose between the path, the senses, the sins, and the emotions. Only the market savvy Parmeswar knew that he had a mini-series up his sleeve - something that the wily man could market well, with OTT platforms and overseas networks, earn a profit and collect a few awards on the way as well. For him, it could be an introspective journey. Having lived in the realm of the senses, he knew that he could justify his experiences most with the number five.

Being positioned outside, he could objectively deconstruct the five senses that dictated life on earth.

He was not sure of the subjects, but he was certain about the five different ways he would tackle his subjects. This was to be his big joke in cinema. He thanked Parmeswar in his mind, for having provided him this rare opportunity in life.

For once, he understood the need for patronage in an artist's life. In ancient times it was either the clergy or the king; in modern times it was the mafia or the big business. The artist needed enough indulgence to forget the needs on earth and create. An artist caught up with his electricity, telephone and fuel bills could never think grand. Gone were the days of Van

Gogh and Keats - of struggle against poverty, consumption and effete idealism. In a decadent consumerist third world, the artist needed his moolah, martini, and Mercedes. What shit, the arrogant self, argued. Even Da Vinci Michelangelo and Shakespeare had people to please. Only he did not have to worry like them, of the threat, - "Off with their heads". He had the ultimate choice of casting Parmeswar off, whenever he deemed it fit. In the meantime, do as you please.

He was burdened with one thought - the need to write. Of late, he had grown accustomed to a human Dictaphone with a 'thought check'. How could he ideate without her? He had promised Aasma that there would never be scripts without her.

Now she had the chance to turn around and tell him in her incisive tone, I told you that you are good enough without me. I am only an excuse. He had no answers to that. His heart ached again and this pleased the perversely vain man.

It pleased him no end to think that she still mattered. His nemesis was too much-acquired knowledge through books and cinema. And all his knowledge seemed to point at one irredeemable fact - it finally did not matter. Why the hell did it not matter?

Aasma was now someone else's wife. Was she by that virtue, someone else's property? "Do not covet they neighbour's wife". But Minal was most certainly not a neighbour. His thoughts were once again impious - goaded by desire, to beget her as property. He banished the thought. The realm of the senses he argued, was indeed my domain.

He wanted to begin with the most palpable - the realm of the touch. The five senses did not need scripts. As jargon would put it, they only deserved treatments.

The Touch would be Soumitro's story told through The Fire Within.

CHAPTER 2

The sixties had tolerated Goddard's childish pranks and polemics as Avant-grade. Jean Luc Goddard was among the unfortunate few, who lived to see his death - in cinema. He decided to play the defunct Goddardian joke of "beginning, middle and end not necessarily in that order", to Soumitro's story.

He again went back to the sea. Not the dull sedate sea skirting the city, but the rough bay resort. This time he was alone. Avinash and Alisha had come back to the city to resume life. Ashutosh's ghost had been buried and their story had wound up in the mundane. He lost interest in their lives. Palpable reality bored him to death. He who was constantly striking poses could not accept the touch of reality. The rough sea was a constant source of rejuvenation in his life. He felt one with that sea. He could feel submerged and become a part of it. By the seaside, he worked on the story of the hills - the terrain where the Dipon - Soumitro romance flourished.

The idea of turning the linear narrative with a proper beginning, middle and end, topsy-turvy was prompted by necessity. He had only known the beginning. To fashion a script, he would have to concoct middle and an ending. To do that, he had to pursue either clairvoyance or imagination. By doing that would he be fair to Soumitro? Could he shape and ruin Soumitro's future? Or else, he would have to wait for the logical ending. That could mean a lifetime and his script would never get written. He was confused. There were no ready answers available.

All his life, he had created complexities and shaped kismet. He was no fly to a wanton god. He made his destiny. Such was the terrifying power of the curse he bore. This vanity was to be his hamartia. Nowhere in the scheme of things did he destine Amrita. Yet she happened one fine day.

He was sitting by the beach at sunset.

Amrita walked out of the sea, almost from the horizon. She was wearing a sarong, had hazel eyes and auburn hair. As she walked past, he looked at her and smiled. Amrita smiled back and walked away. Something inside predicted that he would die in her arms.

How could planet earth allow such a complete fool to carry on? How? How?

As the sun dipped into the sea, he got up and followed

destiny. The thought of the script had vanished.
Amrita realized that he was following her. She stopped in her tracks and turned around. He thought of turning away and leaving. But walking up to her instead, he got over with the statutory introductions and told her that he would lie in her arms one day.
That did not confound Amrita. She just smiled and replied that she believed him. They struck up a friendship in a minute. It seemed that they had known each other in their several previous lives.
They went for a swim by moonlight. By that time, they had known everything they needed to know about each other. If there were any secrets, they did not need telling. They promised never to fall in love with each other and resolved to livetogether, with each having the liberty of their private space - together on the same planet. He composed a poem about her hazel eyes and she offered a solution for the new script.
There was no confusion anymore. A new collaboration started.
The Fire Within was about to begin.

CHAPTER 3

The Fire Within

SCENE 1
An aircraft travelling through the clouds.
The wings glow with the reflection of sunlight from below the clouds, as the beginning titles appear.
A voice-over: My friend, the idle man, had decided to alter the course of destiny. He was walking in the clouds and working towards a relationship that could only exist in the air. The fire was burning within.
The inside of the aircraft.
Soumitro is seated beside the window looking outside, his chin cupped in his palms.
The Narrator is seated by the aisle seat. He looks into the camera.
Narrator: My friend is lost in thought. He knows that Dipon is waiting for him on earth below. He wishes to know nothing beyond that. This love story has begun from the middle. We shall come to the beginning later. A sentimental welcome awaits Soumitro. He seeks Dipon's touch once more.
Bleach out.
Dipon stands with extended hands. Soumitro moves in slow motion to embrace him.
Bleach out.
Inside the aircraft, the Narrator gently nudges Soumitro's but finds no response.
The Narrator turns back to look into the camera.
Narrator: Nothing can break his reverie. Not even my touch. No other touch is real for Soumitro. As this plane lands, the story will head towards an end.
The aircraft lands on the runway, taxies towards the arrival lounge and comes to a halt.
The inside of the aircraft.
Passengers get up and head towards the exit. Soumitro unmindfully pushes the Narrator, without noticing him and heads towards the exit. The Narrator is seated. He smiles knowingly.
Narrator: My friend is in a mad rush to reach. Do not trip over Soumitro. You were not brought up in a barn . . . relax, light your cigar and walk with studied ease. In the eyes of the world, you are still the Boss.

The Arrival Lounge at the Airport.
 Dipon's feet tap anxiously. His hands are crossed behind his back. He is carrying a bunch of wildflowers. Dipon's chinky eyes search through the crowd of passengers. He is casually dressed in jeans and an electric-blue sweatshirt.
Soumitro adjusts his hat, tightens his tie and proceeds languorously pulling the suitcase on a trolley behind him.
Having sighted Soumitro, Dipon lifts his hand with flowers and waves. Soumitro takes off his dark glasses, arches his eyebrows as a smile fleets across his lips. He walks up to Dipon. Dipon hands him the flowers.
Soumitro: Hello!
He gently pats Dipon's shoulders. Dipon takes the trolley and manoeuvres it through the crowd.
Soumitro: How've you been?
Dipon looks askance at Soumitro, smiles and nods his head. Soumitro takes his mouth near Dipon's ear.
Soumitro: My dick missed you!
Dipon smiles widely and runs ahead pushing the trolley vigorously. Soumitro follows.
The Narrator appears in front of the camera.
Narrator: Ugh! I almost feel like throwing up. Such saccharine demonstrations of calf love. To think of it, the sarcastic Soumitro reduced to this level. This is what you call 'falling' in love. What a fall it was!
A fat woman slips and falls with a thud.
The Narrator smirks, abruptly turns, moves away and mingles with the crowd.

SCENE 2
Late Afternoon.
A jeep speeds up the hill roads skirted with tea gardens.
Tight close-ups of Soumitro and Dipon intercut at a frenetic pace. Their lips, eyes, noses, hands, a lit cigar now on Soumitro's lips, now on Dipon's.
The inside of the jeep.
Dipon is driving and Soumitro is seated beside him.
Soumitro: You didn't write to me.
Dipon remains silent and swerves around a bend.
Soumitro: When I called, you did not come to receive my calls. I had to issue special instructions for you to receive me.
 Dipon drives recklessly.
Soumitro: Is this fair? Damn it!

Soumitro places his hand on the steering wheel. Dipon brakes and the jeep screeches to a halt. Dipon turns from the wheel and stares at Soumitro.

Soumitro: Why are you staring at me like that?

Before he can complete, Dipon slides from the driver's seat pounces on Soumitro and is over him. Soumitro's head juts outside the car. Dipon tears open Soumitro's tie and plunges his head inside his shirt. Soumitro starts laughing and places his hand on Dipon's back. Dipon lifts his head and looks into Soumitro's eyes. They heave and pant in silence for a while. Then Dipon fiercely bites into Soumitro's lips.

The Narrator props up from the rear seat and looks into the camera.

Narrator: Such a scene the Indian censors will not allow. Such blasphemy Indian audiences will never digest.

Soumitro and Dipon hug each other and get out of the jeep. They walk towards the edge of the road and look at the crevice down below.

Dipon: Let us jump down!

Soumitro pulls Dipon's hand and retracts.

Soumitro: I want to live with you . . . made all the arrangements ... we'll sell the garden . . . move to Australia.

Soumitro puts his hand into his pocket and fetches a bunch of keys.

Soumitro: Here! Keep your house-keys Mr. Dipon Bezborua. A house in Melbourne.

Soumitro places the keys in Dipon's palm and closes it.

Soumitro: For you this life.

Dipon opens his palm, looks at the keys and suddenly flings the keys down the cliff. Soumitro looks dazed. Dipon moves back to the jeep to start it and drives off. Soumitro looks at him going. The jeep halts round the bend. Soumitro walks up to the jeep.

The Narrator appears at the spot they had left and looks into the camera.

Narrator: If we had wings, we could fly.... So seldom we try

SCENE 3

NIGHT

The bedroom at the Tea-Estate.

Soumitro and Dipon are lying down on the bed nude. Dipon's eyes glow in the light reflected from the bedside lamp. Soumitro's cigar glows and fades in the dimly lit

room. They are both motionless, looking at the ceiling.
Soumitro: Your untold fears I cannot fathom.
Dipon: You will not know.
Soumitro: How will I if you don't let me?
Dipon: I cannot . . . my wings have been clipped
Soumitro: It is possible in today's world for two men . .
Dipon: In your world . . . not mine.
Soumitro: You are my world . . . you taught me what love is.
Dipon: When I was a small kid, I loved a puppy . . . my Naga friends stole him and ate him up . . .
Soumitro: Why will you not go with me? Why?
Dipon: My father never loved my mother.
Soumitro: Why? Why?
Dipon gets up from the bed and reaches the table. He pours a drink in a glass and then pours water.
Dipon: Want some?
Soumitro nods his head in the affirmative. Dipon takes the glass in one hand, the bottle in the other and goes towards the bed. He hands the glass to Soumitro and takes a swig from the bottle.
Soumitro: Why are you afraid?
Dipon: I'm not.
Soumitro: Why then do you drink straight from the bottle?
Dipon: Because you want the undiluted truth.
Soumitro: What more truth can you speak? I am the master and you work for me. Society will scowl at you ... what will happen to your family . . . pour me another.
Dipon pours another drink into Soumitro's glass and takes one more swig.
Dipon: Truth more than anything . . . truth above anything ... the truth that scares the rich . . .
Dipon prances around the room taking swigs from the bottle.
Soumitro: So now we have reduced ourselves to class conflicts? I can sleep with you ... but I can't live with you, huh!
Soumitro pulls the track pants lying on the bed and slips them on.
Dipon: I have to do more than sleeping and living ... I am committed to my people.
Soumitro: I told you that given a choice between my country and you, I'd choose you ... care two hoots....
Dipon sits on the ground beside the bed.
Dipon: You said it in jest.

Soumitro: So, did you
Dipon: I did not ... I did not ...
Dipon starts pacing up and down the room in states of great agitation.
Dipon: Given a choice I have to choose my cause.
Soumitro: And what may that be?
Soumitro gets up from the bed.
Dipon: Our struggle against your government!
Soumitro comes and hugs Dipon. Dipon pushes him away.
Soumitro: Don't be theatrical! You are not a terrorist!
Dipon: You expect a freedom fighter to look like a dacoit?
Dipon points at himself.
Dipon: This is what you've made us . . . nude . . . stripped us of our dignity . . .
Soumitro falters in his steps.
Dipon: What foolish notions your city-folk have ... you do not even know why we are struggling. Do you think I took up a job in your garden just like that?
Dipon wears his underwear and then his trousers.
Soumitro sits down on the bed with a jolt.
Soumitro: You were planted . . . planted to trap me?
An expression of anguish fleets across Soumitro's face. Dipon takes another swig.
Dipon: Not you ... not you ... your class.
Dipon moves towards Soumitro. Soumitro pushes his hand forward to prevent Dipon from coming nearer.
Soumitro: I understand ... I bloody well understand ... you want a ransom ... state the amount.
Dipon fiercely grabs Soumitro's hand and pounces on him, forcing him to fall on the bed. He sits atop Soumitro.
Dipon: What evils your people have perpetrated ... what suffering our people have endured you'll never know ... I am supposed to fight ... I can't ... I can't, I am trapped ... I'm ... my friends ate up my puppy dog . . .
Dipon falls on Soumitro's chest.
Dipon: Why the hell did I fall in love with you? Why? Why?
Dipon clings on to Soumitro and starts sobbing. Soumitro lies motionless, with a blank expression on his face.
The Narrator enters the frame.
Narrator: It is difficult to justify the ways of God to men.......
The bed and the room fade into darkness. Only the Narrator's face is revealed in a shaft of light.
Narrator: This is a very classic situation from the popular

cinema. The seducer falling in love ... only the gender has changed . . . what the heart does to you . . . o bleeding heart ... o bleeding heart..
Fade Out.

CHAPTER 4

Like him, Amrita had loved and lost.

Unlike him, she was not devastated by the experience. On the contrary, she drew strength from it. Love and melancholy had enriched her and helped her blossom as a more fulfilled, mature person. Amrita was no intellectual like him. She acquired vision and knowledge from observing the abundant flow of life all around. She was sweet without being syrupy, virtuous without being moral, perfect by being blemished.

Amrita reacted to his script with scepticism. She felt that despite sundry protestations, he had not yet been able to abandon the melodramatic elements and achieve the much sought-after meditative quality. However, she did not hold him to a fault. That was his ' *Swabhava*' or innate nature. To deny that and choose newer paths would be defying instincts. Emotive opulence was his forte and area of expertise. For effect's sake, if he abandoned it, it would be suicidal.

For the first time, he had met someone who with her commonplace logic could snub and yet bring back a structured reality. That did not mean Amrita lacked poetry. In her heart, she had preserved the candle that shone for her beliefs and let no winds of reason blow it out. In her, he met the ideal match.

She did not allow him to indulge in effete sentimentality. But she was all ears when he proclaimed theories and narrated the fantastic, the absurd and the ethereal. They entered into a real relationship – the correct balance between the emotional and intellectual.

He only resented the fact that she was beyond riling. She left no loopholes. When at last, one blemish was discovered; he spared no effort to run her down on account of her horrible culinary skills. Amrita could not even make simple dal-chaval. And she could not sing. The third, he was to discover later.

She criticized him for finding fault with Aasma. Amrita was convinced that he was equally to blame for the fiasco. He had over-committed and could not fulfill all the expectations Aasma had. He could not contradict her on that count. Amrita reasoned that when he failed to be the superhuman that Aasma believed in, she chose to run away. Aasma was frightened to learn that his heart bled as well.

She already had one bleeding heart to contend with.

159

CHAPTER 5

The Fire Within

SCENE 4
Day.
The office of the tea estate.
Soumitro sits at the head of the table with other officers seated across. They are all quiet. Slogan shouting from outside disturbs the uneasy silence within.
Outside the office, the workers shout unsavoury slogans against Soumitro for conspiring to sell the garden and deprive them of their rights. Far away, Dipon stands alone beside a tree.
Inside the office.
The Manager seated nearest to Soumitro speaks up.
Manager: It must have been him ... we had all kept it a well-guarded secret.
Another person stands up.
Person (1): He's always been instigating them . . . ever since he's come, these people seem to have found a voice in him.
Manager: These illiterates are not even aware of what is called rights ... the militants have poisoned their minds ... causing havoc all over the state.
Yet another person butts in.
Person (2): I suspect he is a part of them ... you should sack him.
Manager: We should do what the others are doing ... declare a lockout. That'll teach them and bring them to book. ... what business do they have in knowing whether you sell or not?
Person (1): You should not have indulged him so much ... you do not know what mischief these tribals can do ... they can even kill a friend. And you are the boss ...
Soumitro looks up sternly and the person is silenced. Soumitro gets up, goes near the window and looks out.
Soumitro: Ask them to place their demands. I want to meet them tomorrow.
He turns and looks at his officers. They are all silent.
Outside the office.
Dipon quietly walks through the tea-bushes down the hills

SCENE 5
Evening by the hills.
A stream trickles down the hills through the foliage and forms a small pool.
Soumitro and Dipon are standing by the pool. Dipon pelts pebbles into the water as Soumitro smokes a cigar. After a while, Soumitro speaks.
Soumitro: If I hand over the garden to the workers would that make you happy?
Dipon keeps on throwing small pebbles silently.
Soumitro: What more can I do? You know that we are making losses, don't you? Yet I'll gladly do it for your sake.
Dipon looks up at him.
Dipon: For my sake?
Soumitro: Yes, for your sake alone ... do you understand ... for your sake. Or else I can declare closure and go off tomorrow ... but damn it, I can't leave without you.
Dipon: I can't go ...
Soumitro: Do you believe anything will come of this meaningless violence, do you? You think it is so easy to break up a country into bits? Didn't you see what happened in Punjab ...that Gill beat the shit out of those terrorists ... is anything happening in Kashmir despite all the bloody blasts throughout the country???
Dipon looks piercingly at Soumitro.
Soumitro: Please Dipon. I can't let you die for a foolish cause. We have a future waiting for us in Australia ... don't you value life damn it!
Soumitro kicks the ground.
Dipon starts walking away.
Soumitro starts yelling.
Soumitro: Why the hell did you give me hope when you were doomed.......Stop Dipon I'll do exactly . . .
Soumitro's voice echoes back from the hills:
The Narrator looks at him and nods his head sadly and moves away.

SCENE 6
NIGHT
The bedroom.
Soumitro sits on a chair blankly looking into space with a letter held in his hand.
The voice-over of the Narrator.

Voice Over: The death-knell had been sounded. As soon as he returned that evening, Soumitro received a threat to his life if he did not pay up. It had been delivered to his bungalow.

A few flash-cut images-still photographs of Soumitro being shot, his head being chopped off, a knife piercing his stomach, being hung by a noose, intercut with slow-motion images of Dipon with a gun shooting, charging with a knife, extreme close-ups of Dipon's face seething with rage, hatred, a cruel smile.

The Narrator stands at the balcony of the bungalow.

Narrator: There was a tragic inevitability to this love story. Had it been a heterosexual story, this was ideal stuff for Bollywood. Even a few songs could have been thrown in to heighten the effect. The viewers must have prepared themselves by now for violins as the coda.

A distraught Dipon rushes down the driveway, up the flight of staircase and runs to the bedroom. He pushes the door open and enters. Soumitro is sitting on the chair and his head bent. Dipon goes to Soumitro and starts shaking him vigorously.

Dipon: You must leave. You must leave now.

Soumitro looks up with a lost look. Dipon sits on his knees.

Dipon: I wanted to prevent this ... but you must leave.

Soumitro looks searchingly into Dipon's eyes.

Dipon: You love me, don't you?

Soumitro weakly nods his head.

Dipon: Then do as I tell you ... leave this very instant. I'll escort you to safety.

Dipon pulls up Soumitro from his chair and drags him from the room, down the balcony, to the flight of stairs.

The Narrator is standing at the edge of the stairs. As Dipon pulls Soumitro down the stairs, the Narrator looks into the camera.

Narrator: Love can make people do the stupidest things... terrorists are trained to be ruthless. One look at Dipon would tell anyone that the whole exercise is a farce. Such is the weird ways of the heart. What Dipon is doing has been celebrated in popular cinema as ' *Yaari*' or friendship. *Cinemawallahs* would shudder at the sexual connotations of the act.

CHAPTER 6

Must you revel at playing demi-god ... Amrita chided as he read out the scene to her ... why have you allowed the Narrator to intrude and pass judgments?

-- That is a neo-Godardian device, he reasoned, tapping the forehead . . . it's also an integral part of the Indian tradition. Don't you remember Mahabharata and Ramayana?

-- Bull shit of a reason she argued ... it's merely an excuse for you to poke your long bloody nose into the narrative. Your friend has already written to you and intimated all the minute details.

-- In Goddardian deconstruction ... he chastised her tapping her shoulder ... such details are not warranted. Even Vyasa poked his nose several times ... so did Valmiki.

-- Such polemics you thrust down more innocent throats ... she countered pushing away his hand.

-- All you must leave me with is rational analyses ... he sighed.

-- Alas you are not meant to be rational ... she relented and walked away down the beach.

Amrita had this penchant for always conceding the truth. He had not known her beyond the seas. Yet she seemed to belong to the elements of the earth. Till now, Amrita had spoken no lies.

 He feared her truths.

Amrita did not quite happen from the seas. She had a past; a rather gory one at that. He knew none of that. For him, Amrita was meant to be picture perfect. It was not correct if she were not. He would feel mortified otherwise. She could not cause him the hurt. Or so, he thought.

CHAPTER 7

The Fire Within

SCENE 7
The forest roads by night.
A jeep rushes down the roads. Inside the jeep, Dipon is driving like a maniac. Soumitro is seated beside him, totally expressionless. The Narrator is seated on the rear seat. He is smoking. He turns to look at the camera.
Narrator: Such meaningful silence can cause extreme anxiety.... especially in moments such as these. Dipon was driving to a destination unknown. Soumitro, my ever-alert friend, was incapable of thought. His passion had driven him to . . .
Soumitro puts his hand on the steering wheel. Dipon pushes it away.
Soumitro: If you let me go, your life will be in danger.
Dipon presses the accelerator and his face is contorted.
Soumitro: They cannot do anything to me . . . I'll agree with whatever they say.
Dipon turns sharply to look at Soumitro.
Dipon: Keep your urban wisdom to yourself. We kill to prove a point. They killed my puppy dog to spite me when I was ten.
Soumitro: The government does not take you seriously ... your point is never proved.
Dipon: I don't wish to argue ... just shut the fuck up.
Soumitro: Why do you want to save a bourgeois?
Soumitro laughs.
Silently, Dipon forms a swear word on his lips.
Narrator: Is love a bourgeois emotion?
The jeep speeds through the jungle. From the other side, the headlights of two speeding motorcycles are seen.
Inside the jeep, Dipon's eyebrows contort.
Dipon: Shit!
Swiftly Dipon swerves the steering wheel and leaves the road and drives recklessly through the trees. Seeing the jeep leave the road, the motorcycles dash into the jungle. Fast flash cuts of the chase – the jeep, Dipon's face, the steering wheel, the leg on the accelerator, Soumitro's expressions as the jeep bumps along, the wheels running through the foliage, the bikes, the riders, the headlights, etc, etc.
The bikes overtake the jeep and screech to a halt in front. The

riders rush to the jeep. They express surprise seeing Dipon at the steering. Dipon hurriedly gets down. The three engage in hushed conversation in the native tongue.
Soumitro is fixed to his seat. The Narrator leans forward and whispers near Soumitro's ears.
Narrator: Run Soumitro run ... can't you see that Dipon is engaging them in conversation to enable you to run away? Don't be a fool ... run!!!
Soumitro remains static, fixed, without batting an eyelid.
Narrator: This is your last chance ... run!!!!
Soumitro: He is my only chance.
Soumitro points at Dipon.
Dipon and the two riders walk up to Soumitro. Dipon laughs nervously.
Dipon: I was telling them that we mistook them for dacoits ... these are my friends, Sir ... this is Bhrigu and this is Anup ... and this is my boss.
Bhrigu nudges Dipon and says something harshly. Dipon winks at Soumitro.
Dipon: Sir, would you mind going to my friends' house?
Soumitro: Am I being taken, hostage?
Anup briskly walks up to Soumitro and clasps his hand tightly.
Anup: Shut up you Bengali bastard!
Dipon rushes and fiercely pulls away Anup's hand.
Dipon: You have no right to behave like this Anup ... I shall complain to the Commander, mind you.
He turns and looks at Soumitro with pleading eyes.
Dipon: I'm sorry Sir ... please don't mind.
Soumitro looks disdainfully at Dipon.
Soumitro: I did not know you were a terrorist ... you will be sacked.

SCENE 8
Day.
A small room in a log cabin.
There is a small cot at one corner, a reading table, and two chairs. A clothesline is hung across the room. On the line, a towel and some clothes are strewn. Soumitro is seated on a chair by the window, smoking a beedi, engrossed in reading a book.
The Narrator stands by the window looking at Soumitro. He looks up and stares into the camera.

Narrator: It is at this stage ... when Soumitro is held hostage ... that the beginning of the story unfolds ... Soumitro's first encounter with Dipon ... the blossoming of their love etc, etc
Flashback begins.
Flash back ends.
Narrator: Since we know all that so we skip all that.

CHAPTER 8

-- But that is the narrative of your life ... Amrita argued ... how would the audience know of it? You must weave it into the script.

-- It is boring to repeat that entire episode ... he said in a dismissive tone ... the readers have read it .... I'd rather know more interesting details of your life.

-- Ah-ha, don't try to be smart with me ... Amrita retorted with a cherry in her mouth ...you promised never to be inquisitive. He bit his tongue. This was no ordinary mortal. This was Amrita. Sharp and stinging; yet ever alert. He coughed apologetically and volunteered a few more stories from his own life instead.

His marriage was a colossal mistake. One of the greatest regrets of his life. Others marry for love or are forced into it. He married out of sympathy. His wife was a dear college friend. He wanted to help a friend in need of a husband for respectability. That was sheer stupidity. He was just out of a love affair and free. She was trapped in an uncomfortable social situation.

Tanya silently bore the torch for him for several years; all through their undergraduate days. When he did not reciprocate, she grew vengeful with herself and became reckless. She left studies because she could not bear the agony of being in his company any longer. She took up a job instead. There she met a much-married man and seduced him. Tanya's body thirsted for his touch. She satisfied herself with her married lover. Their affair grew to become quite a scandal. Abortion chastised her. Tanya understood the need for support in a patriarchal society. He relented out of lethargy. That caused the catastrophe.

-- You made the fatal mistake ... Amrita chided him.

I was only trying to be helpful ... he meekly protested. Tanya agreed to all his terms out of compulsion. When the legitimacy of the marriage confronted them, she revolted and demanded her pound of flesh. This he was not ready to give. That was when the troubles started. Initially, both of them warded it off, as stability was imperative in their respective lives. By that time, however, neither was accustomed to it. They had had enough turbulence in their lives to settle down. They valued stability but could scant afford it. Both he and Tanya were caught in a loveless marriage that had begun on an improbable

premise. Marriages could never work as compromises.
The friendship they shared, suffered in the bargain. No suturing could help.
-- You've never been able to gauge a woman's heart ... Amrita concluded. Despite all your protestations and feminist pretensions, you've not realized that a woman feels insulted when she asks for love and is offered sympathy instead.
-- I am the perpetual villain for you ... he scoffed.
-- Well a rather cute villain .... Amrita chirped back and pinched his nose.
They had arranged for an elaborate bar-be-que with the help of local beach boys, on the beach itself.
He made an ostentatious display of his culinary skills, while Amrita sipped Bacardi with cola and listened to an extended alaap on the Rudraveena recital in her iPod.
After dinner, they ventured into the sea again.
The beach boys thought they were a couple in love
and sang film-songs celebrating eternal love and
lamenting separations.

CHAPTER 9

The Fire Within

SCENE 9
Inside the log cabin.
A montage of sequences.
Morning.
Soumitro stands by the window alone. He has grown a stubble.
Afternoon.
Soumitro paces up and down in the room alone. He goes and opens the window. He peeps down the cliff just below the window.
Evening.
A lantern burns in the room. Soumitro sits at the table and is writing. He tears the sheet he was writing and starts writing afresh. Dipon enters the room and comes and stands beside him. Dipon places his hand on Soumitro's shoulder. Soumitro looks up and a faint smile appears on his face. Dipon fetches a cigar from his pocket and hands it to Soumitro.
Night.
The lantern burns. Soumitro is near the window smoking the cigar. Dipon sits at the table eating from a plate. There is an empty plate beside it.
Late Night
Soumitro lies on the cot. The lantern burns dimly. Soumitro's eyes are wide open. There is the gentle creaking sound of the door. The door opens and a silhouetted figure stealthily enters the room. Soumitro is startled and sits up. The figure tiptoes to the cot and sits down. Dipon's face is hardly visible in the dim light. Dipon holds Soumitro's hand. Soumitro pulls it away, gets up and goes near the window.
Dipon: I'm sorry ... but you know ... they hesitate to allow me to come to you ... they still feel that I'll help you to escape.
Dipon holds Soumitro's palm.
Soumitro: Why should I escape? I'm perfectly happy being held a hostage by my lover and his friends.
Dipon: What can I ...
Soumitro: Say nothing ... after all, I have knowingly reduced myself to this state ... and I find it all very comical.

Dipon: Even my caring?
Soumitro: What the bloody hell do your friends want? ... I'm willing to give everything ... doesn't your Commander have the balls to meet me?...Why doesn't he order my execution ... you can do it... such divine justice – to die in the hands of your lover ... oh sorry I stand corrected ... die at the hands of your fucking gay partner.
Dipon: I'm making arrangements.
Dipon gets up and goes near Soumitro and holds him by the shoulder. Soumitro pushes his hands off.
Soumitro: Won't you offer me another cigar? Chocolate for the miffed kid!
Dipon retracts and walks out of the room.

SCENE 10
Day.
The forest.
Dipon walks through the forests alone. He stops near a clearing. A helpless expression on his face, he looks skywards. Briskly he pulls out a revolver from inside his jacket and fires at the treetops. Birds fly helter-skelter. Dipon starts kicking the tree-trunks ferociously.
Inside the log cabin.
Soumitro sits at the table engrossed in writing. The Narrator enters the room and stands beside Soumitro, leaning over and reading the letter he is writing.
Soumitro's voice-over: Boyo,
I'm not even certain whether this letter will ever reach you or whether I'll be alive when you read this letter. Anyhow, I am compelled to write as I have never kept any secrets from you. I cannot describe what I'm feeling now. I hardly have any feelings left in me. There is only one constant. I do not regret anything. If there is anything correct that I have done with my life, then this is it. Mine was a life spoilt with riches, arrogance, and attitude. When I see Dipon caught in this dilemma between duty and love, the immense suffering he is undergoing, then my torment becomes insignificant. Life is truly tested under trying circumstances such as these. They might shoot me tomorrow, but I'm certain that they will have to shoot one of their own before.
Do not lament for me if I'm gone. If I do die, I'll die a satisfied man. Do you realize my friend there can be no greater bliss?
The Narrator looks into the camera. His eyes are shining and

a smile fleets across his face.
Narrator: I do my friend, I do.

CHAPTER 10

-- You have no right to exploit an emotion as precious and personal as this for purely selfish purposes ... Amrita looked genuinely moved. Tears were shimmering in her eyes.

-- Why do you see it in that light ... he rationalized. It is all a matter of perspective. I'm trying to preserve the purity of Soumitro's emotions in time and space. When it happens on a personal plane, it is grief. Immortalized in art, it becomes a tragedy.

-- Devils like you can turn blasphemy into vision beatific, Amrita sighed. Alas, you are too immersed in yourself to understand that you are dragging an intensely personal moment into the arena for people to relish. That is why I shan't tell you my whole story.

-- I thought there were to be no secrets amongst us?

-- Think again ... Amrita snapped back.

He sensed that the boundary had been crossed. It also made him reassess the initial stance. Could one person with the excuse of being autobiographical bring to the public eye those exclusive moments that deserved to perish? In an attempt to be a faithful historian, he became the artist, a ruthless re-creator? The thought disturbed him.

But he was left with no alternatives now. He had started this dangerous game and could not leave it midway. A fire raged within. The touch had devoured him completely.

-- How do I redeem myself Amrita? He asked her. --------You cannot .... She sighed.

CHAPTER 11

The Fire Within

SCENE 11
Day.
A clearing in the jungle.
A few young men loiter around with guns in their hands. A bearded middle-aged man is seated on a log of wood. Dipon is standing in front of him and is engaged in an animated conversation in the native tongue. The Narrator walks up to them and looks into the camera.
Narrator: They are discussing Soumitro's impending doom. The Commander wants to exterminate Soumitro while Dipon argues that Soumitro has relented and agreed to all terms and conditions. The Commander feels that by killing Soumitro they could instil fear in the hearts of other small tea planters.
For your benefit, they shall now engage in a conversation in your language. Or else, the dramatic impact of the scene will be lost.
The Commander switches language.
Commander: This bastard is conceited ... behaves as if he were an Englishman. His death shall please even his competitors. Bengali *saala...*
Dipon: We are not indulging in a personal vendetta. If he agrees, our purpose is served. We can use the money that he will pay us as ransom.
Commander: But will it send the right signals to the others?
Dipon: You seem to forget that we have another hostage...he has not yet agreed to pay up. Why don't we . . .
Commander: You seem very keen to protect that slimy Bengali . . . bugger you can't shake off your servility as yet.
Dipon: It's not that.... that man is much older. He has a much lesser need in this world.
The Commander starts laughing.
Commander: Some weird logic you have.

SCENE 12
Night.
Inside the cabin, Soumitro is lying on the cot. He hears a few muffled voices and gets up. He listens more intently. There seems to be the sound of shuffling feet and greater commotion

coming from below. Soumitro stands up and then lies on the wooden floor putting his ears to the ground. He swiftly gets up and moves to the door and places his ears on the door again. The latch opens. Gently, Soumitro pulls open the door.

A flight of stairs descends.

Nimbly, Soumitro runs down the stairs. There is a door right below the stairs. Greater sound of commotion comes from inside the door. Soumitro peeps through the door, slightly ajar.

Inside the dimly lit room, a bald man with his hands, mouth, and eyes tied, stands in the middle of the room. He is shivering and guttural yells emanate from his gagged mouth. Surrounding him are four men with daggers drawn. They wear fierce expressions on their faces. The bearded man utters something ferociously under his breath. The four exchanged glances and then stabs the man in unison. In the light of the lantern, Dipon's face becomes visible as blood from the man's guts splashes on his face.

Soumitro pulls back. There is horror written largely across his face. A hand falls on his shoulder. Soumitro turns swiftly to see a guard with a gun, looking at him with cruel eyes. He faints.

The Narrator appears on the top of the flight of stairs.

Narrator: A typical scene from a Hindi film, a high overdose of melodrama. It should satisfy you!

Fade out

SCENE 13

Night.

Soumitro lies unconscious on the floor of the log cabin. Dipon's arms are spread protectively over him. Dipon is seated on the floor. The Commander and three others are standing.

Dipon: You'll have to kill me before you touch him.

Commander: Don't do theatre ... I gave him chance ... he brought death to himself.

Dipon: He'll never know who got killed ... I stand guarantee. He will not speak a word of this.

The Commander kicks Dipon on his thighs.

Commander: Still licking your master's feet ... rise otherwise I'll kill you as well.

The Commander raises his gun. The person beside him pushes the gun in the air.

Person: He is one of us, Commander!
Commander: He was one of us ......no longer.
The Narrator comes and stands in front of the Commander. The Commander does not notice him. The Narrator pulls up his fist.
Narrator: Dare you to kill my friend, you motherfuckin terrorist!

CHAPTER 12

Amrita thought it was wrong on his part to intervene at this point and interrupt the narrative. He took great pains to explain to her the concept of *deux-ex-machina* used by tragedians thousands of years ago. That was the standard device when all human efforts failed. She felt he was trying to bulldoze an opinion.

Amrita vehemently argued that he had failed as a scriptwriter to weave in an interesting twist into the narrative. She was the only one who dared to contradict, despite her ignorance. He prompted her to think again. Vanity took the better off him.

In reality, the Commander was sufficiently inebriated to argue further. Even though he made an uncouth display of his barbaric skills, the Commander was an educated man in his sober moments. He could not jab a knife into a person's guts without a full bottle of rum. If he had been sober, he would sing Bhupen Hazarika's nasal songs, rather than villify Soumitro with his choicest abuses.

Since she had heard her fill, abuses traumatized Amrita. It brought back memories of another day. Those days were still unknown to him. She chose to gloss over such putrid details. Amrita knew that under the professed purity, he had known a share of the vile. No life was pure in this century.

She suffered thinking about a whole century existing and becoming history, without a single pure soul.

CHAPTER 13

The Fire Within

SCENE 14
Night
Inside the log cabin, Soumitro is lying on the floor with his hands and legs tied, his mouth gagged. There is a shaft of moonlight falling from the window, in the unlit room.
A distraught Dipon enters the room in tiptoe. He flashes the torchlight held in his hand to locate Soumitro. Keeping the torch on the ground, Dipon sits down and unties Soumitro. Gently Dipon makes Soumitro sit up. In the silence of the night, with the torchlight casting huge shadows on the wall, both men look at each other for a while as crickets murmur.
Dipon lifts Soumitro to his feet. Furtively, Dipon goes and pulls the door ajar. He peeps out and then signals Soumitro to follow him. Both of them stealthily climb down the flight of stairs and head towards the jungles.
The sound of hurrying footsteps on dried leaves in the silent forest resonates in the air.
Soumitro and Dipon run through the forest looking surreal in the light of the full moon. They come and halt near a stream, panting vigorously.
Dipon fetches a revolver from his pocket and hands it to Soumitro.
Dipon: Just cross the stream and go right ... the highway is about a kilometre.
Soumitro looks incredulously at Dipon who brings out a cigar from his shirt pocket and smiles.
Dipon: The last chocolate for the big boy ... light it . . . let's have a drag together.
Dipon hands the cigar to Soumitro
Soumitro: I don't understand.
Dipon: Simple . . . it's freedom.
Dipon takes out a matchbox, strikes a match and holds it aloft.
Dipon: Hurry ... light the cigar.
Soumitro lights the cigar. The tip of the glowing cigar lights up Soumitro's moist eyes.
Soumitro: I can't leave without you ...
Dipon puts his hand on Soumitro's lips and takes the cigar.

Dipon: If you love me you will ...
Dipon puffs the cigar.
Soumitro: It's so unbecoming to love in a world full of hate ...
I can't leave ... they'll kill you.
Dipon smiles.
Dipon: They won't ... they need a few diehards like me.
Soumitro: I've arranged everything ... we'll fly out... they can't touch you.
Dipon: I can't abandon my *dharma* ... I have to stay back and fight a losing battle like Karna.
Soumitro: How do you expect me to live without you?
Dipon starts laughing.
Soumitro: Why are you ...
Dipon: I guess we Hindus are expected to find sublimation in renunciation ... your friend the film-maker might not otherwise be able to fashion a tragic love story out of this.
Dipon hands Soumitro the cigar.
Soumitro: Cut the bull-crap ... I don't want immortality, I want you.
Dipon: You shall surely have me wherever you are ... your yellow, chinky-eyed pet ...do me one last favour ... shoot me before you leave.
Soumitro's steps falter. Dipon catches him.
Dipon: Shoot at my legs and hands before you run away ... they'll think you've betrayed me.
Soumitro sits down and starts to howl silently. Dipon pulls him up fiercely and snatches the revolver from his hands.
Dipon: Be a man!
Dipon pulls the trigger of the revolver and shoots at his left hand and then his right leg. He falls. Soumitro starts scowling and scampering. Dipon throws the gun towards Soumitro.
Dipon: Run now run and shoot anyone, anybody who comes in sight, before you reach safety.
Soumitro dashes towards Dipon and lifts him in his arms and howls.
Soumitro: Why, why, why.......
Dipon face is contorted with pain.
Dipon: Kiss me before you leave.

CHAPTER 14

-- Cruel, cruel ... he whispered as he read out the last scene. Amrita sat benumbed on the beach.

-- I can't write any further ... he stood up with the sheaf of papers held on the clipboard.

He walks up to the waves and attempts to throw the clipboard into the sea. Amrita comes and stops him. Amrita looks at him and gasps.

-- It's so unbecoming to love in a world full of hate ... this line shall remain engraved in my heart.

-- It's a curse ... he hissed under his breath ... when, when reality becomes fiction in the hands of a butcher.

-- What about the four other senses? Amrita enquired clasping his hand ... what about your resolve to write a series of short films on the senses?

-- They'll never get written ... he spoke with determination ... from now on, I shall stop ideating ... I don't need a story ... I don't need an end.

-- What'll happen to the carrot that your Parmeswar Pandey dangled before you ... she retorted in a lighter vein.

I'll return him the money ... he stuttered vaingloriously ... I shall give up cinema.

What about the cake and champagne you are accustomed to? Amrita queried.

-- I'll live on bread and jam . . . he asserted grandly.

 Later when they went back to their rooms, both he and Amrita resolved to return to the normalcy of a corrupt urban life.

CHAPTER 15

Sometimes he wondered whether this city belonged to him or Aasma. By years, he had lived here longer. But that was not conditioned enough for possession. Serfs always had occupied the land longer than their feudal lords. He felt enslaved in an alien city and sought in earnest to desert it. However, whenever, he ran away, some unknown forces pulled back the strings.

The first call he received was from Soumitro. He wasted no further words and rushed.

There he met a stranger. Soumitro's face was paper-white. The mask had been cast aside forever. Here was a man drained off all his fluids. Soumitro just sat there on his sofa – a spectral figure, a ghastly apparition. He had the temerity to plant a stinging slap on the Almighty's face. The Almighty had lost his might.

-- Hit me harder ... Soumitro faintly answered ... I deserve more ... kick me if you can!

-- You're going over the top . . . he scolded his friend ... what on earth can smoothen your nerves?

-- Nothing! I am beyond hurt.

-- You've even started to emulate me ... he snarled ... you have forsaken your original colour.

-- What is that pray? Soumitro whimpered in discontent.

This was not the Soumitro he had known before. The man before him had none of the haughty, lofty notions of yore. Soumitro of all the people in the universe was sitting in his parlour, smoking beedis. He even seemed to cherish every drag. As he sat down and lit a cigarette and cupped his chin in his palm, Soumitro smiled faintly.

-- You are not accustomed to seeing me without my mask ... your smart, caustic friend, always ready with a repartee . . .

-- It's not that ... he objected ... what you have been doing with your life worries me.

-- You worry too much ... Soumitro spoke in a hushed and ominous tone ... did I die when my parents got knocked off? I have had miraculous escapes.

-- That is a result of your good *karma* in your previous birth ... he replied in jest.

-- Then in my new avatar in the next life, I'll be born a swine ... Soumitro snarled viciously and then suddenly his voice dropped ... the *Karma* of this life is unforgivable ... I abandoned him.

Soumitro walked up to the cupboard, pulled out a drawer, brandished a revolver and pointed it at him.
-- I should have killed myself with this ... he shot himself ... I ran away and kept the gun in the drawer.
He got up and snatched the revolver from Soumitro's hand. He was mortified to find it loaded. With great alacrity, he unloaded the bullets and kept them in his pocket. He pushed the revolver into his jacket. He looked sternly at Soumitro and firmly clasped Soumitro's hand. No words came to his mind or mouth. After a while, he let go. On an occasion like this, he simply could not speak inanities and gentle pieties. He valued this friendship too much. It was an imperfect moment. His words could not change anything. After all these years of knowing, for the first time, he departed without a word.
Soumitro grappled with grief for a while and then made up his mind. After a fortnight Soumitro called him up. He was amazed to hear the usual acerbic tone and immediately guessed all was not right. Soumitro dismissed his doubts and reaffirmed that he had managed to take control and had decided to migrate. He thought it was Australia; Soumitro informed him that he had bought a ticket to Austria. Soumitro wanted to spend the rest of his life as an usher in a Viennese Opera-house.
It was a cumbersome affair because the untying of knots was not so easy after all. It involved property that could not be sold in haste and a hysterical elder sister who could not be handled even at leisure. She freaked out, hearing of Soumitro's grand designs. But Soumitro garnered enough courage for once in his life, asking her simply to keep shut. There were a lot of tears shed and implorations but to no avail. Soumitro was firm in his resolve. Nothing could persuade him to change his mind. The sister finally gave up.
It was to be a late-night flight. He sat at the bar of the airport and downed three whiskeys. He knew a friend was being lost for life. Though Soumitro graciously invited him for the summer season and promised the best seats in the opera house where presumably, he would find employment, his friend knew, they would never meet again. Yet, he could not stop Soumitro from going. What life was left here for the soul devastated by the fire within?
He waited in the departure lounge. Over the phone, Soumitro had asked him to come directly to the airport. Check-in had

been announced and yet there was no sign of Soumitro. As they started to announce the security check, he began to panic. He called Soumitro's residence. No one answered. He did not know what to do. Restlessly, he kept on smoking one cigarette after the other in the smoking zone. Even a regular like him could not stay any longer in the gas chamber. He walked out.

Suddenly, he noticed Soumitro's sister rushing towards him with her timid husband scurrying behind. She screeched to a halt near his toes. He almost tripped. Between her pants and gasps, she informed him that Soumitro had left home before she had gone to pick him up. They were waiting for him to show up near the entrance. When he failed to turn up, they had rushed inside hoping ...

He asked the driver to drive as fast as possible. Soumitro's sister's car followed. They went back to the house. There was no trace. Soumitro's sister sat on the streets and wept uncontrollably. He understood that the poor woman despite her blemishes, loved her brother dearly. It brought back memories and reminded him of Smriti.

As he unlocked the door of the apartment, heaviness burdened him. He felt desperate, lost and guilty. He could have prevented it. Could he? Suddenly on a weird impulse, he rushed to his telephone and pressed the button of the answering machine. There was the answer- crisp and clear in Soumitro's voice.

-- You were the one who kept on goading me to take risks and do the unpredictable. I took the risk and fell in love. Now I shall do the unpredictable and vanish. I am sorry to keep you all stranded at the airport. If you can, try and explain it all to my sister, though I doubt if at all ... anyway, you have a way with words and women. Maybe you can...

I only wish that I had listened to you earlier ... maybe then, the adventure could have come to good use ... if there is anything worthwhile that I have done ... anything . . . then this is it ... at last, I have the freedom to choose my life ... How can I explain those glowing eyes to you ... how ... Dipon taught me the strength of conviction ... Your friend never had faced defeat before ... and so I can never take it lightly ... I have to meet him once more just to ask him one question ... can love give a person so much courage to confront death ... I know he's not dead ... he called up this morning just said "hi" and hung up ... he's somewhere there . . . where I don't

know ... I have to ... I know you'll understand, though to use a favourite expression of yours I've fucked the ending of your film ... hah
Tears started streaming down – tears blasted tears, he thought and the thought was interrupted by Soumitro's hollering after a pause.
-- Don't be a jackass and cry ... or else I'll shout at you . . . Boyo take control ... were you brought up in a barn damn it?
He started laughing silently in the darkroom.
The tide had come in his life as well.

PART SIX

LOVE STINKS – HATE WINKS

"I COUNT RELIGION BUT A CHILDISH TOY

AND HOLD THERE IS NO SIN BUT IGNORANCE"

----THE JEW OF MALTA

MARLOWE

PART VI

CHAPTER 1

Was he to succumb to his impulse and stop his journey of exploring the senses? Or would he remain true to " *Swabhava*" and contradict the fleeting impulse? He was in a quandary. After coming back to the city, Amrita had chosen to distance herself and be remote. He had no one to fall back on. Dabloo was enmeshed in the sordid mess of his marriage. Rukmini had bagged a prestigious contract and left for a recording abroad' Smriti and Srijeet were a million miles away. He loved these exaggerations. Avinash and Alisha were ensconced in silence, and Aasma was out of reach. But not Amma. On an impulse, he called her up.

Being hurt by his neglect, Amma was curt in her replies. He knew her psyche well and tried to warm up. He diligently avoided any reference to Aasma. Amma being Amma, brought up the subject soon enough. She blamed him for the mess. She felt he should have been more assertive and proposed marriage. He could not explain to her that Aasma was in love with Minal.

Amma revealed an interesting detail that made him sit up. The troubles had started and according to Amma, Minal and Aasma had started to drift apart. His vindictive heart leaped with joy. In conspiratorial tones, Amma suggested that he should strike the iron when it is hot. As such Aasma had not left home, to live with Minal. Their marriage had not been consummated, socially at least. For Amma's sake, he should now play the devil's advocate, Amma requested. He was confused. He promised Amma that he would consider the option.

He had called Amma from the office. As he sat brooding, Kalpana knocked at the door. That broke his reverie. She asked for permission to enter. He nodded his consent. She stood awkwardly by the door. He sensed something was the matter. Gently he prodded her to speak. With her head bent, Kalpana spoke falteringly. Her marriage had been settled and she wanted permission. He smiled and expressed happiness. Remembering that she was an orphan, he decided to sponsor the marriage. But that was not the only matter. Kalpana stuttered as she told him that she would have to leave the job. He was taken aback and kept silent. He would miss her endearing presence.

Suddenly Kalpana sat down on the floor and began to weep silently. He could not fathom the reason for her unusual behaviour. In between her tears, Kalpana whispered that he would never know why she was crying. In a jiffy, several incidents of the past flashed past his mind. He realized that the stupid girl had silently borne the torch for him all along, despite understanding the futility of her pursuits. He was stunned. This was a blow he was unprepared for.

Luckily for him, Parmeswar breezed into the room that very moment. Kalpana jumped up and retracted. Parmeswar sat on the floor, clapped his hands in the air and announced his decision to join politics.

-- You mean the bandwagon? He queried disdainfully....... Anyway, it suits your profile.

-- I am doing it for your sake, Sir! If I were there in parliament, wouldn't you feel thrilled? Parmeswar slapped his cheeks and yawned ... how was the sea?

-- Rough, turbulent, unsettling ...

-- And the mermaid?

-- Or she was exquisite ... by now he had mastered the art of countering Parmeswar's googlies.

-- She's right for you ... Parmeswar pulled up a cushion to his lap and started caressing it ... have you proposed?

-- I guess I'll have to return your money, Mr. Pandey ... he pulled a folio by stretching his arms and pulled out a cheque book ... I couldn't ...

-- Don't be juvenile ... Parmeswar waved his right hand dismissively in the air ... it has all the ingredients of a thriller . . . only the homosexual angle ... but not to worry, the international market will lap it up ... summing it all up, Parmeswar smiled like the *Sumitava* Buddha.

This even he found hard to digest. He had come to accept the mind-reading bit as a fact of life though it defied reason. But this astounded him. Was Parmeswar clairvoyant? Or else how would he know about the script. It was certainly not in his mind at the moment. Amrita was. He was at a total loss of words, confounded, confused and angry ...

Parmeswar understood immediately that he had overdone the ostentatious display of his prowess. He pulled out his tongue, bit it, held his ears with both his hands, nodded his head profusely and smiled sheepishly.

-- I promise never to do it again ... I promise ... Forgive me, Sir ... you are truly ...

Abruptly he crawled forwards towards Parmeswar and genuflected. Parmeswar pulled himself back.
-- How will my story end Mr. Pandey? Hollowness resonated from the voice as he looked fiercely into Parmeswar's eyes ... you have to tell me my end.
-- That everyone knows ... everyone ... Parmeswar sounded uncomfortable. You'll have to excuse me sir, but I cannot tell you how you will die. But all of us are eventually going to die. In the great beyond, we shall meet and have coffee for the soul.
Let me make one prediction Mr. Parmeswar Pandey ... he spoke slowly but firmly. Parmeswar's eyes brightened hearing his speech --- You shall die because of me. I shall be the cause of your death.
Parmeswar broke into laughter fraught with nervousness, as beads of perspiration covered his forehead.

CHAPTER 2

He had decided to meet her for breakfast. The early morning was the time when there was no bitterness in the heart as the mind was yet fresh. With the passing of the day . . .

Punctuality was not Aasma. He ordered coffee and waited at their table at Abel's Inn. He had a hunch that she might not turn up. She did.

Aasma smiled nervously and sat down. He looked at her for a long while. Her eyes flitted here and there as he gazed constantly, fixedly, without even batting eyelids. It unnerved her. She fought it back.

-- So ... Aasma managed to speak with great effort ... you've kept a mouche.

-- Does it look weird? He lit a cigarette.

-- Back to cigarettes ...

-- Vices die hard ...

-- Shave it off ...

-- Feels comfortable, cushy ... above the lips I mean, how's your dance ... dance classes I mean ...

-- No longer to your tunes ... she smiled.

-- He felt good. She had learned to repartee.

-- No tunes left I guess ... he suppressed a sigh.

-- Why have you stopped working?

-- Would you be happy to hear if I said only for you ...

-- I always told you, I bring you harm ...

He ordered her cold coffee and breakfast for them.

-- Writing lately? She enquired after a long pause.

He did not know what to say. To spite her, he could have told her the truth. But there was hope still, lying dormant somewhere in the heart, hope yet alive.

-- No ... he faintly replied and thought immediately he would burn up the two scripts. As fire could not burn The Fire Within.

-- Both of them avoided any real conversation for a while. They ate breakfast quietly, sipped their coffee hot and cold. Finally, he had to speak.

-- How is he? He asked hesitantly.

 She looked up and raised her eyebrows.

-- Fine I guess ... Aasma turned to look at the other customers.

-- What is the matter? He hated this inquisition.

-- Nothing, nothing ... she replied casually, to make him feel comfortable. He just left the city. Taken a transfer, I guess.

As they drove down the streets, after moments of extreme sobriety, Aasma broke into silent laughter. He turned to look at her.
-- Your absence played up more than your presence ... she uttered between her clipped laughter ... thought he found your continuous presence in my language ... the way I spoke ... and to think of it, you derided my way of speaking ... such is life, hah!
--Can I hold your hand? He almost curled up inside asking her this.
-- No ... she replied curtly and swiftly withdrew her right hand placed on the seat just beside him.
On the way back, he could not fathom what had brought them back.
No departure seemed final. Was this story never going to end?

CHAPTER 3

Aasma always delayed the moment. As such, she was habitually late. Also, in moments of crisis and coitus, she would dilly-dally. Never want to come ... to the point, directly. Aasma postponed the present. Such was her nature.

She delayed the truth about Minal's eloping for quite a while. Minal was too insignificant to create a social scandal. It had not reached his ears as yet. He innocently believed her version. Not that it was incorrect. Minal had arranged for a transfer a few days before he abducted the hapless, innocent Parsi girl. At least that was how the story went, though, in reality, the girl had forced him to elope with her. Minal was by now sufficiently disgusted with Aasma's lofty stature and preferred a commonplace girl instead. Minal felt that her mentor had corrupted Aasma's mind. She was wife material no longer.

The girl Minal eloped with was a demure little waif, orphaned in childhood. She lived with her maternal uncle whose wife used to beat her up regularly. Minal was an escape route for her. She embraced Islam and married him. This time Minal made no mistakes and involved both Qazi and Quran. Legally, he was entitled to two more wives without uttering the statutory talaq to Aasma.

Though she did not show it, Aasma was shaken by the experience. She put up a brave front. He too played his cards well and avoided any further references to the embarrassing incident. Amma goaded him to broach the subject of divorce. This he did after persistent persuasion. Aasma was averse to the idea. She did not need divorce as she had decided never to marry again ... it was all a circle of deceit she felt.

His heart sank.

Now at least there were no more bindings from her side. He too was footloose and fancy-free. Yet, yet!!!!! It was not to be. To be, was never the question. Not even now. Even now when everything could have been perfect. Their affair was founded on an imperfect premise. If perfection were achieved, the beauty of unpredictability and uncertainties would be stolen. It would become humdrum and result in boredom. To go the family way would sanctify the illicit affair. Aasma could not allow this one relationship to descend to the level of the real, the natural. She wanted to preserve it as a work of art. Something she could interpret through her dance and someday he would transform into a film script.

He sought and thought otherwise. After all the turmoil, he desperately wanted life. She thwarted all his intentions, as she wanted her mentor to create magic until the end. Between the image and the conception, there falls a shadow.

Always.

CHAPTER 4

Over the telephone, Amrita's voice sounded strikingly similar to Aasma's. He was both surprised and pleased to hear her. To his over-enthusiastic overtures, Amrita replied with the monosyllabic ... Hmmm ... Hmmm . . .

When he was driven to the point of exasperation, she broke into laughter. He chided her for having kept quiet for such a long time. She did not pay him much heed. What made him real glad was that Amrita never allowed the persona to interfere in their interaction. To the outside world, he was a social phenomenon and she was a non-entity. When she first met him, she did not know who this man was. She kept it that way. She chose to ignore the rest. That was why their friendship had struck the right balance, the right chord, from the very beginning.

He had known the real Amrita. But she had not revealed the Amrita located geographically or historically. He did not know where she lived, what she did, whether she was married or not. She had assured that whenever he required her, she would sense it and get in touch. He believed her. True to her word, Amrita kept her promise.

He had volunteered all the information about the past to her. He wanted Amrita to be the keeper of secrets. He told her things that even Aasma was unaware of. In a love affair, you need to gift-wrap and then present yourself. In friendships, you simply could walk in naked. Only she was worthy enough to preserve the whole truth.

A woman can never reveal her mystery in totality. It is an intrinsic characteristic of womanhood. He did not mind the stance Amrita took. He respected the mystique Amrita had chosen to wrap around her. The real Amrita was there for him. Her history remained unknown like the depths of the sea from which she had walked out.

Amrita carefully heard whatever he had to say. She expressed a desire to meet him in person. He chose and then cancelled Abel's Inn as a probable venue. That place had too many memories. They met elsewhere. This was the first time they met in the city. Amrita appeared like a different person. The vermilion mark on her forehead gave away her marriage. But he did not probe. They discussed his life instead.

With her indigenous brand of commonplace logic, Amrita argued her case. She felt that his contradictions were unsettling. He was deviating from the chosen path and attaching unnecessary importance to trivialities. Despite all posturing and proclamations, he had yet not discovered the dividing line between sentience and sentimentality. He was a prisoner of passion.

He did not remember any woman telling him off in such a strong measure. Only Soumitro dared to admonish him. Subtly, Amrita substituted his lost friend. He laughed within, recalling the confirmed sceptic turning lachrymose, felled by the bows of Cupid and *Kama-Deva*. Who knew, maybe someday Amrita ...

He immediately dismissed the thought. An affair with Amrita was the last thing in his mind. Horror struck, he realized that a strong sexual attraction to Amrita was growing within.

When he told Amrita about the vile thoughts, she laughed and replied that she had proved her point. He was truly a prisoner of passion. However, in their amoral universe, making love was no big deal. Her body needed its vitamins. Further, she had to test the veracity of his claims to be as good in body language, as the verbal. She proved to be more emancipated than him.

They had abundant opportunities at sea but made no use of it. That was the ethereal arena. The city yielded itself more to the touch of bodies, tongues, and saliva. They made love at a languorous pace, stretching the orgasm to last several hours. It was an odyssey almost. They attempted all the methods – from Germaine Geer to *Kama Sutra*, and succeeded in most. There was extended foreplay with Bach providing the background music. Finally, there was bliss to the chimes of Gregorian chants. Never before had he been so completely satisfied.

As they lay down side-by-side, holding each other's hand and vacantly staring into space, Amrita broke the silence.

-- You are dying to know about the person for whom I wear the mark on my forehead . . .

-- No, I am not dying to know ... he replied feeling slightly affronted with her presumption.

-- My husband had abandoned me and vanished for the past two years and three fifty-eight days ... yet I wear the vermilion mark ...

-- Oh ... he uttered cursorily.

-- I wear it as a mark of shame ... Amrita sighed ... he left me when he discovered me in bed with another man.

Amrita got up and stood by the window. The traffic passed ceaselessly down below.

Amrita stood silhouetted by the sunset.

-- What could I do ... what else could I do ... my body by then had been abused by a million hands ... first, it was by force ... then it became an addiction ... he was pure, he was faithful.

-- All fools are innocent ... he retorted sharply and rushed to hug her. Sadness outlined Amrita's visage.

The sunset across the cityscape. Destiny chartered a new course.

Two helpless souls hugged each other and sought solace.

There was to be none.

There was to be none.

CHAPTER 5

The music awards ceremony was Rukmini's night; a night when she found her much-deserved place in the sun. Feeling nervous, Rukmini had persuaded him to come along. He was reluctant to go as he had opted out of the social circuit for quite some time. He wanted to opt-out of the celebrity status. Even gossip columns had stopped writing about him. Critics had written their obituaries about a misguided genius. He was thrilled to become persona non-grata. But success, albeit erstwhile, had its pitfalls.

When he walked in that night with Rukmini in tow, tongues started yapping too vigorously. This was the carefully guarded secret about his personal life.

Before they went, there was an extended dress rehearsal at his place. He had selected Rukmini's dress for the occasion. He had to even instruct the make-up person and hair-stylist in great details, as he feared that left to her herself, Rukmini might end up dressing like a zombie or a punk. He had little or no trust in her sartorial sense. In fact, except for a voice, she had nothing. She was not a birdbrain but used her brains like a bird. She sang like a bird too. He was confident about her chances of winning. He could not allow the wrong dress or wrong speech to mess it all up.

At these awards ceremonies, the appearances were all. In a televised age, the appearance was reality. Therefore, all the bimbos mugged up so-called meaningful lines and bagged the coveted prizes at beauty pageants. They mouthed their vulgar concerns about the less fortunate, grabbed the cheque and went on to become a film-actresses or tarts. Rukmini did not belong to that genre. But to win an award, she had to behave like one.

Rukmini was all nervous and felt that she did not stand a chance. He had spared no effort to make sure that victory was hers. He had even made her video and wrote out her victory speech. Rukmini argued ferociously about the last lines. He shut her up and insisted that she had to acknowledge her indebtedness to Dabloo in public. That was to be her redemption, as well as Dabloo's. The dominant paternal trait played its bit. To protect her and boost her morale he decided to go to a public function.

What lay in store was beyond his wildest dreams. And to think of it, he dreamt wild.

As he and Rukmini walked into the glare of camera flashes,

his arm around her, the bloodthirsty media went crazy. Rukmini tried to put up a brave front and smiled traditionally. He pulled a poker face. They were offered a special table, as both of them were nominees. Rukmini for her voice and he for best lyrics and video. The other nominee, Dabloo for music, sat just a table away with Brinda.

Dabloo smiled sheepishly at him and smirked when his eyes met Rukmini's. Rukmini scowled back. Underneath, the table he pinched her. She almost yelled but controlled herself right in time. She took sweet revenge through the evening. She clasped his hands-underneath the table again, so tightly with her fingernails biting into his flesh that the handkerchief turned to be a red flag by night. The funniest part was when Brinda and Rukmini exchanged glances. They smiled at each other and then turned their heads in unison and grit their teeth.

The ceremony started with a recital by a budding danseuse. His eyes popped out when he saw Aasma perform the inaugural dance. He looked askance and discovered Amrita sitting five tables away with a respectable socialite. She winked at him. He froze. This was indeed the reworking of a horror story.

Rukmini swept away all the major awards for the singing-best debut, best female, best solo, best song, etc, etc. He was utterly surprised, winning two awards; Dabloo won three. It was all in their extended family.

When Rukmini walked up to receive her final award as the artist of the year, he almost choked. Rukmini delivered her speech in staccato. By then, the wine had gone to her head. She thanked all and sundry in the cheesy Hollywood tradition and summed it up with her salutations to her guru. His lines, her voice.

In a voice choked with emotion, she spoke about Dabloo and how she owed him everything. To you my master ... Rukmini stretched out her hands. Dabloo grimaced within his beard, as Brinda looked at him piercingly, with her eyebrows arched. As per his instructions, Rukmini eulogized the greatness of her master and the gift he bestowed upon her.

He stood up to clap. Dabloo wiped the tears melting into his beard. The audience rose to applause and the fans cheered in gusto, forcing Dabloo to finally get up and acknowledge Rukmini's gesture. Brinda hissed, cursed under her breath and stormed out. He walked towards Dabloo and held him in a tight embrace. The media went hysterical. His deed was done. He felt relieved seeing the dream about Rukmini and Dabloo's joint success coming true. They had made great music together. Nothing else mattered.

Rukmini became a star. Dabloo was crowned the maestro.

Just then, Aasma entered the stage and performed the finale. Such fire in her movements, he had never seen before. She was aflame on stage. He kept stealing glances at Amrita, who smiled back mischievously.

Later at the cocktails, he felt uncomfortable. Everyone was clamouring to be near them. Rukmini by now had gone berserk with an overdose of champagne. Dabloo could not extricate himself from the circle surrounding him to go and placate the sulking, pouting Brinda, standing away.

He was gheraoed by the presswallahs expecting quotes. He simply remained tight-lipped and searched above the encircling heads for Aasma and Amrita.He saw Amrita walking up to Aasma and congratulating her for her performance. This was fast becoming a farce. All the key players were playing by the rules of the game. The permutation combination worked in perfect twos. Amrita – Aasma, Him and Aasma, Amrita and Him, Dabloo and Rukmini, Rukmini and Brinda, Dabloo and Brinda and so it went on.

This was the first social occasion where he met both Aasma and Amrita. He was struck with remorse and guilt and felt he had betrayed Aasma by making love with Amrita, whilst being very much in love with her. He had forgotten the fact that Aasma had regularly kissed Minal in the evenings and then kissed him the same night. She had sex with him immediately after her marriage to Minal. His ego was glad to feel guilty. It satisfied in the middle-class notions of fidelity that he was still burdened with.

This evening had all the ingredients for an absorbing screenplay.

Vignettes and Snippets of conversations:

<u>Aasma – Amrita</u>

Amrita: Hello I'm Amrita … very impressed with your dance.

Aasma: Oh, thank you... do I know.......

Amrita: No, you don't know me ... though we share something in common.

Aasma: What?
Amrita: A man (laughs) . . . catch you later....
Amrita moves away.
Aasma looks bewildered.

<u>Dabloo – Rukmini</u>
Dabloo: (mumbling under his breath and casting fleeting glances at Brinda) You should not have been so theatrical.
Rukmini: I didn't want to ... your friend insisted that I thank you in public and get it off my shoulder once and for all.
Dabloo: So, you did not mean a word ... I thought maybe ... bitch!!!

Rukmini starts to laugh loudly drawing everyone's attention. Dabloo rushes off.
Rukmini: He called me a bitch...he called me a bitch.

<u>Him – Amrita</u>
Amrita: What happened to your guts and sangfroid? Left it home?
He: What did you tell her?
Amrita: That we have had a great time in bed.
He: You're lying.
Amrita: If that satisfies you ... are you afraid?
He: Yes, I am ...

<u>Dabloo – Brinda</u>
Dabloo: Could we argue about this later? People are watching.
Brinda: They've seen what a fool you have made of yourself ... caught with your pants down...your protégé has unmasked you ...
Dabloo: What the bloody hell do you expect from me? You're no less than her.

<u>Him - Aasma</u>
He: So!
Aasma: So?
He: Now you've become a professional?
Aasma: Do you mind?
He: Who am I to . . .
Aasma: No one ... you are nobody to mind
He: How much do I owe you? I'll send the cheque across for

your stenographer's job.
Aasma: Back to basics? You owe me your life. I'll take your crap no more.
He: The docile one learnt to speak huh? You owe me your language.... remember that
Aasma: Only you could be so mean . . .

<u>Rukmini – Brinda</u>
Rukmini: Are you angry with me?
Brinda: No!
Rukmini: Why didn't you congratulate me?
Brinda: Congratulations!
Rukmini: Don't commit my mistakes ... handle him well.
Brinda: You don't have to teach me what I do with my husband.
Rukmini: You seem to forget my dear, that he would not have been your husband if I had agreed ... I gifted you your husband.

<u>Him – Dabloo</u>
He: These women have gobbled us up.
Dabloo: You son of a bitch, you wrote those lines.
He: I was teaching her gratitude.
Dabloo: You wanted to have some fun at my expense ... we're friends no longer.
He: Trot back to your wife... she's unleashed you for long enough ... tell her you've finished your soo, soo ...
Dabloo: You disgust me ... you denigrate ass-hole!
He: Manhole loaded with shit ...
The evening ended in the bathetic.

CHAPTER 6

There were to be scripts no longer. Scripts needed completion. He was too unsettled to complete anything new, mere flotsam. He was encircled by floating incomplete stories. Only the Smriti-Srijeet affair had found anchorage. It did not need completion, as it was complete in itself. The others were unfinished, half-finished lives and love. The Smriti-Srijeet story lacked the dramatic content for a script. It had acquired the quality of a lyric.

Whenever he lay down on the couch, their story flashed in the inward eye. As prescribed, his heart filled with pleasure and danced with the daffodils. There was a rare pleasure, in an otherwise morbid, moribund life. Even thoughts of Aasma inspired passion no longer. He missed her no longer but missed missing her. He felt guilty about it. He missed Smriti, Srijeet, and Pimpu. He wanted to meet them but was stuck here.

Parmeswar suggested that a visit to the USA would do him good. He disagreed to spite Pandey. The masochist worked overtime. Amrita thought it served him right, as negative energies had taken over and reduced the effete man to inaction. In his world of image and sound, "action" was the operative password.

By now Amrita was judgmental about almost anything he did or did not do. Her overbearing presence upset him as she always spoke the unpleasant truth. He was superannuated even before his time was over. She hated this and made sure that she did the pushing around. The pusher was being pushed at last.

Amrita virtually dragged him by the collar and made plans for The Fire Within as a probable film. Parmeswar was elated and wanted a grand launch. He wanted the whole business to be hush-hush. This film had to be shot outdoors and hence did not need to draw attention. He conducted the affair in great secrecy. Parmeswar had no choices left.

The stumbling blocks were actors. No established actor would risk doing this film and get stamped. He was glad that he did not have to start the film and could slink back to lethargy. Amrita pulled him up and forced a beginning. He could offer no further excuses. Parmeswar was thrilled.

Neither of them had met before. Yet both knew about the other. To Parmeswar, Amrita was the mermaid discovered by the sea. To Amrita, Parmeswar was the crazy man wanting to sink his money. When Parmeswar had expressed a desire to meet Amrita, he had warded off the request.

Parmeswar walked up to Amrita and introduced himself at a restaurant where they had gone for lunch. Parmeswar had his uncanny ability to make surprise entries. Amrita was distant and aloof. She did not allow Parmeswar to break the ice or the barrier. They exchanged pleasantries and Amrita carefully sneaked out. She did not wish to be noticed. The wily Parmeswar Pandey found her to be most intriguing. It whetted his appetite.

He sensed that Parmeswar had found a new prey and dismissed all such overtures as luncheon invitations with the mermaid. For once, he felt happy having scored over the fox. Parmeswar pretended to be heartbroken, but could not carry on the act for long. That was the advantage of fickle-minded people. Parmeswar gave up for the time being and waited for the opportune movements to strike back. He knew very well what played in Parmeswar's mind and made sure that Amrita never met Parmeswar again.

By now, the fun of filmmaking had revitalized him. The action was too a sweet word to shun forever. He had to make "The Fire Within" work. It would be his tribute to a lost friend.

In desperation, he turned to Avinash. Only he could adequately portray Soumitro's character. Though Avinash had recovered from the trauma he shied from the camera. Avinash had taken off his mask and resolved not to act again. There was no strength or zest left in life for Avinash, to imitate reality in front of the camera.

He assured Avinash that he would do the needful. Only Avinash had to be ready to surrender. With Alisha's help, he bulldozed Avinash into agreeing, without telling him all the gory details of the script. But that was half the battle won. He still had to find a Dipon.

He decided to cast a newcomer.

CHAPTER 7

He bumped into Tanya at the entrance of the coffee shop where Amrita was scheduled to arrive. Amrita had not yet reached. He was heading towards a table and Tanya was on her way-out. Their eyes met. He could scarcely recognize her. Tanya had aged beyond belief, since the last time he had met her, three years back. There was an awkward moment of silence as they both stared at each other. The gentleman accompanying Tanya was ill at ease and shifted uncomfortably. Tanya took control of her senses and spoke. She introduced the gentleman accompanying her, as her husband. He felt relieved. That was one burden off his chest. Tanya had settled down at last.

He extended the right hand and warmly shook the gentleman's hand. They spoke briefly as Tanya fidgeted continuously with her cell phone. He could sense her discomfiture and bade her farewell.

He sat down at the table and observed that Tanya looked back furtively and then vehemently held her husband's elbow and marched away. He was amused to see her making an effort to drive home a point. That he still mattered to her was obvious and caused sadness. But she mattered to him no longer. He was shocked to realize that she never did matter after they had got married. Before that, he valued her friendship. The reason why he could never bring himself to love her eluded him. If they had stayed married, maybe they would have had children by now. A stable life was not to be his.

Amrita regretted her late arrival. She would have loved to meet Tanya. She had this nasty habit of always finding faults and blamed him for the break-ups.

-- You're the devil! She pronounced sarcastically sipping her coffee.

-- Yeah, but aren't you stretching this thing about women's sisterhood a bit too far.

-- You don't know how to handle a situation ... in a script you do it beautifully, in life you mess it up.

-- Be careful or I might mess up your life...he replied tongue-in-cheek.

-- Oh no, you can't mess up any further ... Amrita replied matter of fact, munching a lemon tart.

-- Someone else can ... there was a mischievous glint in his eyes. Mr. Pandey has taken a fancy on you.

-- Ask your Parmeswar to be careful or else I'll squeeze ...
-- Okay, okay don't get graphic ... he hastily interrupted her.
-- That man is not safe ... one look at his eyes and you can see a killer.
-- I'm not having an affair with him ... he tried to brush off her fears.
-- Mark my words ... Amrita spoke resolutely ... he'll do you harm. Finish the film and dissociate yourself.
-- What film? His nose curled up. We have not found a Dipon as yet and ...
-- Not to worry ... Amrita stopped him midway and hastily opened her bag. She pulled out an envelope and brought out a couple of photographs.
There were six photographs along with the resumes of six aspirants. They all were handsome young men with chinky features. He was adequately impressed.
-- Where did you get them? He asked.
-- You need not worry where I got them from ... Amrita replied ... will they serve your purpose?
-- How am I supposed to know? He sounded a trifle hurt . . . They all are raw.
-- I mean look wise ... we shall examine the acting department later.
He carefully examined the photographs, brought out a pen and sketched spectacles on the faces. Amrita was horrified and protested loudly.
-- What will I tell my friend at the advertising agency? She yelled aloud. I told Titli that I needed photographs of some young chinks...I am supposed to return all these.
-- That solves the mystery ... he smiled jubilantly and picked up three photographs. Ask these three to come for an audition ... and who is Titli, pray?
-- Oh, my friend works in the A/V department an agency ... Amrita retorted sharply and snatched the photographs from his hand.
-- These agency types are extremely repulsive ... he remarked. They are such shallow people, pretending to know everything ... they are little brats who know nothing about nothing. There was acid dripping from his voice.
-- Must you have an opinion about everything and everybody? Disgusting!
-- I have no opinion about you . . . he barked. Consider yourself fortunate.

-- Why the hell did I have to come out of that godamn sea ... Amrita sighed exasperatedly.
-- Or else you would have drowned ... he had the pleasure of mouthing the last line as usual.
As his car turned around the bend, Amrita pulled at the shirtsleeves and asked him to look at the foyer of the hotel. He saw Aasma getting down from the car with a curly-haired man wearing a cowboy hat and leather boots, walking with a swagger. They entered the hotel. His heart missed a beat. Amrita noticed the change of expression on his face. He asked the driver to speed out.

CHAPTER 8

Wicked were the ways of the world. He could not disbelieve Amma. She told him that there was a new man in Aasma's life. Amma had used her detective skills and made discreet inquiries. The gentleman in question – Amma thought he was a ruffian, was an advertising filmmaker with a cowboy's attitude. His name was Neelabh and he hailed from a family of professional cricketers.

Amma admonished him severely and said that she suspected his ardour for her daughter to be not strong enough. There was no other justification for his lackadaisical behaviour. He had made no use of Minal's desertion. Amma went on so far to suggest that he had outgrown her. She once worshipped you like Allah, lamented Amma.

He found the situation to be extremely comical. Here was a mother, in cahoots with her daughter's jilted lover, trying her best to cajole the rejected, dejected lover, to win back her daughter. Was she suspecting him not man enough for Aasma?

He made inquiries and found out that this Neelabh was indeed a ribald person, who loved his share of fun. He was a much-married man with six children and a now frigid wife. Neelabh was a lavish spender and a generous soul otherwise. What was utterly surprising was that, despite the knowledge of the budding affair, he could not garner enough hatred for the fellow. After all, Aasma had volunteered to be with this man.

Even his ego did not take a beating. He could not quite fathom what attracted Aasma towards this man. Maybe he had a legendary dick and could levitate, with a hard-on pinned to the ground. No other reason seemed to work. Only the magical or the absurd seemed to be operational here. Why on earth would the demure, timid child take a fancy to the headstrong, bullish Neelabh and reject him?

In a fit of rage, he did the unseemly and called her up. He demanded to meet her. Aasma tersely replied that she could not because of her hectic schedule. When he abused her and suggested modes of fornication, she took umbrage, cursed him and hung up.

He confronted her at her dance academy. Aasma was aghast to see him in such a situation. She quickly jumped into his car and drove off.

Back home, Aasma stood by the window, stone-like, as he

downed a few more drinks.
Having fuelled the engine, he accelerated to high speed. He spewed venom and charged her with betrayal. She was silent about his accusations. He was virtually a child before her. The violence she inflicted upon him was more studied and penetrating. Like a fool, he indulged in melodrama. She devastated him with her silence.
She had aspired for the God of big things when she placed him on the pedestal. Like the reader, when she discovered him to be the God of nothing, she summarily rejected him out of her system. This, he could not accept. In a trivial world, where smaller Gods were venerated, he proved himself to be a paradox. An effete parody of an icon.
This undid him.

CHAPTER 9

His second stroke, Amrita took care of. Smriti fretted over the telephone and wanted to fly back immediately. Amrita volunteered to do the unexpected. She spoke to Smriti and assuaged her fears. Amrita assured Smriti that she would inform if the slightest need arose.

For some strange reason, Smriti believed Amrita. Maybe, it had something to do with the quality of the voice. Unlike Aasma, Amrita sounded very dutiful. Very surprisingly, Amrita struck up a friendship with Smriti long distance. Even the sceptical Smriti accepted Amrita as a reliable voice as she diligently filled up the sister with the progress charts every second day and had long chats over WhatsApp.

Aasma did not bother to call or visit. Amma did. Amrita chose to be careful and not present herself when Amma was around. Amma wanted to stay back and take care of him. She was obsessed with this son of hers. He persuaded her not to worry and just let things be. Amma cursed her daughter, spent copious tears and departed. This time around, he felt it would have been better to die than be so completely neglected. He refused to believe that the love Aasma professed was not for real. After all, in moments of crisis, minor ideological differences are best forgotten. Even Amma must have persuaded her. Yet she chose to stay away when he needed her the most.

Amrita's caring and dedication were truly touching. He felt burdened with gratitude. There was no love between them and yet how Amrita threw caution to the winds and stayed back to nurse him back to health, defied explanations. Wasn't this act, by itself, an expression of love? Did love have to express itself through conventional proclamations?

This very thought allowed his heart to justify Aasma's behaviour. Simply by not coming to see him, she did not prove that she had stopped loving. Maybe she wept alone. This brought peace to his mind.

Thanks to Amrita's healing touch, he recovered much faster. For the sake of the film, she tried to hasten the process. Amrita also proved to be a hard taskmaster. She made sure he did his homework properly while recuperating. It amused him no end to see her almost behaving like a wife. Even Tanya had never shown such concern and fussed over him. For the time being, she took

control over his life. Fortunately, his normal over-enthusiastic self did not overplay and professes love or propose marriage. He was as irreverent with her, as ever.
-- Your over caring has deprived me of the pleasure of dying in your arms ... he remarked in jest ... well, now that possibility is lost. I shall now die alone.
-- Oh no you shan't ... Amrita quipped back ... I shall murder you before that.
-- That would be bliss ...
-- You sound very much like the filmy dialogues that you detest ...
-- I am the king of kitsch.
-- From my kingdom, you've been banished ... Amrita proclaimed grandly.
-- Art thou my wife? He queried, trying to snatch a cigarette from the packet on the table.
Amrita slapped his wrist, took the packet and threw it out of the window,
-- Not your wife, but the mistress of this house for the time being ... Amrita smirked.
Of the three boys they called for an audition, two proved to be damp squibs. He gladly gave up hope and squarely laid the blame on Amrita's friend Titli.
-- I told you they were good enough for your Titli to seduce ... he remarked with mock disgust ... but acting is different from the ball games your Titli indulges in.
By now, he had made enough enquires about Amrita's friend and found out that Titli was a raving nymphomaniac who had boys for breakfast, lunch, dinner, and supper. Amrita rued her brashness of having disclosed the fact. He would now rile her endlessly for this.
-- Try the third ... she persuaded ... then pass judgment.
The third was an extremely shy person, who refused to speak above a whisper. There was a certain air of disdainfulness about him. He seemed arrogant and hence interesting. His name was Tejen.
He asked Tejen to sport the statutory spectacles and lookup. The boy did it after much persuasion. Tejen wore an attitude, which was impressive and made him resolve to give the fellow a break. The Dipon in his script needed the concealed haughtiness this boy had. He decided to take the risk and cast Tejen as Dipon.
When the character was explained to Tejen, he refused to play

the role. It seemed that he suffered from homophobia. Tejen was scandalized, as he had never heard anything so outrageous in his life before.

Titli could not suppress her inquisitiveness and called up Amrita to find out what kind of a person he was. Tejen had complained to her that he found both Amrita and the Director to be weird. For the first time, someone had thrown in the gauntlet. He had to take up the challenge.

CHAPTER 10

When he heard the script, even Avinash was averse to the idea of playing a homosexual character. Alisha convinced him otherwise. She was more broadminded. She argued that in any case, he had given up his career and had no reputation to worry about. It would also help him to unload his male-chauvinist baggage.

The patriarchy often discounts liberation of thought as a form of perversion and is intolerant to the views of the other.

Attitudes, which do not conform to stereotypical standards stipulated or prescribed by society, are considered deviant. Strangely, all this suppression and intolerance leads to alternate modes of living and being, to become surreptitious, and flourish as an underworld, other world activity. The forbidden indeed becomes the platform for perversion. By attempting to stamp out realities, society encourages the greater lot to flourish and propagate false myths.

Heterosexual behaviours did not need explaining. It was so much a part of a person's life as his profession, his poetry, and his politics. There were simply no questions asked. Why all this intellectual discourse, to justify, to convince a person, to portray a person who just incidentally sleeps with and loves another man?

He felt disgusted with such paranoia. He could not understand the hesitation. In Indian cinema, all the macho men have at some point or other dressed in drag, for vulgar comic effect. What was all the more disgusting was when the leading light of the gay brigade of filmmakers made fun of gaiety in his film. This entire furor seemed unwarranted. He felt like shaking all the dogmatic notions that had stuck on to Avinash. After all, was there no homosexual undertone in the relationship he shared with Ashu?

But the trick did not work with Tejen, the dog-headed fool. Tejen was a virgin until he had met Titli. She had introduced him to the pleasures of the flesh. Tejen was too immersed in Titli to look beyond and discover newer avenues of expression that could make him conquer time and live beyond it.

With great reluctance, he agreed to meet Titli. Only she could convince the guy besotted with her, to play the role. He was left with no other choice.

He hated himself for having scripted Soumitro's predicament

into a film script.

CHAPTER 11

Titli was a restless soul. She smoked endlessly and drank gallons of tea. She could not sit still in one place for more than one minute. He had to suffer fools gladly, with an expression as benign as possible. The moments when Titli turned her face he grimaced. Amrita did most of the talking.
-- Na re baba, na ... Titli protested, moving her hands vigorously ... what will he think of me? Chchi!
-- Can't you do this much for my sake? Amrita pleaded with folded palms.
-- It's not your sake re ... Titli snapped back ... it's for your lover's film.
-- He's not my lover ...
-- Don't you sleep with him? There was a smirk on Titli's lips. He was about to say something nasty. Amrita pinched him to remain quiet and smiled.
-- Okay do it for the sake of my lover's film ... please sweetness ...
O ... Ma ... why do you behave like that ... Titli dramatically positioned herself near Amrita's knees and clenched her hand. You are my best friend. ... I can sacrifice ten boys for you re ... Tejen is so good in bed ... absolutely tatka pineapple ... sweet and sour ... munch him and see ...
He did not know whether to laugh or cry. Titli was comparing her lover to fresh fruit.
-- We won't eat him I promise you ... Amrita reassured Titli ... he listens to you. Just convince him what a big break it will be for him.
-- He'll become a famous porn-star? Titli sounded delighted. He felt pacified. At last, she was relenting.
-- Why don't you make a film with Tejen and me ...Titli propositioned ...I'll do it for free...I don't mind revealing also.
-- Thank you for your offer...he meekly replied ... I should surely consider it. You are surely a very interesting character.
-- Does he have to kiss another man?
-- Well not exactly ... he answered hesitantly.
-- He'll be comfortable don't you worry ... Amrita butted in ... do you know he'll be playing opposite Avinash. Even Avinash the star has accepted.
-- Owwwwww ... Titli's jaws fell ... you mean Avinash? I've always desired him ... Will, you give me an intro? ...
-- Sure, sure ... he assured her.

-- Okay then ... Titli answered with a tinge of regret in her voice ... for the sake of an art-film, I shall sacrifice my little lamb ... he won't stop making love to me after all this bullshit na re? He makes such good love.
Titli's innocence made him laugh. He could not control himself any further. Titli blushed.
Your lover is quite sexy ... she whispered into Amrita's ears ... If you don't mind, I'd love to go to bed with him.
Amrita threw up her hands in exasperation.

CHAPTER 12

With Neelabh, there was no bondage. Aasma relished her newfound freedom. Life with him and Minal were just claustrophobic. One enforced his opinions on her, the other imposed authority. Neelabh was a free bird without the shackles of a moral order. He did not chain those who happened in his life.

The chance encounter occurred when Aasma accepted the offer to dance for an advertising film on sanitary napkins. The message of the film was simple – a girl could even dance during her periods. Amma was dead against the idea. She felt the concept was against decency and religion. Aasma promptly agreed. The money in question was ten times the amount he had paid her for her services. Amma wailed that her writing was much more respectable and would enrich Aasma morally. Amma's protestations fell on deaf ears.

Aasma was convinced that all the protestations of love were a sham. If she had to prostitute her talent, she would rather do it for money, than the hocus pocus of lofty notions which were as valuable as a fart. With Neelabh, the equation was simple. The accountants would deal with cold cash. Giving and taking were to reduce to the body and the joy of mere words. Nothing more permanent than the night.

Having ironed out the rules, the game became easier, more hassle-free. Aasma relished every bit of it after the heavy overdoes of "emotions abstracted from the substantiality of circumstance" and its accompanying dog shit. Real bulls were a rare species in these days of wrath.

Neelabh took Aasma out for a long, long drive. Driving was his only enduring passion. He smoked grass and drank rum. He did not bully her with his philosophies. She felt relaxed. From the locker, Neelabh fetched out an audio CD and asked her mischievously what mysterious music the CD contained. Neelabh got out of the car, went and opened the door for Aasma. She climbed down. They were parked at a huge barren beach. Neelabh put the CD in the car stereo. Aasma was taken aback to hear the music that usually accompanied her dance. Neelabh smiled enigmatically and with a broad gesture of his hands asked her to dance.

On the seaside, with the backdrop of a starlit night sky, Aasma released her energies and danced like a dream. Her body became pure form, pure motion. She found herself at peace, in harmony with the elements.

CHAPTER 13

Somehow Smriti felt that all was not right with her brother. Pimpu's uncanny behaviour seemed to confirm her fears. The normally effusive and bubbly girl had been morose for about five days. Pimpu kept on going to the window looking looked at the sky and then emulating a flight with her hands. Across the glass pane, her hands glided upwards and took a swift turn to jump off into the air. She kept on mumbling Mam . . . Ma . . . Mam . . . Ma . . . in her soft, sibilant voice.

When Srijeet came back from work, Smriti confided her fears to him and they called up their dear Dada. He seemed to be in ebullient spirits. He told them that he was rearing to go to the hills to start the new film. Smriti kept on fretting and ordering him to take medicines on time, smoke and drink less. For the first time, Smriti intruded into his private life and observed that she had quite liked Amrita. When he informed them that this film was going to be a shocker, Smriti scoffed and replied that nothing he did could shock them any further.

Did he seem to be in love, Srijeet inquired heaving a sigh of relief? That's what I find strange Smriti replied, tucking Pimpu in the bed. For a change, he seemed to be in a happy frame of mind and not obsessed with all the heady vapours floating around his head. Well then, I think you should talk to this Amrita, Srijeet commented. Then we can all go to India for the wedding in spring. I missed his last wedding. I am told it was grand.

Oh yes, it was, Smriti sighed. Though neither Ma nor I were comfortable with Tanya, we were happy for his sake. He had just come out of a disastrous affair with a tart who even stole money from him. Ma wanted the wedding to be an event on the social calendar of the year. She simply would not listen to poor Dada's protestations. Smriti laughed and cushioned herself by Srijeet's side. She held his hand.

Even the broken marriage could not chastise him. There was a tinge of sadness in Smriti's voice as she remembered the past. After Ma's going away, he gave himself up totally. She looked into Srijeet's eyes. You know, I sometimes feel guilty about our happiness. I made one choice and am happy with it. Why couldn't my brother make one correct choice?

That is because Srijeet commented with a poker face, your brother is not as scheming and calculating as you are. You fished well and have me dangling on the hook ever since. Smriti swiftly turned to look at Srijeet smiling silently. Smriti lifted her hands, ready to punch Srijeet's face. Srijeet gently held her uplifted hand and whispered into her ears – still head over heels for you. Smriti pondered for a while, looked furtively at Srijeet and then broke into a grin. Life was so simple and pure with them. They were regular people.

CHAPTER 14

Parmeswar Pandey played a nasty prank. He was livid with the newspaper report about a mystery woman and an even more mysterious film in his life. He was certain that only Parmeswar was capable of such mischief. He stopped taking his telephone calls.

When he accosted Parmeswar, the man laughed. He accused Parmeswar of being a gossipmonger. Parmeswar readily accepted the accusation and replied that he did it to simply add some spice to life. In the end, he gave up. After all, he had volunteered to surrender to the devil.

Amrita repeatedly warned him to steer clear of this man. She sensed that in the long run, Parmeswar Pandey could do him great harm. He had to disagree. Or else, he would be defying nature. He requested her to come along with them for the shoot.

-- But what good will I do? Amrita protested.

-- You'll inspire me ... he stated grandly.

-- Isn't that a cliché? Haven't you used it before?

-- Well you'll ... you'll design our production ... he changed the stance . . ..

-- Precious little I know of that ... Amrita did not swallow the bait ... stop looking for support systems. Don't you realize that you are perfect by yourself? Why do you have to delude yourself into believing that you need people? You need no one ... not even me.

-- You speak like Smriti ... he pouted ... I feel comfy only with you.

-- But you're not my lover, remember that ... Amrita smiled ... we promised never to fall in love.

-- Will you marry me? He suddenly turned around and propositioned.

Amrita fell on the sofa.

-- Well my sister thinks you're excellent wife-material ... he piped sheepishly.

-- Will you?

Amrita's jaws hardened.

-- No ... she replied firmly ... I can't marry you. I am still married. Don't you see my vermilion mark ... besides, that is another excuse for you to seek a shoulder ... I find this contradiction in you the most intriguing. You are such a strong man of ideas ... why do you reduce yourself to becoming weak? You have no right to be weak.

He kept quiet and stared at her without any expression whatsoever. In his mind he kept on mumbling – Do not make a God of me … I am a normal mortal like the rest of them....

"do not mock me aye . . .
do not do mock me"

CHAPTER 15

Only Titli knew Amrita's history. This was a secret she held close to her heart. That was why Amrita respected Titli despite her blemishes. Maybe whatever Titli was and did, was because of the lessons Amrita's life taught her. It was a life from which many lessons could be learnt.

Amrita's handsome father did not like the smell of his wife. Hence, he sought different smells. The smell of liquor, smoke, and flesh. Amrita's mother started hating the smell of the male flesh altogether. By then, she had been burdened with three daughters and a son. These were a product of those days when her handsome husband liked her body odour.

Amrita's mother expressed her wrath on her children. They brought back memories of a stench she detested. The children had a tough time growing up. Amrita and her siblings coped with the situation and grew up in trying circumstances. They had a childhood deprived of fairy tales and pink ribbons.

Amrita blossomed to be an attractive and intelligent woman. Hers was not a beauty that poets could praise, painters reproduce on canvas and filmmakers capture on celluloid. It grew within her. Only those who knew her well could catch an occasional glimpse of it.

Her father needed no beauties after his drinks. He only needed bodies. It did not matter even if he had produced them. One night when he tried to touch Amrita, she jumped up and was frozen with fear. Amrita's mother shrieked and brought the whole neighbourhood to their courtyard. They beat up the inebriated man mercilessly and threw him out of the locality. The next morning, Amrita's mother turned mad. Amrita blamed herself for all this.

In Pranesh, Amrita discovered sobriety that was opposed to all that her father signified. She liked his looklessness and worshipped his intellect She was very comfortable in his presence, though he was a decade her senior. She agreed immediately when he proposed to her. It did not matter that there was no statutory romance serving as a prelude. Pranesh was to be the epicentre of her existence.

By then Amrita had a job to fall back on. Therefore, she did not pay any heed to her mother's apprehensions. She dismissed them like a mad woman's imaginary fears. Even her sisters and brothers were sceptical, but they chose to remain neutral. At least, the firstborn in the family was attempting the happiness the eluded them all their lives.

Pranesh proved to be every inch the devoted and dutiful husband that he promised to be. They set up home and Amrita found tranquillity in the lull before the storm.

She met Titli at work, and soon the two of them struck up a friendship. Titli was a shy and tongue-tied girl in those days of yore. Amrita was happy that even Pranesh took a liking to Titli, in his undemonstrative way. They spend the evenings playing scrabble and cooking.

It all happened one night.

Amrita, Titli and Pranesh were returning after a late-night show. In the middle of a dark deserted street, their car stopped. They had run out of fuel. For the first time in her life, Amrita found Pranesh using cuss words and cursing himself. She was slightly surprised to see him buckling under so little pressure. To reassure him, she suggested that the three of them walk back home.

Just then, five men appeared out of nowhere. Exactly as it happens in Hindi films, they wore lewd expressions on their faces. The trio tried to avoid them and walk past. But these men formed a circle around them. Pranesh started yelling and then howling like a little child, as the men laughed.

They pounced on Amrita and Titli. Three targeted Amrita, two ran after Titli. Luckily for Titli, her athletic records stood her in good stead. But Amrita was overpowered. They took turns to intimidate a cowering Pranesh and rape Amrita in twos. Her father's failed attempts found fruition in this attack by strangers.

By this time Titli returned with help, Amrita had been ravaged and Pranesh had fainted.

Titli screamed aloud in sheer helplessness.

Titli's shrieks and Amrita's silence went unheard in the courts of law as well. A dumb Pranesh stood as a mute witness in the box, unable to recount the monstrosity.

Amrita lost all will to live and die. Pranesh was reduced to silence. Only Titli attempted in vain, to bring normalcy back to their lives. She took great care of Amrita. For six months Amrita stopped having periods. Doctors ascribed it to her trauma. Anyway, in these months, Pranesh had not even dared to touch her.

After a while, Titli lost patience and consulted a psychiatrist. The psychiatrist was a young person well versed in modern schools of thought. He suggested that the husband and wife should try and reinvigorate their sex life. For Pranesh, it was an idea too frightening, to even attempt. It brought back memories.

Though they resumed their respective lives, Titli could not bear to see Amrita's face. She blamed herself for having run away. Titli was a new woman now. She started having sex randomly for catharsis. To expiate her sins, she brought a new man into Amrita's life.

Pranesh was away on tour. One evening, Titli dropped by with a stranger. Amrita seemed to be oblivious of his existence. She had taken to drinking heavily. When Titli sensed the time to be right, she quietly slipped out. The stranger took care of the rest. He was gentle enough not to unnerve Amrita, over-wrought with her fears.

By the third night, the stranger brought Amrita to an orgasm. She wept bitterly after that, as Titli smiled contentedly and hugged her. Amrita bled profusely for four continuous days and still, there was no sign of Pranesh. He had called up to say that he would not be back for five more days as he was stuck with some work.

In her sober moments, Amrita blamed Titli for bringing a curse to her life. Titli shot back, saying it was better to fuck rather than be frigid. Such cuss words scared Amrita. She rushed to fetch her drink.

That evening, when the stranger appeared, Titli introduced the two of them. The man with the cowboy hat was a person who went by the name of Neelabh and was not in the least blue when Amrita blushed red after intoxication.

Unfortunately, that very night Pranesh returned two days before schedule, unlocked the door with his spare keys, discovered his wife in bed with Neelabh and left.

Was Pranesh all that pure as Amrita had vouchsafed him to be?

CHAPTER 16

-- Your mermaid was raped by five men and slept with seventy before she landed in your arms Sir ... Parmeswar said in a sing-song voice.
He remained quiet.
-- You want more details? Parmeswar chimed ... her husband is someone called Pranesh and her sundry lovers include Neelabh the ad-film maker, who gave her the first after rape fuck. Besides ...
-- Stop! He shouted ... stop you mean bastard Parmeswar ... he gasped for breath ... were you born of one bitch or two?
-- Hey Ram! ... Parmeswar pronounced Gandhi-like ... where has your morality evaporated ... has this mermaid sucked off your senses?
-- You almost did, you devil ... he snapped back ... I shan't do this film with you anymore.
-- Oh no! Parmeswar retorted, ever so sweetly ... you can't ... you're contract bound, you know.
--Eventually the mask has come off Mr. Pandey ... he replied coldly ... all those fancy Londonings were for this purpose?
-- I still respect your talent, Sir ... I want to keep it mine ...
He deciphered a concealed threat somewhere.
-- You need not be bothered ... Parmeswar continued ... you need money to produce films and I'll provide it. Your work will go on uninterrupted ... when does the unit leave for location?
As he hung up, a cold wave crept up the spine. It was no longer a mere game of words. Parmeswar was turning out to be a dangerous man in reality. He felt that there was no need to worry, as he had played the cards well. This man could not hold him to ransom. Little did he know what cards the opponent held closely to his chest.
When Amrita called, he asked her to meet him immediately. She came across after a while. He was restlessly pacing up and down in the living room when the bell rang. He rushed to open the door and almost tripped over her. She steadied him with her hands and entered the apartment. He did not know how to broach the subject. Amrita could not fathom what had happened to him. She apprehended; it must be something concerning Aasma that had an overworked turn to such states of frenzy. She hesitated to mention it. Suddenly, he remembered that it was Amrita, who had spotted Aasma's entering the hotel with Neelabh.

-- You didn't mention to me that you knew Neelabh ... he spoke after much deliberation.
Amrita was taken aback, though she did not show it.
-- You never asked me, was all she replied. Again, there was silence. He had given up smoking. That made him more restless. After a while, Amrita spoke again.
-- You called me here, to ask me whether I knew Neelabh.
-- No, no. ... he replied quickly.
He wiped the face and glasses with the handkerchief and came to sit beside her. He held her hand and caressed it gently. Then he looked up, to look deeply into her eyes. His eyes reflected great concern. The wall of resentment that had built itself around Amrita, crumbled down when he had asked the cruel question,
-- I can't say everything to you ... he spoke haltingly . . . I don't think it is safe for you alone over here ... come with me.
-- You were never supposed to keep any secrets remember? Amrita observed there was a nervous tension building within him.
-- Has Parmeswar done any mischief?
She nodded her head in the negative.
-- Not yet ... but he just might ... he blurted out the truth ... he's made inquiries about you.
It took a while for the truth to sink in. Amrita gasped, and then laughed.
Now there are no further mysteries left? With great difficulty, she managed to put up a brave front. He observed that her eyes were gleaming in the shaft of light that fell across her face. The vermilion mark on the forehead was glowing. He went behind and embraced her. Amrita turned to face him and stared blankly. The looks penetrated him.
Didn't he tell you how many hands embraced me before? Amrita fought her tears as she spoke. I've stored within me a thousand smells ... different odours of different men ... no fragrances, only odours ... you know ... every time a new hand touches me, I feel my father's touch ... in the darkness, he touched my breasts once ... those rapists ...when they touched me ... I could smell my father in them ... each one of them ...
He silenced her by putting a hand on her mouth. Amrita rested her head on his chest and cried silently. That night, he heard the story of her damaged life.
As she finished, he held her in a tight embrace and then, did

the boldest thing in life. He wiped out the vermilion mark on Amrita's forehead.
-- You've not been touched ... he whispered into her ears ... even I have not touched you. But I will. After this film is over, I shall touch you and make you mine.
In Amrita, he found the woman of his unfinished script with Aasma. She was the woman in the devastated landscape with pyres burning all around. He was the man lying in her arms. He would surely kiss her before his death.
Wherever; however.

CHAPTER 17

It occurred that his life and films were too verbose. The power of language had corrupted him completely. Now to overcome the temptations of the spoken word was difficult. He could admire silence in the works of other filmmakers but never emulate it. Whenever he conceived a screenplay it was words, words, and words. The wordy man regretted that he could never attain the dignity in the piety of silence. He drew solace from Amrita's observations that words were his " *Swabhava*" ... the real self. Here was a man who hated his words and yet spoke more and more.

If there was any one colour that characterized him, it was red. After all, he was made of fire, hate, and desire. All he could search for was the colour red.

He refused to learn any lessons from the life and world around. If only he willed it, life would be otherwise.

But then, by his admission, the man inside was unchangeable. He had to confront the inevitable, eventually.

228

PART – SEVEN

FAULT LINES OF LOVE

"BIRTH OR DEATH?   THERE WAS A BIRTH,

CERTAINLY, WE HAD EVIDENCE AND NO DOUBT. I HAD SEEN BIRTH AND DEATH"

---- JOURNEY OF THE MAGI

T.S.ELIOT

PART – VII

CHAPTER 1

Tejen did not dare to say no to Titli. Though he resented the idea, Tejen came to hear the script.

They were only the two of them at his office.

 He had arranged it that way. In front of others, it would be difficult to break the boy's inhibitions. Only Dilip the peon was around to serve tea. By then Kalpana had left work and settled into domesticity. He could not go for the marriage. However, he had sent the cheque. The burden had been lifted from his heart. He was scared realizing that Kalpana had harboured romantic thoughts. But girls like Kalpana knew very well how to cope with life and accept reality. He had decided not to employ another secretary. As such, the workload had been reduced over the last year and his assistants Pico, Tico or the twins, could manage the show adequately.

In his usual style, the script reading was a fervently animated exercise. He was sure that Tejen did not understand it. At the same time, he was certain that Tejen was floored by the style. He always had this electric effect on people while reading out scripts. Or so he thought.

-- Why do you wave your hands so much when you read? Tejen questioned sharply. After all, you are not going to act. Your reading might influence your actor.

He did not quite expect this out of a boy who hailed from the tribes and had chinky features. Chinks were supposed to be dumb. He was in for a surprise learning that, Tejen was the son of a chief minister of a north-eastern state, and had studied abroad. He had seen Kurosawa, Kieslowski Almodóvar, and even Wong Kar Wai.

-- Why were you modelling, he inquired rather haughtily.

-- Because Titli wanted me to ... Tejen replied matter of fact ... this Dipon character of yours ... what is his social class?

-- Oh L. M. C. ... he remarked casually.

-- You seem to know next to nothing about tribal society ... Tejen commented sarcastically ... we are not divided by your standards ... We have chieftains, warriors, etc. etc.

-- That's unimportant to my script ... he felt affronted by such arrogance....... Dipon's parents were poor, yet they managed to provide him an education. His father was a schoolteacher.

-- Were they converts? Tejen questioned again.

-- What do you mean by that?
He felt a trifle annoyed. This boy had too many wrong questions.
-- I mean if he was a Christian, he would behave differently... his aggression would be toned down.......
-- Well I'm not so sure ... he decided to put the boy back in his place. Most tribals from that region feel themselves to be outside the Indian mainstream.
-- You Indians have given them enough reason to feel that way ... Tejen was quick to point out.
-- You Indians? He found Tejen's statement bordering on blasphemy. Do you not consider yourself to be an Indian?
-- Of course, I do ... Tejen asserted. Only the rest of you Indians deny our role in the freedom struggle. You conveniently label us as pro-Chinese, because of our mongoloid roots.
Tejen seemed to be an opinionated upstart.
-- You are missing the tree for the woods ... he pursued a different line of argument. My focus is on the unusual love story.
But you seem to forget that your story is set against a backdrop of political activism ... Tejen shot back. You cannot tamper with contemporary history. Or else your story will not sound authentic.
He had never met such an argumentative actor before; that too a newcomer. Tejen contradicted everything and yet could not be made to shut up, as his logic was irrefutable. There was truth in what Tejen said.
-- If I may suggest so ... Tejen continued ... we should read up some of their literature. I have a friend who is in their think-tank. He can provide us the clues. Otherwise, we would reduce the insurgents to becoming villains in the mould of popular cinema. Can you afford such clichés in a serious film?
He could not. Though the ego took a beating, he had to concede that more homework on the subject was essential. Grudgingly, he had to admire Tejen's clear-sightedness. He felt convinced that Tejen could do proper justice to Dipon's character. As he nodded in consent and smiled warmly at Tejen; the ice was broken.
-- I am a great admirer of your work ... Tejen spoke reverentially ... you use melodrama so poetically ... and before you stop me, believe me; I am not saying it for effect's sake. I

loved the ending of your script.
-- Has it changed your attitude?
-- Well you see, I'm not exactly homophobic . . . I've never given alternate forms of sexuality much thought. Anyway, one can always begin somewhere. I have never kissed a man before.
He laughed. Tejen had not lost his boyish charm despite his strong opinions.
--But in the film, you have to ... there was a mischievous glint in his eyes. Even Avinash has not kissed a man. You two need to know each other better, to overcome the discomfiture.
 --My father's political image will surely take a beating ... Tejen smiled absentmindedly. The Chief Minister's son in a gay film...
--Is it politically incorrect to be gay? He bantered. Well, I shall be hanged too ... the critics will tear me apart and the militants will lust after my blood.
Life ahead had so many surprises in store.

CHAPTER 2

The following week was hectic. So many odd jobs to be done before the unit left for location. He was informed that they needed protection to shoot in the jungles. As such there was the threat of the militants. Moreover, they had a big star and a chief minister's son acting in the film. Tejen proved to be a big help. He arranged for everything, using his father's good offices. Little did the Chief Minister realize that he was helping those very people for whom his image might be tarnished soon enough.

For the first time, he decided to act. It was not a wish-fulfillment in the tradition of Hitchcock. He was to play himself – the Narrator in the film. Amrita laughed at his presumptuousness. Only Parmeswar provided him moral support.

It was surprising to see that all the members of the unit resented Parmeswar. Whenever Parmeswar was present, be it rehearsals or production meetings, everyone behaved cold and distant. Not that Parmeswar cared for the responses. True to his eccentricities, Parmeswar always rubbed people the wrong way. He revelled in irking and irritating people.

Amrita assiduously avoided any interaction with Parmeswar. Whenever Parmeswar met her by accident – barging in unannounced, he would fall all over her and smother her with a vulgar display of his rakish charms. Amrita stopped coming over when people were around.

He wanted to make their togetherness public, but Amrita opposed the idea primarily because of Parmeswar. Whenever he would get worked up over this and threaten to stop, she would try to pacify him commenting that it was more important for him to complete the film than to fall prey to Parmeswar's ploys. Amrita felt that Parmeswar was the ultimate sadist who derived pleasure by annoying people. By not getting angry, he could deny the man pleasure and thwart all evil intentions.

On the flip side, he was happy to see Avinash and Tejen get along famously, from the very first encounter. Avinash got into the decadent outfit of languor – the hallmark of the Soumitro Sanyal character, rather well. Tejen quickly acquired the quicksilver aspect of Dipon. Jokingly, the duo would behave wildly, using pronouncedly effeminate gestures and camping with élan. When he protested and told them that he did not want them to behave like pansies, they would overdo do their bit and melt into each other's arms. He would give up after a while and laugh. After all, they meant no harm and when it came to serious business, they would behave like studs. He wanted to explode the myth of gays as dandy men dressed in drag. He was surprised to find himself fast turning into a gay activist. For a change, he stopped being belligerent and did not dread the idea. At last, he was espousing one cause at least, in this otherwise, causeless life.

Aasma fitted nowhere into the scheme of things. She was almost forgotten. Well, not totally. At nights, he thought of her. The heart did not ache any longer. But a thousand memories flashed across the mind. He missed her innocence. He had not yet been able to flush her out of the system. It took great courage and a good deal of convincing himself, to call her up. It was so different from the first call from the airport. There were no words left for either of them to speak. Not even their statutory "So".

She had come to know that he was starting this mysterious film, through newspaper reports. He could not deny having written a script without her. When he volunteered to tell her what it was all about, she stopped him. She was not interested in knowing. It did not hurt him to hear her so blunt. When he expressed a desire to meet her, Aasma refused. He insisted on one final meeting. He was very particular about endings. She relented.

At Abel's Inn, everything was the same, except them. He had promised her that the business would be over in fifteen minutes flat. Five had already past and both had finished their coffees. Aasma was dressed in black. He commented on her looks. She accepted his compliments gracefully.

There were eight minutes left.

He inquired about her dance. She briefed him.

There were five minutes now.

He told her that he was seeing someone. Aasma told him she was glad to hear that.

Three more minutes.

He hoped that she would see the film, once it was completed. She said that she would consider the option.

Only a minute and a half.

There was silence.

Forty seconds ticked off from the last minute.

He coughed, hemmed and hawed and then was about to ask,
couldn't we ... when the time ran out.
Aasma got up, looked at him straight and announced that she
was pregnant. Then she glided out.
She stole the last line from him.
Whose child was she rearing in her womb?

CHAPTER 3

He insisted that Amrita come to see them off at the airport. Alisha was going to see off Avinash, Titli would be there for Tejen. So why not her?

The junior technicians and the equipment had left two days earlier. The actors, senior crewmembers and Parmeswar were travelling together, by flight. Everyone but Parmeswar had arrived. Vipul, the production manager had taken their boarding passes. They were scattered across the lobby. The three couples stood together.

-- So, you are going to be men without women for a whole month baap re . . . Titli made a wisecrack.

-- Well, for the period of this film we are off women ... Tejen butted in saucily.

-- We'll form a nice cuddly threesome ... Avinash said in jest ... hey, why don't the three of you form a *ménage-et-trios* while we are away ... a steamy lesbian affair.

-- That shall be the subject of the next film ... Alisha remarked.

-- Come to think of it ... he observed ... this is my first film without women.

-- Well you still have time to rework the script and incorporate a woman militant who has the hots for Dipon ... Amrita suggested.

-- That will be a marvellous idea............ Tejen piped eagerly. It will allow me ...

Don't you dare or else I'll chew you aasto ... Titli threatened. They all laughed heartily.

He was on top of the world. All charged up. It almost seemed like old times.

--Well where is your producer? Avinash nudged him . . . the prankster Pandey.

-- I hope he arrives at the last moment ... Amrita commented. Then he shall no longer have the opportunity of chatting up with us. I find him so slimy.

-- Me too re ... Titli twittered.

-- Don't be uncharitable ... Alisha observed sagely. After all, he had shown great guts to fund such a film.

-- Indeed, Mr. Pandey is a man of great guts ... he wryly reassured them.

Just then, Parmeswar Pandey breezed in. Vipul rushed towards him and collected his ticket and baggage and ran towards the check-in counter.

-- What a pity ... Parmeswar panted as he spoke ... had I known the ladies would be here, I could have arranged for some cakes and croissants. There's still time, I shall go and fetch some.
-- There is no time Mr. Pandey ... he butted in ... they have announced security.
-- What nonsense! Parmeswar waved his hand dismissively ... they can't leave without me.
Saying this Parmeswar rushed off to the pastry shop. This man was simply beyond control. The sight of three women had thrown him into a tizzy. The others laughed it off as foolish pursuit. Except for Amrita. She sensed something eerie. She curtly refused the croissants. Parmeswar was not ready for such a reaction.
--I shall leave you to say your goodbyes . . . Parmeswar mumbled weakly ... see you on the flight, Sir!
As Parmeswar withdrew, he held Amrita's hand firmly and looked into her eyes.
--A new life when I am back ... he whispered.
--Live in your present and make a great film ... Amrita advised him ... the future would take care of itself.
--*Kismet*? He laughed and turned to the security check.
When he took off the seat belt and looked around, Parmeswar was not to be seen onboard the flight.
His heart missed a beat.

CHAPTER 4

They were staying at a tea planter's bungalow. It was a spacious and luxurious affair, set on a cliff. Parmeswar had arranged for it. Something urgent had cropped up at the very last minute, making it imperative for Parmeswar to stay back. He would join them in two days, he assured over the phone.

On the third day, the shoot began. It started smoothly. They had chosen to film the silent scenes in the log cabin, to begin with. Tejen warmed up before the camera with amazing dexterity. When they returned to the bungalow that evening, he discovered Parmeswar sitting on the balcony and sipping tea. He felt relieved seeing the man. He dismissed his fear about Parmeswar as unwarranted and even felt guilty for harbouring negative thoughts. He spoke to Amrita that night and had a sound sleep after a tiring day's work.

Work progressed as per schedule. Parmeswar left after three days and promised to be back in a fortnight. As such, Parmeswar had very little to do on location. Before leaving, Parmeswar entrusted him with the money and wished good luck. Parmeswar also asked for forgiveness for his cranky ways. He felt touched and apologized for the abuses.

With Parmeswar's departure, the entire unit felt more relaxed. Now they could all work in peace. Only one thing disturbed him now. He discovered that somehow Avinash had lost the electric responses. He took great effort to warm up his friend. Tejen was a great help. This was the first time he was handling the dual responsibilities of an actor and director. That proved to be taxing. He could accurately point out the mistakes of the actors. Was he being able to be judgmental about his acting prowess?

He rehearsed at night. The normal routine was shooting by the day. At nights, they would first work out the schedules of the next day and then relax over drinks. Avinash had to be given his medicines and put to bed early. He and Tejen would then sit and chat. They soon struck up an intimate friendship. He confided to Tejen that this film was based on the real-life experiences of a friend.

One night, the security guard came and informed that a stranger wanted to meet him. After some hesitation, curiosity got the better of him, and the guard was asked to show the stranger in. They had finished dinner and he was alone in the room.

The stranger limped in, with a shawl covering the face. He asked the person to sit down. The stranger opened the shawl and he saw that the man had lost one arm -- the left one to be precise. The man was a native and wore glasses and a beard. He was startled when the stranger introduced himself as Dipon Bezborua. He did not know what to say.

I know you are making a film about Soumitro and me... Dipon spoke softly.

He was aghast. He still could not gather the courage to speak.

-- Word travels fast in the jungle. ... Dipon continued ... but be rest assured; no one can touch you or do any harm. I was aware that someday you would make a film about us. I had predicted this before.

-- Where is Soumitro? He questioned after much trepidation.

-- You should know that ... Dipon suppressed a sigh.

-- Didn't you know? It was his turn to get agitated ... don't you know?

-- Know what? Dipon looked up.

-- Soumitro came back here to look for you ... he gasped.

Dipon's eyes lit up. He looked at Dipon, wonderstruck. Dipon limped forward and held his hand.

-- Are you telling me the truth?

He nodded in assent. Dipon left his hand and restlessly paced up and down the room.

--He came back ... he came back ... Dipon muttered almost prayer-like.

-- He received your call and cancelled his departure ...

Do you think I can find him? Dipon asked helplessly.

He was overcome with pity.

Of course, you can ... he chanted.

Thank you . . . Dipon whispered. You have given me hope to live. Good-bye and best of luck ... will your film end on a happy note?

-- It wasn't supposed to ... he remarked ... but now, I'm not so sure.

Dipon melted into the quietness of the night.

CHAPTER 5

The next morning over breakfast, he recounted the incident of the previous night to Tejen. The boy rued his decision to go to bed early that night. An encounter with Dipon would have provided Tejen the ideal opportunity to observe the character he was portraying, first hand. This was a chance of a lifetime, for any actor. But the bus had been missed. So Tejen had to be satisfied with the graphic description of the incident.

That day, they shot the scene where Dipon begs for Soumitro's life, in front of the Commander. A much-enthused Tejen outdid himself. Even the perpetual sceptic he, could not help but applaud. Tejen felt elated at having satisfied the director.

The next day, they were supposed to film the scene of the first seduction. That night, Tejen was extremely nervous and worked up. He arranged for a rehearsal. Avinash and Tejen were both on tenterhooks. He administered two sleeping pills to Avinash to soothe the overwrought nerves. When he came back to the room, he found Tejen sitting on the sofa and drinking. Tejen's eyes were bloodshot by now. He fixed himself a drink and sat on the bed deciding to assuage the fear.

-- In moments of great passion and intoxication you often forget your immediate context and do things on an impulse.... he rationalized. For you, the moment becomes supreme.

-- But how far can you pretend and play-act? Tejen questioned innocuously. After all, there is a thing called a biological impulse, when you touch fire, there is a burning sensation ... when a pin pricks you, it pains.

-- That is the litmus test for an actor ... he propounded ... that is the time when you separate the mind from the body. Your flesh is merely a vehicle that is driven by an alert, objective mind. So, you are beyond conventional notions of pleasure, pain, and hate. All these sensations are created because of emotional resonances.

-- You ask me to become a machine? Tejen's speech was slurred by now. It is easy for you to sit afar and direct. When an actor has to physically enact ...

-- You seem to forget ... he interrupted Tejen ... I am also an actor in this film.

-- Yes ... Tejen stood and swayed towards him seated on the bed ... but you don't have to do the kissing and making love,

in front of the camera. Tejen came and sat beside him and looked up, with intoxicated eyes. He gently placed his hands on Tejen's shoulder.
-- You have to dispossess yourself when acting ... your emotions have to be controlled by logic ... by your mind. You have to be calculative.
-- That means you will feel nothing physical at that moment? Tejen's question made him uncomfortable. For instance, imagine we are doing that scene right now ... you will feel nothing if I kiss you?
He knew this was a dangerous game and yet nodded in the negative. Tejen leaned forward and kissed his lips softly. He felt awkward.
Did you feel anything?
To prove a point, he nodded in the negative again. Tejen leaned forward, held him in a tight embrace and bit into the lips. His jaws hardened as a severe sensation swept across the whole body.
He began to shiver.
-- Even nothing now? Tejen could not quite believe him.
Again, he repeated his actions. Tejen held on firmly and pushed him on the bed and smothered kisses all over the body. He shivered uncontrollably as Tejen looked searchingly into the eyes.
-- Are you being truthful? Tejen's voice quivered . . . are you?
He lay motionless on the bed, praying fervently for this to be a dream. Yet there was the immediate reality of the touch. Tejen put the head on his chest and whispered almost inaudibly.
-- Why do I like it then? I was always afraid I might ... don't you like it?
He had no answers. This seemed to be a moment beyond time and space. Yet he could not deny it. He hated the pleasure it evoked. He decided to switch off the mind, as the present could no longer be prevented.
Both he and Tejen evaporated into a different sphere of existence. There was only darkness and fire.
Nothing was impossible.
Forests walked and fishes flew.
Tigers chirped and birds growled.
All that was possible exhausted itself by dawn.

CHAPTER 6

When Amrita opened the door, she was shocked to see Pranesh standing there with Parmeswar. She stood frozen, unable to react. It took a while for the situation to sink in. It was worse than a nightmare.

-- Haven't we brought good tidings ... Parmeswar chirped gladly. You always thought ill of me. See, I've brought happiness back to your life.

-- Won't you ask us in? Pranesh spoke in a voice drained of all emotions.

The voice from the past broke her reverie.

-- Sure, sure ... come in.

In her mind, Amrita kept on praying for this to be a dream. It was her sub-conscious fears about Parmeswar that had resulted in this fantasy. She kept on pinching herself and her body responded with great alacrity.

-- I had such a tough time locating your husband Madam ... Parmeswar heaved a sigh of relief as he plunked himself on the sofa.

Parmeswar did most of the talking, as Pranesh and Amrita remained silent. They could not even look into each other's eyes.

-- I sensed you must be very unhappy without him . . . Parmeswar pointed at Pranesh. After all, for a Hindu wife, her husband is the be-all and end-all . . . there was a tinge of vindictive glee in Parmeswar's voice. It's okay to stray for a while, but marriage is sacrosanct. You are bound by the seven pheras you took around the fire, for life. It's best to forget and forgive. As for me, I've done my bit to secure my place in heaven. The Gods will bless me for sure ... the sinner refused to stop ... now that the two of you are settled in your love-nest, I shall take your leave ... Parmeswar got up, walked towards the door and turned.

-- Both of you are cordially invited for lunch tomorrow . . . and just in case you need anything, don't hesitate to call me up ... bye . . .

As the door closed behind Parmeswar, Amrita knew it was not a dream. Though Pranesh's reappearance was a bit too weird to be real, Amrita was left with no choice but to accept it, as a moment that had already happened. She could not undo the coming.

As Pranesh sat mummified on the sofa, she tried in vain, to figure out how Parmeswar had got hold of him. However,

Amrita was certain about Parmeswar's intentions. This was his way of getting back at her for playing hard to get. The scheming Pandey had dug Pranesh out from her past and resurrected him, to take sweet revenge. It was done to trap her into a situation from which it would be impossible for her to escape.

Amrita was determined to thwart Parmeswar's evil designs. She was no longer burdened with the guilt of infidelity and could gather the courage to confront a mute Pranesh. By now, the enormity of his guilt had caught up with Pranesh and he was a broken man. He meekly admitted that Parmeshwar had coerced him into returning and threatened with death if he dared to leave.

Titli was aghast when she saw Pranesh at Amrita's apartment. Amrita had called her up in desperation. When she heard the full story, Titli was seething with rage. She decided to confront Parmeswar head-on, Amrita advised her against it. Parmeswar was anticipating this move and would be able to tackle it deftly. Their adversary was no fool. They had to plot a counter move. The whole situation reeked of a horror story.

Pranesh was too much a coward to be a party to the plan that Titli and Amrita were working out. However, he agreed to maintain the status quo and silence. In the new scheme of things, his life and work had been disturbed. He had been bulldozed and blackmailed to come back. Given a choice, he would prefer the life he lived alone. Pranesh took great care never to come in the way and blended with the furniture. To lighten up the bizarre situation occasionally, Titli would feign drunkenness and holler at him. He would go scampering back to his room wearing the expression of a petrified pig. Even Amrita had learnt to shed her inhibitions and began enjoying a laugh. That was the only way to cope with the grotesque situation.

When they met Parmeswar for tea, both Titli and Amrita wore their charmed amulets. They flirted with him just enough. If they had come on any stronger, their intentions might have been suspect. They dangled their respective carrots and set him up in hope. But Parmeswar being Parmeswar did not give up suspicion. Though he pretended to get carried away, in actuality, he was as alert as ever.

Amrita and Titli had resolved that they could tackle the circumstances locally, and did not need to worry the boys on location. They were adventurous enough to even accept a dinner invitation. That night, Amrita was dressed to kill. Titli was dressed to mourn the dead.

They deliberately drank themselves silly and embarrassed Parmeswar by falling all over him, at the restaurant. Heads started to turn and Parmeswar began to feel uneasy. He reminded Amrita that her husband was waiting for her. Amrita scandalized him by buggering off her husband. Titli egged him on to drive them through the deserted streets by night. The ever-effusive Parmeswar was too polite to refuse.

As he drove, the fire in him seemed dimmed. Titli and Amrita took turns to paw him shamelessly and set him on fire. He was human after all. After a while, even he started to pant. By that time, Titli had managed to pull his pants down and Amrita had ripped open his shirt. The tie was dangling from his neck. They drove him to a point where he had to stop driving.

Both Titli and Amrita stepped down from the car and started to dance to the music playing in the car stereo. Titli pulled Parmeswar out and started dirty dancing on the deserted streets. Parmeswar was unmindful of the fact that he was in his jockeys. Diligently, Amrita untied the tie-knot and took off his shirt. By then, even the wily, scheming man had let himself go berserk. Very carefully Titli pulled down his jockeys and passed them on to Amrita. Amrita flung it far away. Here was Parmeswar Pandey in the raw.

As soon as they saw the headlights from the opposite direction, both Amrita and Titli started to shriek. Titli's hands were on Parmeswar's eyes. He thought the women were shrieking with delight.

When the police baton hit his hard-on, Parmeswar opened his eyes. Everything seemed to happen in fast motion though he was not drunk. He understood that he had been drugged. As the police dragged him away, the two women stood smiling. He yelled at them, abused them. The cops kicked him hard and abused him further. Parmeswar tried hard to exude authority but the cops refused to listen to a nude man, drugged out of his wits. They kicked him, slapped him and even made fun of his size.

Before he fainted, Parmeswar swore revenge.

CHAPTER 7

It was beyond anyone's wildest imagination that a first-time actor could essay a role so convincingly. Even Avinash resented Tejen's virtuoso performance. It goaded Avinash to shake off his lethargy and made him try to compete. The conservative members of the crew ignored the sexual connotations and marvelled at the passion the actors displayed. This was indeed turning out to be "the film" of their lives. All of them relished every moment. It was work no longer. No one calculated shifts and kilowatts of lights.

Tejen felt that "he" was the best of the lot. Both as an actor and as a director. He discounted the kid's proposition as idolatry. After that night, Tejen was no longer argumentative. Though neither of them spoke about it afterward, he observed that Tejen and had become submissive. This submissiveness was in no way servile – it was more of giving in to a big brother, respecting the elder. There was no escape from inspiring the paternal and fraternal. He never got tired of fathering people.

Shooting on location was always more fun. It was an extended picnic, a Boy Scout camp. Often, they would light a bonfire on the lawns of the bungalow at night and sit around it. Sometimes he would volunteer to cook for the unit. Even there, Pico, Tico were the forever willing attendants in that. They would chop the vegetables, peel the onions, and de-skin the chicken. Finally, when the table was laid will all the ingredients, the chef would arrive with much pomp and ceremony and stir things in the giant *haandi*. The unit would have to be content romancing the food as there were no women around.

One night, the local people caught the slimy Vipul with his pants down with a tribal woman. All hell had broken loose.

A petrified Vipul cringed and shat in his pants. None of them knew how to tackle the situation. Tejen volunteered to meditate. He pulled the chief aside and spoke in the native tongue. A simple bribe of two bottles of scotch did the trick. Tejen disapproved of the notion that things such as bribes were unworkable in tribal societies. Consumerism had conquered all spheres of existence. When admonished for his errant ways, Vipul solemnly vowed to remain celibate for the rest of his life.

Nothing remarkable happened after that incident. For the rest of the days, shooting went on as per schedule. Only

Avinash seemed slightly off colour. He sensed that Avinash did not take too kindly to his proximity with Tejen. Over the years Avinash had been habituated to his undivided attention. To extract better performance out of Avinash, he adopted a different strategy. He would henceforth run down Tejen and rave about Avinash. That did the trick. Tejen was clever to understand the move.

One thing bothered him though. Would he alter the ending? Dipon's visit had shaken him up. When he pondered about whether to let art imitate life, he found no ready answers. He needed Amrita's help. When he called her up, her phone kept on ringing. Even Titli had not called Tejen for quite a while. This was beginning to cause anxiety. He brushed off the thought and attributed it all to the innate nature of getting hyper at any minor aberration. He began thinking about his portrayal as the Narrator in the film instead.

He had begun to relish playing God. It unleashed his energies and proved to be exhausting. He was so caught up with acting and directing, that other things ceased to matter. The Narrator was a departure from the real story. After all, why did he have to stick to the real story? He only needed the essence for the right dramatic impact. He found a solution regarding the ending. Whatever happened in Dipon's or Soumitro's life could not alter his interpretation. The story was just the take-off point. The beginning middle and ending had assumed their places. Strangely, the extended joke on the new wave was being played back on him. The film was no longer a travesty of the neo-Godardian structure. It was creating its shape, which was way beyond his control. The master was now the slave.

Life was playing its jokes, in its inexorable ways.

CHAPTER 8

Amma's outburst at Aasma's confession of her pregnancy was very much in the tradition of Chinese opera. Great raving and ranting in prolonged cadences, screeches, punctuated by silence and then the high pitch again. First were the gentle inaudible sobs and then gutturals yell that brought the neighbourhood to their windows. After all such a display of melodrama, Amma fainted.

When she regained her consciousness, Amma wanted to reach out but he was not available. Amma cursed him for having deserted her. She pounced on Aasma and wanted to extract the name of the father. When Aasma replied resolutely that she did not know, Amma shrieked and fainted again.

After three bouts, Amma recovered and resolved to go against the conventions and have the child aborted. Aasma refused to co-operate and insisted on having the baby. Amma's protestations, threats, and pleadings fell on deaf ears. Strangely, Aasma thought the child was to be her proclamation of victory over men. Only she knew exactly who the father was. She had counted the periods precisely.

In a fit of rage, Amma threw Aasma out of the house.

Though it broke her heart, Amma knew there was no other way. She failed to understand the inexplicable horrors of an alien world. In Amma's universe, faith, fidelity, and purity were still the three important passwords. She could not accept the multiplicity and co-existence of different truths.

Neelabh arranged for a shelter. Aasma was unwilling to accept help. She was petrified of being burdened with gratitude any more. In the end, all men wanted her to be grateful for their small mercies, Minal had clamoured for gratitude for having loved her. So, had He. She did not want Neelabh to do the same, in the long run.

With Neelima's help, she made her arrangements. Aasma's only concern was to rear the child in her womb with utmost care. She wanted to gift her child a life without identity. She desired that the child be born outside the convention. All conventional notions had ceased to be important for her.

The ever-alert unborn child cried in Aasma's womb, pleading to be given birth. I shall ask you no questions mother-just give me birth. I want to be the testimony of love, in a world full of hate.

The lessons the child taught her made Aasma truly wise. She learnt to forget knowledge as a historical phenomenon. From now on it would be an abstraction – pure and undefined. Aasma waited for the child to be born and give her the freedom from choices.

CHAPTER 9

Parmeswar sat brooding at his office. The horrors and the humiliation of the night haunted him still. Using his connections, he had managed to keep the scandal undercover. No one came to know about it. The policemen on duty had been transferred to a remote district and no records were maintained. Yet the fire did not cease to burn.

There was no one in the office. Parmeswar preferred it that way. His staff sat elsewhere. From this place, Parmeswar controlled everything by remote control. He even made his coffee and dusted the place himself. It was a one-room affair on the fifth floor. Parmeswar was a great stickler for details. He took great care to maintain everything in perfect order. The lighting suited his dull grey mood. Despite a great display of mirth to the outside world, Parmeswar was essentially a melancholy man.

Parmeswar's troubled childhood was responsible for what he had become. His mother was an unrelenting, overpowering harridan, who kept her son on a leash. She was extremely critical of whatever he did and spared no effort to spank the madness out of him, whenever he indulged in harmless boyish pranks. This resulted in the madness increasing manifold. The aberration had its roots in the Oedipal. Parmeswar grew up to oppose every rule in the book and become a misogynist.

He hated a woman's mind but relished her flesh. In his pursuit of physical gratification, he isolated himself completely. One fine day, he realized that he was a friendless man. By now, his opinions had solidified into beliefs and he found no one worthy of friendship. As he was switching channels unmindfully, a dialogue from a TV show hit his ears
–

We cannot hate with the purity of thought.

Our energies are dissipated and hatred fails to create an impact

You have to be pure when hating

Parmeswar watched the remainder of the episode carefully and was moved by the villain's evil charm. All the impure characters spoke with such haunting conviction. He decided to locate the maker and befriend him. Here, at last, was a man after his heart. He even decided to go into film production to purchase a friend. Everything was hunky-dory and things were progressing according to his pre-planned designs, till such time when a woman intervened. She came and stood between Parmeswar and his friend. The friend started paying her greater attention, Parmeswar had to usurp her. After all, women were his forte. When the woman resented, Parmeswar became vengeful. Parmeswar felt that the man who inspired in him such pure passion of hatred would surely understand his move. It was his duty to reciprocate the gesture and evoke hatred in his friend's heart. Parmeswar loved to wear a mask, to hide his real self from his mother. He did not realize that after prolonged usage, the mask became his face. He had become a consummate actor who deserved a chance in the movies. Only one day, the mask came off and his face fell. Two women, whose sleeping records beat all whores hollow, stripped him in the middle of the streets at midnight.

How could he forgive them? How? Hatred was his vocation and these women inspired him to succeed professionally.

Parmeswar knew well that villains were vanquished only on screen.

CHAPTER 10

Not hearing from Amrita for ten days, he started to panic. So did Tejen. Even Titli had not called up. And to crown it all, Parmeswar had not arrived after a fortnight, as promised. Though Parmeswar had sent across a message and money, the coincidence was causing enough for alarm. He could not concentrate on work. Nor could he abandon everything and rush back. He had responsibilities to fulfill. The climax was yet to be filmed.

When Avinash called up Alisha, he requested her to find out about Amrita. Alisha called back to say that both Amrita and Titli had left town for some work and were expected to be back after a week. After she failed to get Amrita on the phone, Alisha had called up Titli's office and found out the details. When she had visited Amrita's apartment, she met a man who failed to give her Amrita's whereabouts. When he enquired who the man was, Alisha replied that the man had introduced himself as Pranesh.

That solved the mystery and explained everything. Though it shattered the dreams of an ordered future, he felt relieved to hear that at least Amrita was safe. He had dreaded that Parmeswar might have done her some harm. Amrita had got back her husband. The vermilion mark that he had erased was back in its place. The red dot on Amrita's forehead sealed his destiny. His thoughts turned to Aasma and he felt miserable for having forgotten her completely. How quickly did fickle minded men like him change horses, despite protestations of undying love?

That indeed was the supreme irony of his age and times.

On a hasty impulse, he called up Aasma. Amma answered the phone. Her voice was hollow, cold and distant. Initially, he thought it was the long-distance connection that affected the quality of the voice. When Amma informed him about the situation, he knew it was otherwise. He could not speak for a while. Amma cursed him under her breath and hung up.

Destiny had played its game well. It had allowed his share of manoeuvres. When he failed to make the right move, it struck right back. Now it was only fair that he conceded defeat and accept everything in the right spirit. The twin fold blow benumbed him. In a strangely perverse way, he found the matter amusing. All alone in the room, he even started to laugh aloud. A situation potent with the possibility of the tragedy was reduced to the bathetic.

He picturized the climax with great aplomb.

His enthusiasm was so infectious that Tejen got all charged up and asked for a loaded revolver to get himself shot. The pain reflected on the face would then be authentic. It took great persuasion on his part to prevent suicide. Despite an appetite for the bizarre, he controlled Tejen and the grand plan was abandoned. Though crestfallen, Tejen excelled in the climax, virtually stealing the thunder from Avinash. The normally petulant Avinash was too deeply impressed, to throw a tantrum.

As he shouted 'cut' and looked up, he saw two pairs of eyes gleaming from behind the foliage. Before he could focus attention, the eyes disappeared. He was not sure whether it was an apparition. Those eyes seemed to belong to two people he knew. Though they denied him the comfort of knowledge, he believed that eventually, they had met in the jungles, and two of them were living happily, at least in the now. At least this one story found fruition.

Now that the shooting was finally over, the unit went berserk. Even the reticent Avinash let himself go and danced with gay abandon. He chuckled when Tejen pointed out the irony of the usage.

Just then Avinash propped in a pertinently naughty question – in the Soumitro-Dipon affair who slept under whom? To this, there was no answer, as he never dreamt of asking Soumitro that question. We have to re-shoot the entire film, Tejen proposed teasingly. Our characterizations have gone all awry. You mean, the characterization would depend on sleeping positions, was all that he could ask. Indeed, it would, his rational mind asserted. But now there was simply no other choice. The film would suffer from this blemish forever. He felt disturbed having acquired the new knowledge.

But of course, it would, Avinash butted in, with a sardonic expression.

He understood that both these guys were playing a prank. He hollered back . . . I'll shove bayonets up yours . . .

That'll hurt ... ouch, Tejen protested in a mischievous vain.

That is most unbecoming of a gentleman . . . Avinash said haughtily ... Boyo were you brought up in a barn???

He laughed. Finally, Avinash had indeed become Soumitro.

That night, the men became boys and he enjoyed the last lap of happiness with gaiety.

CHAPTER 11

Parmeswar received them at the airport. Though Parmeswar was his usual effusive self, he noticed an imperceptible change in the man. He did not mention anything, but the heartbeat became faster.

He rushed back home, took a shower and sat down with the telephone. No one answered at Amrita's house. Tejen called up to inform him that Titli was not back as yet.

The panic button had been pressed. He resolved to go over to Amrita's house and confront the errant husband. Pranesh would surely know where the woman, who wore the vermilion for her husband, had gone. He requested Tejen to come along. In the new scheme of things, Tejen had become a buddy. Just as he was leaving his house, he stopped and walked back to his bedroom. He opened the cupboard and pulled a drawer. There was the gun and the bullets he had snatched off from Soumitro's hand not so long ago. He loaded the revolver and put it in the inside pocket of his jacket.

When they accosted a moribund Pranesh, the man had no answers. Amrita had told Pranesh that she and Titli were going on a business trip and would be back soon. They could not believe a man who was content with his wife's "will be back soon". Either he was not man enough, or else he was lying. Tejen deduced that Pranesh was doing both. Though he chose to be civil, Tejen's tribal instincts came to the fore and Pranesh went pale in the face seeing Tejen seethe with rage.

Tejen grabbed Pranesh by the collar and demanded an explanation for his sudden reappearance. Pranesh stammered a few unsatisfactory replies. He felt that such investigations would come to no avail and forced Tejen to leave the effete man.

All the roads were closed. Except one.

He succumbed and asked Parmeswar for help.

-- Your mermaid has disappeared? Parmeswar asked incredulously. Maybe she had found better bait.

-- Please help me ... he hated asking the devil for help.

-- For you my life.... Parmeswar pronounced ... why don't you meet me at five? We shall find her out ... I promise you we shall ... honey and sympathy were dripping from the vile voice.

Tejen was averse to the idea of him going alone. But he knew that nothing would emerge if Tejen accompanied. He furnished the revolver from inside his jacket. He patted Tejen's shoulder and bidding Tejen a peremptory farewell, he assured the anxious boy, "I'll get back as soon as . . .

Alone in the apartment, he sensed the ending. He called up Neelima. After much convincing, she gave him Aasma's address. He drove recklessly and reached in fifteen minutes. When he pressed the calling bell and loitered in front of the door in the states of great agitation, the image of the dove flashed past his mind.

He had opened the palm. Aasma opened the door.

She was visibly pregnant. Seeing him, Aasma took a few steps back. He still did affect her, after all. Aasma imagined trouble. He assuaged her fears, promising not to interfere with her life.

He sat down and spoke about the last few months of life without her. He even mustered courage enough to speak about Amrita and his present predicament. He was too engrossed in the story, to see the geography of Aasma's face changing with the mention of Amrita. He recounted how Amrita had inspired when Aasma had deserted.

 Aasma cringed when he mentioned that the woman in the unfinished script was none other than Amrita. As he fretted for Amrita, Aasma felt dizzy and wanted to die.

He told Aasma that they had to meet her once before the curtains went down. This was the moment. He apologized profusely for the intrusion and got up to leave.

He stepped out but halted in the steps and turned to ask her two more questions.

Are you happy?

Whose child is it going to be?

Aasma chose not to answer and closed the door, gently on his face. She knew this was the last time she saw him and felt weak.

Though there was a month left, she suddenly felt a kick within.

The child within her had started to revolt

CHAPTER 12

When they met, Parmeswar expressed a desire to go for a drive. He had no other choice. Parmeswar drove at a leisurely pace, whistling a tune from an old Hindi movie.

-- You remember the film? Parmeswar asked without turning from the steering ... it's very silly of me to ask you the obvious. Generations have been brought up on this melody ... Lata Bai's hauntingly beautiful voice ... Parmeswar began to sing the refrain ...*alvida,alvida* , the farewell dirge ... uff it still gives me goose bumps...Bina Rai's eyes were full of pathos ... who did you think made a better *Anarkali, Madhubala* or *Bina Rai?*

He did not reply. He could not make out where all this gibberish was leading. What connection the apocryphal myth about the legendary love affair between the emperor *Akbar's* dandy son *Salim* and the courtesan popularized by Hindi cinema, had to do with his search for Amrita, evaded him.

He understood Parmeswar was playing a prank yet again. He wanted to get down from the car.

-- But where will you search her? Who will give you the clue?

-- Does that mean you have some connection with Amrita's disappearance? He put a hand on the steering.

Parmeswar patted his hand and laughed gently. They were on the highway. Parmeswar glided down the road and parked near a culvert. Gracious as ever, Parmeswar got down from the driver's seat, crossed over to his side and opened the door. He stepped out and inhaled deeply. He needed cigarettes for this occasion, but since he had stopped smoking there were no cigarettes at hand. Parmeswar rushed back to the car, opened the dashboard and swiftly fetched out a packet and a box of matches. Running back to him, Parmeswar bowed as he held out the packet on his palm.

-- Your wish is my command, Sir! Parmeswar chimed ... only you don't value my friendship. I can do anything for you.

-- Find me Amrita ... he blurted out.

Parmeswar's expressions changed.

-- Please Mr. Pandey don't do this to me ... he pleaded fervently.

He looked helplessly into Parmeswar's eyes. He could not find any trace of sympathy in those cruel eyes, though Parmeswar constantly wore a benign smile. His despair inspired Parmeswar to again break into the same song from

the classic film *Anarkali.*
She was in love with the Emperor's son. The Mughal monarch could not allow the blasphemy, as it would set a bad precedent. So, he ordered her death. This story had no basis in history, though folklore had immortalized it as a story of unrequited love. The love story of the Prince and a nautch girl caught the fancy of *Cinemawallahs* and two films were made in a row, on the same subject.
One was called *Mughal-e-Azam,*the other *Anarkali .* Both of them went to break all box office records. The entire nation hummed songs from these films. The central image in both these films was the courtesan. To this day, people debate about who essayed the role better. No one however debated about the best song. Though *Naushad* was the music mogul of those times, the credit for composing the best tune went to *C Ramchandra. Lata Mangeshkar's* rendering of *Anarkali's* dirge had generations weeping. The final lines, the refrain in which *Lata* kept on wailing....... *Alvida* or farewell as *Anarkali* was being buried alive, by a perverse twist in the tale, was now, being hummed by Parmeswar.
-- Why don't you make a film like that Sir? Parmeswar turned to ask. Something that will touch people's hearts ... no intellectual masturbation ... only love, pure love ... don't mind my saying it but you have the streak of a pervert in you ... making films on birds and homos ...
He lost patience.
He knew by now, Parmeswar had driven this far only to play some stupid trick of his. He did not even feel like replying to the insult and turned to go. He had to locate Amrita. Despite all grandiose assertions, Parmeswar could not help him. The slime was simply wasting his time. As he walked a few steps ahead, Parmeswar caught up and nabbed his shoulder.
-- You are mistaken, Sir ... Parmeswar hissed behind his ears ... all this preface was needed to prepare you. After all, you have a weak heart. I know where Amrita is. I have sent her there.
He turned sharply and held Parmeswar by the collar. Parmeswar smiled briefly and shook his hands off firmly.
--- If you try a trick, you shall never know.
The snake had eventually appeared out of the man's shadow.
-- I meant no harm you see ... Parmeswar spoke in his usual singsong ... she and her friend provoked me. Those two

bitches paraded me nude on the streets ... they thought they could get away with it . . . but I am Parmeswar, the supreme God ... by now Pandey had almost got into a trance. As I was contemplating modes of revenge, the song came to my mind ... *alvida,alvida...* farewell, farewell ... and I was reminded of *Anarkali's* fate. She sang the song as she was being buried alive in the wall; brick by brick ... Amrita was such a spoilsport. She fainted.
His heart started to swirl. He could not believe the monster. Such things never happened in life. Only in cinema . . .
-- Exactly ... Parmeswar cooed . . . I wanted it to end like a film ... but your mermaid behaved un-heroine like....... her friend, that butterfly even peed ... but not to worry... I did not bury that lesser mortal . . . I shot that Titli. After all, how could I give the same death to your girl and that bitch? Your Amrita will now become immortal like *Anarkali.* Why don't you make a film on this subject ...? I don't mind playing the villain ... Parmeswar's voice was human no more.
He was beyond reaction.
He fell on the ground in slow motion, with eyes closed. He genuflected and prayed that the present is rendered as a nightmare.
Oh God, that madest this beautiful earth... o Lord ... make my life untrue, the atheist prayed.
-- That is not all Sir ... Parmeswar descended, as he spoke with great concern ... please, Sir, hear the end. ... I'm helping you ... try and understand that I am helping you to achieve the pinnacle . . .
His eyes opened to stare at Parmeswar. Parmeswar's eyes were moist. Parmeswar was genuflecting with folded hands.
-- I'm your friend sir ... Parmeswar murmured ... even *Ram* needed a *Raavan* to redeem him ... I am only helping you achieve your Zen of hate . . .
In that desolate landscape, he was sitting motionless on the ground.
Parmeswar sat beside him, whelping like a child.
He went near Parmeshwar and genuflected beside him. Parmeshwar's eyes were closed. He swiftly brandished the revolver out of his pocket and held it on Parmeshwar's temple.
Parmeshwar quickly opened his eyes and saw the unbelievable sight.

A smirk appeared on his visage as Parmeshwar started whining. It was the first time in his life, he had brandished a gun. Parmeshwar folded his palms and asked for forgiveness. This was a prank on the reverse. The prankster was finally robbed of the perverse pleasure he got by holding people to ransom.

With the gun held by both his palms, he let out a short, contrived laugh. Mr. Pandey, if you care to remember, not very long ago, I had assured you, that I shall kill you. You should have taken adequate precautions. But now it's too late in the day. Before your hand moves to the pocket that has a gun, I will fire. Saying this, with all his might, he pulled the trigger.

Particles of Parmeshwar's brain and skull flew around in myriad little bits, as the body fell to the ground. He was still holding the smoking gun. All passion spent, he kept on shooting the corpse till he exhausted the bullets. Or so, he thought. The surreal merged with reality.

Life was playing its trick. He could not fathom what was true anymore.

CHAPTER 13

Aasma's child was born premature, after great pain and suffering. The child was held in Amma's caring arms. As Aasma battled for life, she wanted to make that final call but eventually could not. Her time was over before the spoken words were about to be formulated. He remained a wordy man forever, as her eyes shut nimbly, gazing at her baby. She could see the truth in her baby's face. That calmed her. She had made her choice. She could finally sleep.

He could not figure out where the real Amrita was. He felt restless and helpless. He realized that the narrative of his life had come to an abrupt end. Yet his soul was not ready to exit his body. He could hear the faint gurgling chant of Pimpu, from a distance. He waved his flying arms, desperately seeking reality veering away from the monstrous dream that had enveloped him for so long. At last he chanced upon the truth. Unpalatable yet resilient.

He wandered whether he would be redeemed. The Maker provided no ready answers. He resolved to smile. To be or not to be was no longer a question. The answers were finally provided.

260

PART – EIGHT

ZEN OF THEN

"LIVING TO LIVE IN A WORLD OF TIME BEYOND ME;

LET ME RESIGN MY LIFE FOR THIS LIFE, MY SPEECH

FOR THAT UNSPOKEN, THE AWAKENED, LIPS PARTED,

THE HOPE, THE NEW SHIPS"

----- MARINA

T.S.ELIOT

PART VIII

CHAPTER 1

Did he ever function outside the matrix of the mind?
Did he ever seek birth outside his thoughts?
Did Amrita and Aasma even ever die?
Did he will the dream child to be born, to give the narrative circularity?
Did the great pretender he, conjure all this in the mind, for the sake of a mere dramatic end?
Did hate ever need a theory?
Can we truly learn to love after this extended orgy of hatred?
No answers.
We leave him alone in the darkroom, groping and conjuring clever words in the mind; ideating and expounding upon a non-plausible theory full of flaws.
Was he, where he was, in the beginning?
A Nowhere Man.

About the Author

Sudipto Chattopadhyay is an author, film-maker, screenplay writer, poet, lyricist, a creative director, an engaging chat show host, a social commentator and a film director and television producer with over 28 years of experience. He has produced and directed over 1500 hours of television shows in the fiction and non-fiction categories. He has written successful films like Dus Kahaniyan, Alibag, and Acid Factory. His feature films as the Writer and Director include, Pankh, Terrorist Uncle, Shobhna's Seven Nights (in Hindi) and Highway (in Bengali). They have been critically acclaimed, winning several awards at various international film festivals including the Houston, Chicago, New York, Seoul, Busan and London film festivals. He has made award winning documentaries like Overture, The Play Is the Thing and Even Gods Lived Here and also made advertising films. He is currently working on his three new feature films in Hindi, Bengali and English as a writer and director. He has also been the editor of a monthly magazine on entertainment and a cultural columnist with a leading English daily. He writes extensively on society, literature, art, culture and cinema. He has written lyrics for feature films in English, Bengali and Hindi and independent albums as well.

His anthology of essays, poems and a play --The Day I Stopped Lying (published in 2019), has been received extremely well and won critical acclaim.

He is single and lives with his mother, in Mumbai.

A Nowhere Man is his debut novel.